Realists

ALSO BY BISHOP & FULLER

Co-Creation: Fifty Years in the Making

Rash Acts: 35 Snapshots for the Stage

Mythic Plays: from Inanna to Frankenstein

Damned Fool: a Year in the Life

Full Hookup

Frankenstein: DVD

The Tempest: DVD

Descent of the Goddess Inanna: DVD

Available at

www.independenteye.org

Conrad Bishop & Elizabeth Fuller

Realists
— a novel —

WordWorkers Press
Sebastopol, CA

Realists

ISBN: 978-0-9745664-8-1

Contents

Part One: Realities

Chapter 1
Before Stuff Happened

Eddie Grabowski got off work at seven a.m. and walked out of the sweaty coliseum into the chill of reality. He hated working concerts at the Deepak, he hated Washington DC, and he hated "heavy-melt." Programmed guitars, subsonics, hiss and hum, samplings of Lawrence Welk and machine guns, lyrics like "Buzz mah fuzz, butt buddies," and loud, loud, loud.

Last week he'd worked a great gig: some bands still played music. When they hit the groove, he could go on all night, lost in wonderland. One gal had a weird gravelly voice but with something supple in its roughness. Eddie played with the board to bring her forward, adding just a touch of cross-delay to give her space. She heard it, grinned, crammed herself up against the mic, and started really playing with the phrasing, trusting him to help her ride on top. The voice went from honey to rock salt and back again. Eddie felt like a proud dad, or maybe more like a midwife.

But that was last week. This week he'd turned thirty-four, a supremely qualified audio engineer working sound crew for morons. Everything went late. The concert died at three a.m., and it took four hours to load out. With all-wireless you didn't need cables, you just needed the system to work, which it never did. So you ran cables to bypass the gizmos, slapped it all down with gaff tape, just like the old days. Then you tore it all out, restored the state-of-the-art wireless units to their inert condition, and packed it in. Eddie hummed a few bars of some old Springsteen cut — not sure what, as he could never carry a tune himself — just to clear his head.

He shivered, zipped his jacket, tugged the bill of his cap to start himself moving, and walked three blocks to the Stadium-Armory Metro. A few shops were still in business behind barred windows. Mom's Hot Dogs specialized in good old-fashioned crystal meth, and Best Hardware fenced guns. The economy was booming, said the news, so everybody was broke. He passed the huge animated billboard that rose above the buildings for half a city block. Gigantic hog faces twinkled across it, jaws set firm, eyes on the future, grinning with rage. Ah, the candidates. He'd almost forgotten. Two weeks before the election you could smell the whole country hot from the oven, ready to be served up.

He stopped to read a protest poster glued to an unbarred window.

ROCK AGAINST REALITY!

How dumb could people get? It was common knowledge that the Realists funded protests against themselves, knowing that everybody hated protesters. But voters forgot stuff once it was common knowledge. He peeled a flap of the bogus poster, ripped it off the window, folded it into a cockeyed paper airplane to see if he still remembered how. It crashed on launch. Ah, stop with the politics, feel the breeze. The chill felt good.

He caught his own reflection in the window, slapped at the hair bursting all directions from under his baseball cap. Weird hair, too short to be long, too long to be short. He'd mash it down on top, only to have it sprout out the sides like the crazy thoughts he could muffle but never kill. Distant sirens howled. His T-shirt said *Not Right Now*.

Eddie jerked himself awake. He'd been up twenty-five hours straight and nearly fell into his reflection. Thirty-four. Look on the bright side, he thought, you're a full year older than Jesus ever got. But he knew from his dad, a sardonic trombonist, deceased, that with age the music either got better or it got worse, and some day you'd be forty, fifty, then more, then dead. And how could he stand to live so long with someone as depressing as himself?

No, he thought, that was only the verdict of his last girlfriend Dot. *Dottie, no, don't take me seriously when I call myself a cynical nihilist. I'm kidding. Haven't you heard me on the mixing console trying to cut down on the hiss and the feedback and make the world sound better. Dottie, Dottie, Dottie, remember that weekend we had?*

He glanced at his watch. How did it get to be 8:30 already? He thought about breakfast, hitched up his worn chinos, slapped his hair again, tugged at his cap. No improvement. Ahead, the rush-hour crowd streamed into the subway maw like shave water running down the sink. He lunged into the flood, zipped his UniQard through the slot, crammed himself into a car. The ads were blasting eighty decibels, exact. The old liquid-crystal flats, you could smash the screen, but these were indestructible plastic steel that blared and chirped and grinned. The Gallup Poll told you you loved these ads.

The subway jerked, and a heavy, muffled lady with an armful of parcels slammed against Eddie. She grabbed a hand-hold, lost her grip on the load, clutched the top box with her chin. Eddie reached out to help.

"Hands off!"

Thick glasses glinted under her red-tasseled stocking cap. She sized him up.

"You okay?" Eddie shouted over the subway roar.

"Not enough." She fumbled the packages. "Grab these, willya? I got an itch." Eddie held the boxes. She dug into her ribs. "Oh that hits the spot." She reclaimed her burden. "Mabel McClafferty. Two F's in McClafferty. You going to work?"

"Coming from work. Worked all night."

"Whatta you do?"

"Sound." Did she understand? "Audio."

"Like noise?"

"Lots."

Over the blare, Mabel McClafferty launched into her own work history. Snack bar, dry cleaners, parking garage, "all the places the big-shot bozos go to act like big-shot bozos." Briefly she'd owned her own business, an electrostatic hair-wash stand ("Don't ask!"), but it didn't work out. "Worst job was being wife to McClafferty, moving his butt from the couch to the dinner table and then back to the couch. What stop we at?"

"Seventh."

More passengers wedged into the aisle. Mabel jerked around, muttered to an anonymous hulk, "If that's your elbow you wanta keep it?" In a shouted whisper she confided, "I gotta mail these before they boot out the government, in case they change the stamps. I still use stamps. The ones with the ads are cheaper. Free enterprise, sell everything. I'm sending these Special Delivery to shoot'em off fast." She tapped a package. "This one, I'm sending a toothbrush to my uncle. I'm making a statement there."

Mabel glanced around suspiciously, then continued. "Big one, that's a waffle iron. That's an antique. That goes to the

President if they elect him some more. Cause he oughta have waffles so he'll understand the common people. He's a crook, but I'm gonna vote for him cause he knows how stupid people are. Least you know what to expect."

Eddie watched for his stop. He never liked talking to strangers. For sure they'd start talking politics. Why not just have an auction for President and the richest guy wins? That'd put some bucks in the till.

Suddenly the ad-flats flared, swollen music filled the car, and over it the voice of one very tough guy:

> OTHER GUYS BABBLE ABOUT THE ISSUES.
>
> BUD PERT SAYS: GET REAL!
>
> VOTE REALISTS AND GIVE IT TO'EM!
>
> HARD!

Echoes of *Hard, hard, hard* . . . and it flipped to a Happy-Jox blurb. Too much reverb, Eddie thought, and they need to roll off the bass. No excuse for bad audio, even for fascists. "That was the post office," he said. "You shoulda got off there."

"I go the next stop past, in case they got a tail on me. There's lotsa ears around here." She pointed to a man at the far end of the car whispering into his own lapel.

The subway screamed to a halt, and the human flux drained. Mabel streaked for the stairway. Eddie was sorry to see her go. It was nice to remember that people could still be stark nuts in sweet, harmless ways. He'd keep watch for that red-tasseled stocking cap.

The doors rasped shut, and the ad-flats showed the sobbing face of a little boy.

> LAST YEAR, TEN MILLION KIDS LIKE ME HAD
>   DREAMS OF SEXUAL PENETRATION.
>
> THOSE OTHER GUYS SAY, "GEE WHIZ."
>
> BUD PERT SAYS, "GET REAL."
>
> VOTE REALISTS.

The camera zoomed in on the President's mad grin as the back-up girls swung into an up-tempo "No narcoflix, no narcoflix!"

The stop wasn't Eddie's, but he had to get off before he blew his cool and started pounding on anything breakable. He stood on the platform, absorbing the roar. Images started to play behind his open eyes. He jerked his brain back into its groove, slid his UniQard through the exit gate, and climbed a dead escalator to the street.

The streets were bare. If he went home he'd be too exhausted to sleep. His mind chewed on some lyric about dead frogs on caffeine as he walked the six blocks to the Mall. The barricades there were temporary but still in place, five years running. Tourists ventured up to the stun wire, took snapshots of the bristling black-helmeted cops, who smiled and waved. Eddie missed walking in the Mall, even missed the army of derelicts who had once speckled the meadow. He saw the cops eyeing him, realized he looked pretty scroungy himself, flipped them a Boy Scout salute, then went numb. Restrain your humor, Eddie. From that range they might miscount the fingers. Last week, a guy had started to peel a banana and died in a fusillade.

Still, the grass was green. There was that. Some things don't change. He still watered the geranium that Dottie had left on the windowsill over the sink.

Eddie walked west along the Mall, looking for something he couldn't define. He hated that. Lately he'd read three novels about guys moping around the city looking for something they couldn't define, then meeting women who took four hundred pages to define that what they longed for was not those guys. He could write that one. Years back, they'd made a big thing of the New Millennium, and for freshman English he had to write a paper on what the New Millennium would bring. He worked all night, logging into every Futurist website, skimming his shelves of science fiction. He wrote forty pages of dystopian extravagance, then boiled it down to four words:

MORE OF THE SAME.

He tried to keep politics out of his brain, but nobody cleaned up their doggie droppings any more. Girls used to tell him he had a great grin, but it was hard to grin for real when the candidates had trademarked the grins. Still, dammit, he was looking for the indefinable — what? — life mission, hot babe, Holy Grail, or perfect cardioid mike? Thirty-four was only a third of a hundred, not so far along. He liked trees, he liked sunsets, he liked kids, he liked music when it wasn't too loud to hear, and women when they really saw him. So why did he walk around with this bubble over his head saying *Blech!*?

Eddie took the crossing point and walked back southeast. He hadn't gone there since the last round of riots. Before, it was a slum. Now, the bombed-out waste was freckled with gated communities that looked like the Magic Kingdom: Disney was big into real estate. But there were still a few scattered blocks of old buildings, mostly vacant, where the artists were starting to squat. They'd squat anywhere. No electrical service, but it wasn't hard to jimmy the panels and hook up enough juice to set your loft on fire.

One block was a string of funky bars. Beer? He glanced at his watch: beer at ten a.m.? No, better start home. But as he passed the Melody Box, the door banged open, and a taut blue-jeaned rump thrust out.

"You're outa here, you sonofabitch! You want a front-loading asshole you just come right back!"

And Eddie saw Pepper. The drunk was a hairy three-hundred-pounder but never knew what hit him. She'd jerked down the front of his pants, throwing him off balance as she pulled him through the door, then yanked his collar sideways, planted a foot in his kidney, and propelled the great bleary bull into a streetlamp. She pivoted, face-to-face with Eddie. Bleach-blonde. Taut lips. Fox eyes. Pretty, the way chisels are pretty.

"Christ, where you from, lady?"

"Oklahoma." She disappeared.

For a moment he watched the drunk taking inventory of his delicate parts, then followed her into the bar. He could feel that rump. That was a cutting-edge rump, all muscle and appetite. He could do right by that rump. That rump might be the solution to all his woes and the source of serious new ones. The indefinable suddenly defined itself. Why not give it a try?

She was already behind the bar, two mugs filling. He approached. She gave him a sharp glance, and Eddie took a quick breath, confident that the right words would come. But suddenly the news popped onto the vid. He tried not to look, tried to hold the moment, but his eyes couldn't resist the suck of flickering fools.

> AT THE TOP OF THE NEWS. ROSALIE, ALL
> POLLS SHOW THE REALISTS ARE REALLY
> ON THE ROPES. APPROVAL RATINGS AT
> HISTORIC LOWS.

AND YOU KNOW, HAROLD, FIVE FORMER
U.S. PRESIDENTS SAY ANOTHER REALIST
VICTORY WOULD SPELL DOOM.

TO WHICH BUD PERT REPLIES, "DOOM FOR
YOU, PUSSIES."

A splash of cold water on the dog. Eddie turned away. She's probably past forty, Bible Belt, brain-dead, married to some Marine. Reality Land, Eddie. He went outside. The drunk was still standing there like a huge misdelivered refrigerator, muttering "Fuckin' bitch" to the parking meter.

Eddie walked east. Where to? To his apartment? Flip on the vid and watch the pond scum, otherwise known as pundits? Two weeks before election, but no suspense this time around. These pigs were down to eleven percent in the polls. Things were bad enough now. They couldn't get any worse.

He kept slogging through wasteland, his brain on life support but drifting like smoke back to the Melody Box. Yeh, kids, trees, sunsets, and he'd almost forgotten: fox eyes, taut buttocks, and jazz.

Chapter 2
Narkies and Eggy-Pops

Jessie dawdled at her cereal. She'd picked out the raisins to eat, and now it was just sweet flaky goo. Milk dribbled from her spoon onto the table. She should wipe it up with her napkin so Mommy wouldn't have to, but that would mess up the napkin. She'd dribbled milk at school and Miss Edsel said, "Jessie, you're dribbling," and the children laughed. If things were so hard now, how would it be when she had to grow up?

She looked up at the tube. On the tube they were killing people. Mommy called it the tube, even though it was a vid. Mommy said none of the people on the tube were real, but if they weren't real what were they? She wanted to ask at school, but at school they didn't like questions.

Harold and Rosalie came on the vid. Jessie thought they were funny. They always looked happy even when people were screaming.

> BIG DAY, ROSALIE.
>
> SURE IS, HAROLD. POLLS OPENED AT SEVEN A.M. THEY'RE PREDICTING A TOUGH BATTLE FOR THE REALISTS.
>
> WILL LIGHTNING STRIKE TWICE, ROSIE?
>
> HEAVY TURN-OUT EXPECTED. COULD BE AS HIGH AS FIFTEEN PERCENT.
>
> IN OTHER NEWS: THAT BROOKLYN WOMAN WHO BLEW OUT HER BRAINS ON THE HOME SHOPPING CHANNEL WAS REPORTED BY NEIGHBORS TO BE UNHAPPY.
>
> HERE'S ONE. THE DEATH OF A SEVENTEEN-YEAR-OLD COED PUSHED THE NUMBER OF UNDERAGE SUICIDES TO A RECORD HIGH. POLICE GAVE NO DETAILS, DESCRIBING IT AS "ROUTINE."
>
> AND DON'T FORGET, ROSALIE, IT'S FIRST TUESDAY, AND YOU KNOW WHAT THAT IS.
>
> YOU TELL US, HAROLD.
>
> IT'S . . . PEE-DAY!

Harold pulled out a zip whistle and made a zip. That was funny. Jessie heard sirens. That wasn't on the vid.

> THANKS FOR THAT, HAROLD. SO, ALL OVER
> THE COUNTRY, WE'RE LINING UP TO MAKE
> SURE WE'RE FREE FROM NARCOFLIX.

> DID YOU PEE, ROSALIE?

> SURE DID, HAROLD. AND DON'T FORGET: YOU
> CAN PEE AT THE POLLS. TESTING STATIONS
> RIGHT IN THE VOTING BOOTHS.

> FIRE AWAY.

Mommy clicked off the vid, then dug through her purse, getting her feet into her shoes while drying her hair with a towel in her other hand. Jessie liked the way Mommy could do three things at once, but she didn't like the ugly dress Mommy called business drag. She liked her in blue jeans, or at night when Mommy was very tired, but smiled.

Pepper ransacked her purse. "Jessie, were you playing with my keys? The school bus comes in ten minutes, put on your shoes. We miss it, we'll have to catch MUNI and they'll dock me an hour."

She liked tending bar, but she'd had to quit. Daytime tips were zilch, and her only night babysitter Richelle was shacking up with a meth head. Mom called, said move back to Oklahoma. Sure, Mom, so you can fuck up another generation. Some things never change. Moms full of bullshit never change. Politicians never change. Crappy jobs never change. And love never changes, Jessie, not for you, never. You're what love is.

Jessie looked up from her cereal. "Mommy, what are you thinking about?"

Pepper stared at her. No kid ever asked stuff like that. Kids didn't know their mothers ever had a brain to think with. "Finish your cereal."

"It's too sweet."

"It's what you asked for."

"The box had Baby Mickey."

"Well you just learned something, didn't you?" Pepper ripped the seal of an Eggy-Pop.

"What are you thinking about, Mommy?"

What was with this kid? She must have heard it on TV. Pepper plopped the Eggy-Pop on Jessie's plate. Ever since she had told her that baby chicks came from eggs, Jessie wouldn't eat eggs, but Eggy-Pops weren't exactly eggs. Why couldn't she ever keep her mouth shut? "Nothing. Come on. Five minutes."

"You said ten."

Right now, Pepper's mission in life was to get out the door. They'd dock her an hour if she was a minute late, and that hour would buy two boxes of goddamned Eggy-Pops. Last night she'd made the mistake of reading the supermarket tabloid she'd picked up on an impulse, seeing the headline, "NUTTY GAL BLOWS IT." She read about the nutty gal who blew it, and she couldn't stop seeing the face. It probably wasn't even the real woman's face. They just stuck any old nutty gal on the cover. Get rid of dreams and make all the nightmares real.

"What are you thinking about?" Jessie persisted.

"Just a story, honey."

"What story?"

"Three Little Pigs."

"Tell it."

"Finish your food!" Pepper was packing Jessie's lunch and scribbling a grocery list. "You know Mommy has to be at work on time. Mr. Henry's a sonofabitch."

Pepper was seeing the face of Myra, the nutty gal named Myra, what the tabloid said about Myra, the dream she had about Myra, and now she had a blinding headache. The dream scurried through her mind like roaches.

She was still having dreams. Besides the meds in the tap water, she was taking her NoNarx, but it wasn't working, none of it. She was scared that somehow they'd find out.

"Mommy?"

"What!"

"Does everybody talk like you in Oklahoma?"

"Come on, get your damn shoes on." Jessie hopped down and trotted across the floor. "Hold on, honey, I better check the weather. You might need bundle-ups." She flicked the vid. Harold and Rosalie, still with the fucking news.

> THE NATION'S DRUG CZAR REPORTS GRIM
> DATA ON NARCOFLIX. THE NATIONAL
> PSYCHOSIS RATE IS THIRTY-THREE PERCENT
> AND RISING. THE PRESIDENT SAYS THAT'S A
> SMALL PRICE TO PAY.

> LOOKS LIKE IT'S TIME TO GET SERIOUS ABOUT
> THIS, HAROLD. MAYBE, AS THEY SAY, "GET
> REAL."
> BUT ON THE BRIGHT SIDE, ROSALIE: LAST
> WEEK, A RECORD NUMBER OF AMERICANS
> TRIED TO SHOOT THEMSELVES . . . AND
> MISSED.
> NEW REVELATIONS, HAROLD, ABOUT THAT
> CANNIBAL NURSE—

She flicked it off. "Thanks, guys, just what I needed to know." Jessie struggled to get her arm into her pink coat sleeve. Pepper tried to help. Jessie pushed her hand away. Right, she wants to do it herself. Let her. Don't try to beat it out of her. You know about that.

"Mommy, Jeff says there's a monster."

"A monster. Where?"

"When we color pictures. He says there's a monster in there and he draws a circle around the monster and that makes a hole for it to crawl out."

"So what does the monster do?" Okay, button up now. What the hell happened to her mittens?

"It eats him up."

"Honey, don't worry about that. There's bad people in the world, but we'll make sure they don't hurt you."

"How?"

Pepper ran out of dumb things to say. Maybe if she'd stayed longer with her mom she'd have a bigger stock of bullshit to pass along to her kid. "Mittens now."

"But it does."

"So if he's eaten up, how does he come to school? Okay, boots."

"He's dead. He said so."

"Hon, we gotta go. Listen, it's okay to tell Mommy that stuff, but you shouldn't talk like that to other people. They'll think you're having narkies."

"It's not a narkie."

"They'll think it is, and they'll think I'm doing something wrong and we'll get in a lot of trouble." Pepper didn't need this conversation. Not right now. Why did such a cute little kid make her so mad sometimes?

"But what about Jeff?" The little girl was desperate. Oh Christ, she's gonna cry.

"Don't worry, hon, he's just teasing. Sometimes boys try to scare you just cause you're a girl. Other boot." Oh damn, and the keys.

Jessie's voice was different now. "But I saw him do it."

"Saw what? Honey, other boot now. We're going to miss the bus and then I'm really f— messed up." Pepper pulled the boot on with a jerk. Jessie's face started to wrinkle.

"But I saw the monster eat Jeff."

"When?"

"Last night."

"When you were asleep?" Pepper stopped dead. Jessie saw terror fill her mother's eyes. Mommy's fingers dug into her arms. Really strong. They hurt.

"You didn't drink your water last night, did you?" Jessie pulled away. Pepper jerked her back. "No, you didn't. Now listen. Now you have to drink your water, honey, because you can't have narkies. That's bad. You're a bad girl. And you know Mommy loves you, hon, but you listen to me now!" Oh God, she's gonna cry. Don't grab her so hard, you're hurting her.

Pepper smoothed the pink coat sleeves, trying to pet her little girl into a better world. Forget the bus, forget the boss. She spoke quietly to her child's frightened heart.

"Now you don't tell anybody else about Jeff and the monster, you hear me? You don't tell Jeff, and you don't tell your friends, or Miss Edsel, or your babysitter Chrissy, nobody! That was a narkie, hon. You hear me? That was a narkie." And they'd think it was Mommy's fault and they could hurt Mommy, they could take Jessie away from Mommy, and she'd never see Mommy again. No, soften the hands. This wasn't a lumbering drunk, this was the six-year-old girl-child she loved. So sweet in her little pink coat and stocking cap.

"Don't cry, Jessie!" Pepper took a deep breath. "Now listen to me," she said, trying to be gentle. "Now what are you supposed to do?"

"Don't tell," Jessie whimpered.

"Okay. I'm sorry to scare you, honey. But it's okay to tell me because I can make it okay. We can be sure you drink your water." Pepper gave a deep sigh.

"What's the matter, Mommy?"

"Nothing, honey. My bottom dropped out." Then, about to harangue her daughter for the keys, Pepper felt them in her pocket. For half a breath she thought of screaming, but then she was past the last straw and into the rest of the day.

She pulled up Jessie's collar, opened the door to the cold. They walked out the rear door into the alley, cut across the vacant lot to the school bus stop. There might still be time.

"Mommy?" Jessie asked. "What's wrong with it?"

"Dreams? C'mon, Jessie, you're in first grade, they teach you that. It's because dreams are scary, and you sort of escape from reality, and they give you bad ideas. Besides, they're against the law."

They stumbled along the path through dying weeds. "Hey, you know the thing about monsters," Pepper said in her best attempt at good cheer, "if you draw a really beautiful picture, trees and flowers and maybe some bluebirds, and there's a rainbow in the sky, you know what? That picture's so beautiful, why, that old monster, when he comes out, he just says, 'What a beautiful day! I'm not gonna be a monster anymore. I think I'll be a chicken.' And that's what he does. He lays an egg. Hey, there's the bus!"

The bus was just turning the corner. Jessie didn't like the bus. Mommy said school buses used to have windows. Now, because kids got shot, they had heavy armor and it felt like riding in a lunch box. The bus had bright colors, with bunnies and flowers, so the mommies would think it was fun.

The bus pulled up. "Mommy," Jessie asked, "How does a chicken make eggs?"

"Well, they just sit down and . . . poop'em out."

"Why is Mr. Henry so mean?"

"His mommy doesn't fix him breakfast."

Jessie climbed up the stairs of the armored vehicle. The door clanged shut. The bunnies bared their teeth.

Chapter 3
Pee-Day at the Polls

The first Tuesday of each month was a test of national purpose known for the past four years as REAL Day. REAL — renal emulsified agglutinin locator — was the critical urinalysis tool for determining the presence of NoNarx in the bloodstream indicating compliance with narcoflix laws. The slogan was *Get REAL*. The acronym never caught on with the public. They just called it Pee-Day.

Dream suppression was the key issue that had raised the Realist Party from a mocked band of fringe wingnuts to the highest levels of power — one of those happy accidents that have given American politics the trajectory of a drunken sailor. Its precursors, of course, were the Red Menace, the War on Drugs, the War on Terror, each new war spawning the next, convincing us that someone, somewhere, set the alarm a half hour early every day to plan our destruction and could only be foiled by heavy explosives and lots of laws. We needed to be convinced that something was being done about anything.

Now, the ultimate enemy was an enemy within: dreams. We'd all been chased by the hairy monster. We'd all felt the lust of the succubus. We'd all gone naked to algebra class. We'd survived it, of course, but our kids might not. The prospect that our children might be unsettled, might cry for Mommy, might ever taste fear — this was worse than property values falling.

It required the right adjustment of language. *Dreams* had a lilt to it, a sweetness, a longing. *Narcoflix* suggested narcotics, skin flicks, snot. The Realists offered no redeeming social value, but they had one distinct advantage: they sounded real. They were honest. They told us precisely what they were going to do, and they did it. The Realists saw the world as it was, or as they were going to make it. Not that rational, educated Americans were fooled for a minute. They all saw it for the cheap trick that it was and stayed home from the polls in droves.

This Pee-Day, as every Pee-Day, most raw data was flushed. Some random sampling was done and a few exemplars punished with confiscation of property, children, and pets. Their

UniQards were wiped to prevent the malefactors from working, banking, buying, traveling, phoning, entering buildings, or using public toilets ever again. Fear was the best deterrent.

But on this particular Tuesday, as Democracy ground its molars, the fluids from a select cadre of citizens — whose interconnected metadata formed a suspicious pattern — were meticulously tested, the containers fingerprinted, and the data filed in a log of international terrorist conspiracies. A special team of analysts was assigned, with a backup team to analyze the analysts. Of course, all suspects were presumed innocent until accused.

Pepper caught the city bus to work. Crammed to the gills, it sounded like a cement mixer, grinding its gears and wheezing into traffic. She used to take the subway, but eleven bucks now was too much for a trip downtown. Guess it kept the riffraff out. The bus hit a pothole, and passengers caromed off one another. Right now, bus rides were Pepper's only social life.

She scanned the passengers, their noses and bulges, and tried to see them at Jessie's age. What had that walking corpse looked like at age six? What was the point of starting out so sweet and cute? Wasn't that just asking for it? In her mind, a sudden flash of Brian.

Sometimes she did think of moving back to Oklahoma. Safer there, maybe, simpler to know who to be careful with. Or was it? Alec, who raped her in the bathroom? Dad beating Mom every Saturday night, at least till she cut him up? The grim hungry guys at the bar, and the hard-ass bitches like that bleach-blonde coyote named Pepper, who could be just as mean as any man?

No. Not back home.

Two inches from her face, a bundled figure with mittened hands fumbled under a red-tasseled stocking cap to find an ear. "Where is that damned thing?" demanded her querulous gravel voice. "Never can find it when you need it." Mabel McClafferty lurched at Pepper, jerked back as she found her ear and wrung its neck.

"Scratching my ear," said Mabel, fumbling her parcels. Pepper steadied the heap to forestall an avalanche. "I ain't built to carry stuff. My tits are too big. They shove stuff off the top. Even worse in the voting booth, damn touch-screens, I'm voting for one guy up here and some other guy down there. My neighbor down the hall, she don't vote, but she tries to give me a cat. A damn cat. Too many animals in the world. My niece in Chattanooga, she's got five cats and she's divorced."

Music enveloped the bus as the ad-flats flickered. "Here we go," muttered Mabel. The voice of everyone's kindergarten teacher, tender but firm:

> MOMMIES AND DADDIES, REMEMBER:
>
> REALITY IS MORE THAN A PLACE TO HANG
>   YOUR HAT.
>
> IT'S THE LAW.
>
> NO NARCOFLIX.

Pepper gnawed her chapped lips. She couldn't get Jessie's tearful face out of her mind. Her daughter's questions rose up like a flutter of geese, black against the sky, and Pepper's daddy would have answered that flight with a shotgun blast of ridicule. She never talked to strangers, not these days, but sometimes you had to speak the way you had to spit. "My daughter asked me what's wrong with dreams," Pepper muttered.

"No, that's one law I support," Mabel shrugged. "Get rid of the pornography. Pornography all over the place. Don't dare look up zip codes any more, you never know what you're gonna find in there. My husband McClafferty, always reading pornography, and he got hit by a bus. My cousin, she married this guy, he'd go out on the street and expose himself, cause he'd get a big laugh."

Great start to the day, Pepper thought. "You know they did away with the Bible," Mabel continued, "but I like to read it anyway. The clean parts. That other stuff, that's the Philistines, they were like the Communists, kinda smarty-mouth, I can't stand that, so I'm all for the Jews. I mean the ancient ones. These new ones, I had one come in my apartment, little ratty guy with a roach fogger. What does a Jew know about a roach fogger?"

Mabel's eyes were dark pinpoints. Pepper flashed on a wounded hawk she'd tried to nurse till Daddy killed it. Its eyes pierced a world it couldn't fathom, nor could she.

"Only I don't believe in putting drugs in the water. That fluoride, they tried to put toothpaste in our drinking water to make the teeth hard, that's what happened to the kids, their whole head is one big tooth. Not to mention the President." Mabel glanced sharply up to the security vids. "No, nothing wrong with the government. Government's great. President, he's a peach. They oughta write him up in the Bible."

Abruptly, a young man in sunglasses and an army jacket shoved to the front of the bus. "Okay, friends and neighbors, just a minute of your time, freedom of speech, okay? I'm not asking money, I'm asking just for you to think how you put up with these fascists for four years. Whatta we got, we got—"

"Shut up!" the driver yelled.

"We got selling off Yellowstone, we got privatizing the Supreme Court, we got nukes on fucking Albania. Hey, we got the War on Dreams. War on Dreams, we're all going insane, scientific evidence, and now the Realists saying that's not good enough, let's try harder. Well, fuck'em!"

A shout from the rear, "Shut up, faggot!"

"Who are they kidding? Dreams scare little kids! Dreams are fulla sex! Dreams escape reality, blah blah fucking blah! That's bullshit and you know it! Number one campaign donor is the pharmaceuticals! Big Pharma, raking it in from NoNarx! You all know it! You know it!"

The bus pulled to a stop. A burly man in a trench coat grabbed the young troublemaker and dragged him down the steps. "Dreams are my constitutional right!" he screamed. "Dreams are in the Bible! Martin Luther King said 'I have a dream' and nobody asked him for a urine test!"

The bus rumbled on. Pepper didn't look back to see what was happening curbside. That wasn't her business. If you want to go nuts the world will provide lots of opportunity. "They say it's gonna get a lot worse before it gets better," mumbled Mabel, "so it looks like we're making progress."

Pepper turned away. She still saw Jessie's face, scared to death. Amazing what a little terror could accomplish. Images ran in her head: the nutty gal, the hawk, the rising geese, the memory of Brian. Separating dreams from reality had been easier in Oklahoma. She needed to take more NoNarx.

Amazingly, she was five minutes early to work. She shoved her UniQard into the elevator slot, but it didn't work, so she punched in her code and rode the grunting lift to the seventh floor. Now if she could only get past the alcove. Her boss couldn't stand the idea of someone having a couple of minutes free if he could possibly prevent it. She scooted down the hall to the employees' lounge.

Some lounge. No seats, just a high Formica counter where you could stand and a line of vend-its along the wall, emitting their frantic buzz. A little glassed-in closet for one smoker at a time. And a big chintzy painting of a barefoot boy and girl standing by a mountain stream. Didn't that make you feel ducky around mid-afternoon?

Five minutes to catch her breath. She punched her code on the SlurpIt and drew a cup of coffee. When had they started giving machines these childish names? Maybe we want the illusion of control, like we're playing with toys. Maybe we want to be little babies sucking the rubber tit of the SlurpIt.

Pepper sipped her coffee. She tried to remember when you started having to punch your code into everything. Security was the name of the game — the gates to the park, your car, your desk, your apartment, your dishwasher, your vid, the ladies' room. Shutters on the shitters. No big deal, just swipe your UniQard through the slots — only it never worked. You had to punch in your code. Twelve-digit codes, and half the time even that didn't work. Car doors flew open on the freeway, bank accounts were blitzed, people locked out of their houses. Sirens went off all day. They blamed it on terrorists, but Pepper had a hunch that this stuff was built and run by people who loved their job exactly as much as she did.

Two minutes. Don't think about the job. A whole week in Customer Service and name one customer you've served. Granny Bell's market research showed that customers wanted to feel that Granny cares, like back in the Good Old Days. So they create the cool slogan *Granny Cares* and hire a bunch of slaves at sub-shit wages to care. You get the call, let the poor sap take out his rage on you for twelve seconds, then switch him to voicemail. The customers catch on quick and know better than to call. So mostly it's old ladies who just natter on or guys jerking off.

The lounge was a bad idea. Five minutes of thinking was not the best way to start the day. Pepper glanced up to the vid. The sound never worked. The newscasters babbled mutely, trying to tell her things she didn't want to know. It seemed to be the same two people, all hours of the day. Did they write the news a couple of weeks ahead, just make it up, and then send out a crew to make it happen?

"Stop thinking," Pepper said aloud. She crumpled her cup. Of course they make it up.

Tonya Brown was making up the news. Sitting in her cubicle, she jabbed the keyboard, cursing her third cup of coffee. If America ruled the world, she wondered, why did we still have lousy coffee? Those peasants who grew the stuff must grind their dead kids into it. Tonya was in a black mood.

She killed a few minutes hacking out some good-news fluff. A nun had won the Pillsbury Bake-Off, and the President ate a piece of pie. That was actually true, but the rest had come up from Creative, pure slop but harmless. A granny who played the drums in her grandson's band. A family of all-blue Druids. The sole survivor of a crash that killed three hundred people, thanking God for sparing him and fuck the other dudes.

The big story was the election. She hadn't been given clear orders how to slant it, but she could guess, and she wasn't ready for that. Up at five doing her meditation — the last vestige of her old goddess-worship days with Joy — then getting Loki ready for school, she kept thinking this was the day she'd shove it. But as she'd driven to work, the pungent invective in her head was gradually replaced by columns of numbers: the serious bucks she made writing lies.

"What do you do with the news, Mom?" Loki had asked. I process it, she thought. I spice it. I put it through the blender, add sugared bile, and then I wipe its ass.

"I just write the words the newscaster speaks, hon."

"Is it all true? It always sounds fishy." That kid was too smart for his own good.

Ten minutes till deadline. Plug your nose and swallow. Polls open at seven, and we project the results by noon. Deadline at ten a.m., so it goes through channels to the top, half hour for rewrites, channels again, and at noon Harold and Rosalie proclaim—

A STUNNING REPEAT VICTORY FOR THE
REALIST PARTY, FROM THE STATE HOUSES

TO CONGRESS TO THE PRESIDENCY, THE
NATION HAS SPOKEN: IT'S THE REALISTS.

That's as far as she'd got. She was stuck. She gulped her coffee, batted out *Pro Dom Says Fuck Action News!* Her thumb hovered over SEND, then she zipped it.

She had liked sex work, actually, though she knew her BDSM specialty was the white-collar level of an otherwise grim profession. Her tough stubby frame put the guys at ease: she was the girl you never thought of dating in high school, but you'd go over to her place and play ping-pong. Yet, for her white-bread clients, her mocha complexion added edginess.

"Whatta you do for work, Mommy?" Loki had asked when he was about four.

"I help people work out their problems, honey."

"That's good." And in fact the faces who left did look a lot more human than the faces who arrived. But then her spine went wacko, so her journalism degree came in handy, as well as her experience catering to fantasy, and she joined Action News.

She sat in her cubicle, adjusted her back support, and tried to blank her mind. Every day it was harder to get out of bed. This morning she'd walked from the garage through the park. She rarely did that. She didn't like what it did to her to notice trees and then plunge herself into concrete boxes. In the park she passed the old man who wandered the streets looking for Moby Dick, mumbling that he'd kill him when he found him. "You evah read *Moby Dick*?" he asked as Tonya passed him. "You know who I talkn bout, sista, yeh? Fin'im, kill'im! One a these days!"

And she still had to run down to the test booth in the lobby to give her sample. She worried that she hadn't taken enough NoNarx to pass. The stuff made her crazy, like a mad rodent in a cluttered maze, so she would lay off taking it until about three days before the test, then dose herself silly.

For ten years she'd fed her head every drug offered, but since Loki's conception had never done anything stronger than coffee. In fact it was widely known that a generous line of cocaine would mimic the chemistry of NoNarx and breeze you through the test, but she didn't want to hook up again with that old lecher. Instead, she'd taken a triple dose of the dream suppressant and laid wide-eyed all night, seeing herself through thousands of eyes as a flat cut-out paper-doll Tonya, folded on her pillow.

She touched her face again to reassure herself that she wasn't a flat cut-out, imagined the eleven million gallons of urine surging toward Washington, DC, then clicked her terminal. The nasty part of the job was knowing news that nobody else knew. The wire services were still pretty reliable, so the news came in and the editor filtered out "what doesn't work for us." She absorbed the toxins daily, with truth crying to be spoken while the news media dribbled baby food out the side of its maw.

What the hell, the election news was probably true. The only people who'd vote today were the knuckledraggers and the billionaires. The rest saved their calories. However gross the Gross National Product, nobody made a squeak. The Realists' first term was a parade of scandal and atrocity, mitigated only by sheer incompetence. In fact, for much of the voting public, nauseated by government, their main appeal seemed to be as bumblers. In a flurry, Tonya finished the copy, hit SEND, groped for her cane, and hobbled off to the SlurpIt.

Ten minutes later, a memo was on the vid: *See me*. Tonya left her cane in the cubicle, walked down the hallway. In the studio, Harold was perched at the anchor desk. He seemed to pass most of the day there, doing nothing except when they taped the five-minute hourly segments four at a time. Rosalie, on the other hand, spent most of her off-camera time being sick in the ladies' room. She had her own private dressing-room but seemed to prefer barfing with the staff.

Harold looked up from his clipboard, grinned at Tonya. "Tonya, great," he said expansively. "You like the logo?"

On the wall behind him was a large cartoon of Earth smiling and wearing a party hat. "Is that new?" Tonya asked. She never watched the news.

"Election special," he said. "Okay, couple questions on the copy?" She waited. "Okay, yeh, very good writing. Pungent, bouncy, funny but serious. You really catch the style. Rosalie and me, we love you."

"Thanks."

"So I wonder if we can do a little tweaking?"

"Tweaking?"

Harold's grin frayed at the corners. "Well, it's good, it's very good—" *Harold, it's bullshit,* she thought, *we both know it, just tell me what you want changed, no sweat.* "Well," he fumbled for words, "the stunning victory stuff is great, very up-beat, and so on, but then Rosalie says—

"Harold, there must be lots of celebrating in Reality Land," Tonya quoted. She had an eidetic memory for the drivel she wrote. "What's wrong with it?"

"Well," Harold floundered, "it's kind of . . . objective."

"Objective? It's the news."

"Well, it sounds like we don't like it. *There must be lots of celebrating.* That sounds like we're not celebrating."

"Are we?"

Harold hated confrontation. He saw his role as a mediator between grim reality and the billion sick souls who watched him convert the world's horror into nutritious entertainment. It was a calling, like the priesthood but better paid. And Tonya made him nervous. Her slanted black eyes, light-brown skin, and sturdy fireplug physique were of some indefinable ethnicity. He approved of ethnic people, of course, but preferred to approve from a distance.

He pressed on. "Tonya, look," refreshing his grin, "it's an amazing saga. It's a new American Revolution. First time, everybody said it's a fluke, against all odds, candidates from the zoo. Whole campaign says *Get Real,* but it's totally scripted. So everybody stays home except the crackpots, and they win! How could they win? They win!"

"Are you asking me or telling me?"

"So they stumble through four years, piss off everybody, prove that not only are they fascists, they're not even efficient fascists, and here they hit another bases-loaded home run."

"But how do we know that, Harold? It's ten-thirty in the morning."

"Because that's the story," he said. Tonya smirked, or at least to Harold it looked like a smirk. "So we want to hear the announcer get excited, okay?"

She nodded too enthusiastically, Harold thought. "Okay, more the sports angle," she said perkily. "I'll work on it. We're tight on time. Think sports."

Was she mocking him? No, she seemed understanding. She really was very talented. And strangely attractive.

"Great," he sighed. "And Tonya, look. Third line. *Lowest voter turn-out in history.* Let's take that out. That's not relevant. I mean, Tonya, I mean, look— You know they monitor this. I mean, these guys are vicious. It's my face out there."

Tonya stood for a moment. "So let's see," she said quietly, "basically you're saying lie and kiss ass and totally compromise our journalistic integrity."

"You got it!" He smiled with relief and walked away.

Mabel McClafferty climbed the stairs to the third-floor office of Med-OK to give her sample. The elevator hadn't worked for months, but that cut down the HMO's patient load. If you had trouble climbing those three flights, you could either decide to feel better or die: freedom of choice. She trudged down the hallway to the bright pink door with the vibrant blue letters OK.

That was supposed to make you feel okay. Life expectancy was going down fast, with people starving to death or getting shot, and doctors spending about ninety seconds with patients and forty minutes filling out forms. Since faith healing and placebos were getting better results than doctors, it only made sense to bring faith-based placebos into Med-OK, which they called a public/private initiative: the public sector put up the bucks, the private sector took'em.

Around the office were little tracts about Sin, Hell, and Florida timeshares, but Mabel picked up a *People Magazine* with a spread of President Pert shaking hands with movie stars and crippled children of all races and creeds. Everybody had nice hair-dos. Great thing about this country, Mabel thought, we've got the hair-dos. Her name was called, she took her plastic cup, went into the booth, returned to the desk, and handed it to the nurse. The nurse asked her how she felt. "Oh, I feel okay," said Mabel. You didn't dare feel anything else.

Eddie Grabowski used a city facility. They processed people pretty fast, though you took your chances with being mislabeled by minimum-wage employees who'd dropped out of school before they'd got all the way through the alphabet. He knew half a dozen ways to fake out the test, but they weren't foolproof, and it wasn't worth the risk. He didn't really mind the NoNarx. It gave a purple color shift to his dreams and added a bit of reverb, which was kinda sexy.

Pepper McBride welcomed the monthly tests for the extra ten-minute break. Her supervisor ordered them to hurry, but she could trot to the bathroom, drop the sealed cup in the rack, stop at the lounge for coffee, joking with the other women, and zoom to her station with precisely five seconds to spare. She loved the look on his face.

Late afternoon, Tonya stopped by the water cooler, popped a couple of Prozacs, one of those old traditional remedies her grandma swore by. Something had to give. The stats were seeping out slowly, like toddlers emerging from death camps, on the number of psychoses the suppressants were causing, though the President maintained that people were just going nuts because they felt like it. Regulatory testing by the drug companies themselves — they being the most qualified — confirmed this conclusion but suggested stricter enforcement plus new additives to the basic dosage: an anti-psychotic, a relaxant, a stimulant, an anti-hypertensive, and something for body odor. In the *Washington Post*, it was reported back among the classifieds.

She thought of the trash science fiction she'd read as a teenager, all the technological wonders of the future. Instead, we had nine lanes of the Beltway moving like cement through the guts of a whale. We had corporations buying green-energy patents for the purpose of shelving them. We had toxins spewing from Emission Decontrol to keep us Number One. We had wars to provide employment for our underclass while copping the last dribbles of petrol for the good ol' USA. And we had millions of livid consumers who had just voted to keep it all the same.

This is like from another planet, she thought. All afternoon it ran in her head. *Another planet. . . Another planet. . .*

Chapter 4
Another Planet

Recess. Loki leaned against the scraggly catalpa tree at the edge of the asphalt and watched the other kids play. It was all elephant color — the sky, the playground, the faces — but the tree still had a little green. He liked its broad leaves and its long seedpods. Artie said you could smoke them like cigars and that's how Artie's big brother got girls to take their clothes off. Loki didn't follow the logic.

Sometimes Artie played with him, but now Dennis was back. Dennis was out of school a lot. His father beat up his mother, then she'd beat up Dennis and Dennis would be out of school. But Dennis was back, and Loki was just the retard.

It was a bad day. Mom was cranky and gave him a peanut butter jelly sandwich. She thought it was nutritious or something. Then Mrs. Clemson started reading one of the Dr. Doolittle books for story time, and he liked those old books, but he'd read them all before he was three. That was the only good thing about being retarded: they knew you couldn't do the things the other kids could, so they didn't hold you back.

Then Artie had punched him in the kidney to entertain Dennis and called him "Harry Potter." Loki hated Harry Potter. Harry Potter did all these magical things, and by the time Loki got to be the same age everything would already have been done by Harry Potter. And Harry Potter wasn't even real.

Tracing his finger down the tree's smooth bark, he started playing Another Planet. "Another planet, another planet. . ." he mumbled. Then, looking through the chain-link fence across the drive to the high school, he saw something was happening. Police cars had pulled up in the driveway, but nobody was in a hurry, so it must be just a suicide. He tried to imagine how it would feel to die but could only envision his nose falling off. Mrs. Clemson said people killed themselves because they were crazy, but that wasn't the same as being retarded so he shouldn't worry. He touched his nose, and it sobbed.

No. It wasn't his nose. He turned and saw a little girl in a pink cap. She'd fallen on the asphalt.

"What happened?" he called out.

"I fell," she sobbed.

"I thought you were my nose," he said.

She looked at him and sniffled. Loki glanced around to make sure nobody saw him talking to a little kid. He didn't mind being teased, but Dennis and Artie could never think of anything clever to say, so he'd be embarrassed for them and that was boring. He walked over to her as she brushed her knee.

"What's your name?" he asked. What else could he say?

"Jessie."

"I'm Loki."

"What kind of a name is that?"

"Mine." Loki rubbed his nose. "I was reading a book about synchronistic illusion, which is this idea that things that happen simultaneously seem connected, like when I touched my nose. Because you think they are, but they're not, although there is a connection except that it's backwards from the way we think it goes. Cause and effect are reversed. Except that I can't follow the mathematics because I'm retarded. Except you're supposed to call me challenged, which means retarded."

"You talk funny."

"Well that's why."

They stood silent. "Why?" Jessie said at last. Loki looked toward the high school. The police cars were still there.

"I'm in third grade, Mrs. Clemson's class, so they give you a test that tells what's wrong with everybody. So they found out I'm retarded because I can't learn stuff that's wrong. Although maybe I'm retarded because I took the test. So I can't follow what Mrs. Clemson teaches, so I get to bring my own books to school, and I can't read the right way but. . ." He waited for her to say something. "I read backwards," he explained.

Jessie raised her eyes. "I saw you before. At the park."

"My mom takes me to the park," he said. He walked back to the tree, depressed. Why had he started talking? She didn't understand a word of it. After a moment she followed.

"You like to play games?" he asked, to be polite.

"In class we play soldiers and office and restaurant," she reported listlessly. "It teaches us stuff."

"How about turning into animals?" He'd never asked anybody that before.

"Animals aren't real, except dogs and cats. They only let us play real stuff. Cause if you pretend you have to sit in the Bad Girl's Seat. I had to once."

Surprise. She could talk. Her blue eyes were fixed on his. He wondered if he could tell her things. When you grew up and fell in love, then you told each other everything. He wasn't sure it was okay to do that when you were kids, but her eyes were open to him.

"I don't mean pretend to be animals," he said, "I mean really be animals. I do it but Mom doesn't know."

"It's bad if she doesn't know it."

He didn't want to frighten those eyes away. "Well," he ventured, "you want to play trees?"

"How?"

"Be a tree."

He struck a pose, arms outstretched. He wished he hadn't said it. The tree game scared him. After a few seconds he'd begin to feel hot spasms shooting down his legs rootward and out his arms blossomwise, and he'd stop. But now Jessie's wide eyes held him, and he felt the first stirrings of roots.

A siren whined. He broke free and staggered to regain his balance. At the high school, another squad car pulled into the driveway. A boy was being walked between two portly policemen out to a car. He had little black rabbit eyes, and somehow Loki knew his name was Billy and what he'd done.

"What's the matter?" Jessie asked.

"Nothing," he said. "They had a spelling contest, and he won a trip to Disney World."

"No he didn't. You told a lie."

No one had ever said that. At school they didn't think he was smart enough to lie, and at home he could tell his mother anything and she'd just say, "Whatever." But this tiny pink girl had nailed him.

"No, well, I think his name's Billy, and he hurt somebody," he mumbled. "It was a girl in his class, and she sat in front of him, and he kinda went crazy. I don't know if that's true or not, but— I saw a movie once where you could stop stuff by going back in time. It was at my babysitter's. It was scary."

"Loki?" Jessie asked.

"What?"

"What if we go back to before he hurt the girl and tell him not to?"

"We can't, because that's the past and this is the present. And lots of stuff happened to get us from there to here. Like if I drop my jelly toast on the rug it makes a stain, but before that there was jelly and toasting the toast and the people who wove the rug, but then Mom comes in and sees the rug and I'm definitely in the present."

He watched Jessie as she thought about it. Was she too young to be entrusted with the secrets of the universe? It was lonely sometimes, knowing the secrets of the universe and not having anyone to tell. Of course he didn't know any secrets for sure. He'd read all the science fiction in the school library, plus Mom's mystical stuff, mostly while Mrs. Clemson was telling lies about history. He didn't blame her for that. He knew she had to tell lies, that was her job, and grownups needed jobs. So he didn't know if he was right, but he thought so.

He knew about wormholes. You're in one space-time and you go through a black hole and you're in another space-time. You don't need rocket ships. It's like when he and Mom visited New York, where there were three subway lines. You could walk through a tunnel and transfer from one to another. So maybe you could go forward or backward in time if you just had the subway map. Only what would happen if you jumped to the other tracks and there was a train coming right at you? He'd read a story about that. The hero wound up in another space-time with mice running around inside him. So you can't just walk into another universe and bring along your own physics. Land there, you might be somebody's ham sandwich for lunch.

He started to explain why they couldn't go back in time, but Jessie looked at him the way she might look at a kitten playing with its tail. Then he saw — human behavior confused him sometimes — that she just didn't want to be told no.

"Okay, so here's one way we could do it, okay?" She scowled at him, then softened. "So like I can't read forwards, I have to read backwards. But you can't understand it backwards. So I read a sentence, memorize the syllables, then I've made up a code for how the last syllable goes to the front, so I see it in my mind and I move it there, then I say it back to myself backwards and I understand it. Get it?"

She looked intrigued.

"So if we could like take a core sample from where we are, like in geology, down through all the layers and up through the alternate space-times, and past and future and sideways, okay? And then we locate a universe where something good happens, say if your mom might give you something, like a—"

"A baby brother."

"Okay, baby brother. So you've got the butterfly effect, where there's just a butterfly in China, but his wing flutter makes something happen, and this chain of events, and either some fat guy drops dead in Alaska or you get a baby brother."

"Butterflies don't make babies."

"Indirectly, okay? Feed this in and the computer figures it backwards, all the different ways it could have got from there to here. But it's a really big computer, say a CM, that's a carbon molecule computer, but the size of the Milky Way, all the matter in a whole galaxy linked up, and it figures all probabilities of everything you might do and shoots out the answer, so you ask your mom to take you to see the dinosaurs and pretty soon you've got a baby brother."

Jessie looked at him. "We already saw the dinosaurs."

She was honest. Loki liked that. "Well," he said, "that's one idea."

As it happened, the nearest wormhole was in a standpipe three feet away, accessing a space-time that had already put Loki's hypothesis into practice. "I saw a movie with little green men," Jessie said, trying to make Loki feel better.

And as it happened, that adjacent wormhole opened directly into the ninth subquantum string dimension of the Planet Gruk2BIC, whose inhabitants were the original Little Green Men. And every third Tuesday, one of them, Johnny by name, sent out messages to Planet Earth, though no one on Planet Earth could hear them. Not yet.

ONK ONK. We are Little Green Men. I say hello. I am Johnny. Remember me. I am green and little. I title me Secretary of Killing in Planet Gruk2BIC, hello. I tell it ask no why.

Tell works this doohicky here? This happens now. We live inside our planet wow. Once we were smart and sane. Now computers are smart and sane and we are Little Green Men.

I waddle tell Boss all stuff. Boss is busy picking his nose. Boss will kill me when he likes to. He looks up his red eyes. Maybe today I die.

RUCKFRUMUCK, he says.

EXEPOTEET, I tell him truth.

He calls to get a girl for sex at lunch. I do not have sex at lunch. I have sex at breakfast on my wife. Odd but good with coffee. He laughs at my joke. Maybe he does not kill me. Boss cannot get right girl. It is old girl with twenty years. He likes a bitty girl. He screams. Maybe today I die.

Hello to you out there. Hear me? I am saying English.

We go to big room. We put hands together and shake and slap our face. We mean business, bub. The Boss kills one of us now but he does not do it but the killers do. We hop up and down when they do. We not know why we do. We know we are insane.

Please understanding on Planet Earth. We know we are insane. Some day maybe we kill you. Some day Boss kill me. The cookie crumbles.

This is the facts, ma'am. Little Green Men rule fifty-six galaxies bunch. We seek intelligent life. Finding none is terror. We must defend us. We make Biloxi3. Big whole galaxy computer. Talk about big.

We wait for Boss. He under table got a girl. She is loud. We laugh ho ho. Boss crawls out wipes off. But he does not do it but the wipers do. I could kill him if I could. We are insane we know. You are nice guys I bet.

I tell on computer Biloxi3. It is great big. Works hard the butterfly in China. We use your Planet Earth as test. We do storm in Kansas. We do snail crawl days in spiral but squash in street. We made President do sex, wow wow. Your whales come out of water. Stuff costs chunk but we do not pay but the taxpayers do. You clap my English here? We were smart once but now big dumb. Brain does hardly not almost work. I am bad to tell you I am Johnny, remember me. Maybe Boss not kill me but cut off pieces. But he does not do it but the cutters do. We are royally screwed.

Now Boss is wiped I make report. Goodbye if they kill me. You my kind of people Planet Earth when the cookie crumbles. RICKIMORFT, I say. You clap my English here:

WE ARE DANGER BIG.

HAPPY ARE KILLERS, CUTTERS, WIPERS AND
    BOSS. OTHERS STARVE BUT IF WE KILL
    THEM NO MORE GIRLS AND FOOD.

WE ARE UP SHIT CREEK, AN EARTH JOKE.

All at table wave arms and scream at joke of shit creek. Boss is not killing me yet. We are so dumb I start to weep which I do not. BOOLYBOOLYGEEK, I say.

THE ANSWER I FOUND IT, BOYS.

ON PLANET EARTH ARE ENERGY CAPTURE
    PANELS. THESE ARE THE VID TV AND TUBE.
    HUMANS WATCH THE VID. IT SAYS BE HAPPY
    THEY HAPPY. IT SAYS BE MAD THEY MAD.

IT IS FUCKIN HOT STUFF SHERLOCK, AN EARTH
    JOKE.

They scream and flap. The Boss gets it. Vid will might make us happy. We get a bunch vids for Gruk2BIC. Boss is pink to flap. We are all pink. They bring in girls and food. I guess I will have some. Boss get first pick, I get next. Hide eyes.

We all wipe off or the wipers do. I say NUP to Boss. It is thank you Boss that you not kill me. FIC, he says. We are short of hands. This is joke I scream. Thanks Boss. Thanks Johnny.

I am Johnny. Remember me. I am green and little. Tell do you hear? Tell works this doohicky here? This what happens now. Remember I am Johnny. Remember even some more. I love you Earth I do.

The whistle ended recess. Jessie gave a faint wave toward Loki and ran across the asphalt to the little kids' side. Loki watched her go. "Maybe I'll see you at the park," he whispered, but she probably didn't hear.

He turned and slouched toward the line for Mrs. Clemson's class. First they'd have to go to the nurse's office for Pee-Day. Mrs. Clemson walked at the end of the line, and the class tried not to look at Mrs. Clemson. They couldn't bear to imagine Mrs. Clemson doing it.

And then this afternoon they'd watch the vid about great Americans drinking Coca-Cola, and tomorrow the news about Billy would be all over the place, and the school counselor would give a lecture that there was no excuse for sticking a pencil four inches into the carotid artery of the girl in front of you, and if you ever felt like doing that you should ask the counselor for a pill. Mom said that when she was young kids got tattoos, now they kill people. Can't stop progress, said Mom. Loki thought she was joking but he wasn't sure.

The whistle blew again. Loki's mind was jumbled with thrusting roots, with wormholes, with Billy's eyes, and then it all went blank and he saw only Jessie, Jessie, Jessie. *Butterflies don't make babies.* Wow.

Chapter 5
Granny Cares

Tuesday. He might have known. Eddie had the firm conviction that the most bizarre life incidents happened on Tuesdays, and not just urine tests. He had come up with that idea as a quirky opener for picking up women, but gradually he'd started to believe it.

The day had been weird from the start. He'd spent the day helping some jerk finish building a recording studio for the Pizzle Wartz, who'd just signed a recording contract with Fox/Exxon. State-of-the-art: cryosonic pads at $1,100 a square foot, vitrohelix resonance baffles, radiant sourcing. Then they'd be recording entirely onto chips, never through a mike, and for vocals they'd clone Al Jolson or Eleanor Roosevelt. So why did they need a recording studio? For the image.

Coming back to his apartment, he noticed flags all up and down the block. Must be a war on, he thought. Eddie had stopped checking the news two years ago, mostly. He tried not to glance at the headlines or watch the vid. At the first whiff of politics he'd cut off a conversation, even with a blonde. It took real work to stay ignorant, and even so, a few atrocities got past his guard. Overall he felt better, but under all there was some unscratchable itch.

He shuffled through the weekly mail delivery. Why did they even bother with mail anymore? So that during elections you could get ten glossy turds a day? So they could misdeliver your bills and charge penalty fees? Phone bill. Open it.

"Shit!"

This was the fourth billing for August. He'd already paid it. He'd called to straighten it out, and he'd been assured that it was just an error because he'd moved and that now it was taken care of. He asked the name of the clerk to whom he spoke on the phone. Jeremy. "Thanks, Jeremy." The second billing he just ignored, assuming that the computer had already passed the point of inevitability and had spewed his billing into the mail before Jeremy had rushed to stop it, a valiant goalie hurling himself across the mailroom. When the Final Notice arrived,

Eddie called Customer Service once again. This time he spoke with Susan. He gave her the numbers and codes she asked for, including blood type and mother's maiden name, and received fulsome assurances. He thanked Susan, asked her to convey his best wishes to Jeremy, hung up, his faith restored.

Now he stared at the bill. Zero balance, but attached was a check for $8,225.40. No explanation. The check was made payable to Edie Grabots. He considered his options. He thought about calling a lawyer to ask whether he could legally cash a check to which he had no claim and with his name misspelled. Could he charge Granny Bell a consultant's fee for time spent straightening out their affairs? Could he just ignore the check without risking that the IRS would drone-strike him for unreported income?

He decided to call Customer Service and ask for Susan. She'd been sweet and more than a little bit sexy. But the androgynous creature who answered wasn't sweet or funny or the least bit fuckable. It didn't know a Susan. It had a headache, too much caffeine, and only six years to go before retirement. It asked for his retro number. Eddie didn't know his retro number or what the hell that was. He asked for Jeremy. He was asked for Jeremy's transpo number. He had not a clue. The thin raspy voice that might have been male or female — fat chance anyone cared — snarled that there were lots of Susans and Jeremys, that this was a company, after all, not a barber shop, and those weren't their names anyway, because who'd give their name to a total stranger?

Eddie said, as calmly as possible, that he himself had done just that. And that he was actually trying to give money back to the company to the tune of $8,225.40, but that he didn't want to send it back unless he had some assurance that this could be straightened out. "I mean, what if I send it back, and then you discover you'd sent it to me and ask me to send it back, but I'd already sent it back?"

"I'm sorry," the voice rasped, "but we simply provide a public service. We don't have control over what we do." It was so perfectly phrased that it ran in his head for days.

Eddie was stymied. Then suddenly he knew precisely what to do. Hang up. He hung up. As the creature said, it's a company. Call back, you'll get someone entirely new, with a totally different perspective on reality. They train them in nonlinear response. Company policy is an organic Dionysian entity, not some stuffy librarian. He redialed. In Pepper McBride's cubicle, the light throbbed.

"Pepper, get on Five," her supervisor bleated.

"Mr. Henry, I'm answering a call."

"Please get on Five."

"I am on Five."

"Now!"

She punched RECEIVE. From another cubicle she heard old Francine.

> SIR, WE UNDERSTAND YOUR CONCERN. I'M
> TRANSFERRING YOU TO OUR SUICIDE LINE.
> THANKS FOR CALLING.

Carry on. "Hello, Granny Bell, we care. This is Pepper. How may I help you?"

"Like who am I talking to?"

Young knucklehead. Take a breath. These guys are too much like the pricks she grew up with. Except that in Oklahoma you could depend on his hard-on.

"Hello, this is Pepper. How may I help you?" she repeated, hearing the ice creep into her voice.

"That ain't your real name."

"Matter of fact it is. Do you have a problem?"

"Well yeh, why you think I call? Is this a human?"

"Yes sir, I'm not a machine till about ten a.m." Two more lines were blinking. Get rid of this guy. One minute a call is the quota. From another cubicle she heard Jeremy. Jeremy was very sweet but threw Pepsi cans at the wall.

> WE UNDERSTAND YOUR CONCERN, MA'AM. I
> WOULD DO THAT IF IT WERE PHYSICALLY
> POSSIBLE.

"You care, okay, Granny," the guy continued. "Yeh, so what happened, I paid my bill, that was last August, and then next month I get the same bill. But I already paid it."

"Yes sir, that does happen. Could I have your name?"

"Eddie! So I call up you guys and you fix it, sure. You bill me again, with interest!"

"Sir, could you give me your customer number, please?" Finish this guy off.

"Zero! Look, I called three times, three different people plus machines. And now, surprise: you send me a refund. Eight thousand bucks. If I tried to cash that, they'd fry my butt."

Four lines were lit, and Mr. Henry was hovering. "Eddie, listen, I think if you send it back—"

"Look, I wanta bring it down to your office and—"

"Eddie, sorry, you can't do that. We're national. We're not located anywhere. Could I transfer you to Voice Mail?"

"Who answers that?"

"Nobody."

Susan's voice leaked through the divider. Susan was on heavy meds and barely fit her cubicle.

> YES SIR, MICROWAVES MAY CAUSE BRAIN
> TUMORS, BUT VERY TINY ONES, AND WE DO
> SUPPORT THE SIERRA CLUB.

Eddie was breathing heavily. "Okay, so lemme talk to your supervisor."

"He doesn't talk, he barks." Better change tactics. "Look, Eddie, I'm backed up five calls, and he's a total you-know-what, and I really need this job, okay?" Damsel in distress, it sometimes works.

"Look," Eddie went on, "if I send it they'll screw it up again. So I'm gonna come down, give you this check, and you're gonna give me a receipt that says Eddie Grabowski paid his phone bill."

No no no. She punched a button, checked the screen. "Where are you? DC Northwest? Look, it's just by accident I'm talking to you in DC. We handle calls from Atlanta to Boston. My only function is to sit here and tell you that Granny cares!" She was shouting. Seven lights blinking, Mr. Henry panting through pinched nostrils. "Sorry, Eddie, it's been a long day."

"It's 9:15 in the morning."

"Right."

"Then is there anybody down there that's smarter than you?"

That was it. Pepper lost it. She stood up, muscles tensed to grab the ponderous drunk. "Listen, shithead! Put your pecker back in your pocket before I toss the little squirt in the blender! I'm Room 1342 in the Hanreddy Building, 23rd and Vermont. Come on down and kiss my ass!"

She punched GONE, heard a gasp, turned around. Mr. Henry stared at her, red-faced, his hand tangled in his necktie, strangling himself. She glared at him. "Don't say a word. I used to be a bartender. There comes a point."

Pepper turned away, adjusted her headset. She had to remember that with all she'd been through she could handle anything. Skinny bleached blondes had the element of surprise. She punched RECEIVE. "Hello, Granny Bell. We care."

Pepper expected at least a demerit from Mr. Henry if not dismissal, but he looked at her now with a strange respect. Mid-morning she got up to go to the ladies' room, and he gave her a playful wave and contorted his face into what might be his virgin attempt at a smile.

After her fifteen-minute lunch hour, she was back in her cubicle, listening to a sweet old man ramble about hidden charges while obviously trying to jerk off. Which was fine if he didn't take more than a minute. She had a weekly bet with Jeremy on who'd get the most sex calls. Finally she had to cut it short.

"Sorry, sir, only one to a customer. Bye-bye."

Someone was standing outside her cubicle. She looked up. Repairman or something? He looked at her as if he knew her. Bright hazel eyes, kinda bloodshot, deep-set in an angular face that hadn't seen a razor for a week. Coppery cast to the stubble, two shades lighter than his shaggy hair.

"Hi, I'm Eddie Grabowski. I talked to you before on the phone."

Pepper gaped at him. Two lines lit up. "Scuse me," she mumbled, punched RECEIVE. "Hello, this is Granny— I mean Granny cares—" Her eyes were fixed on Eddie. His T-shirt said BAD VIBES. "Yes ma'am, live personal service just like in the good old days, so I'm switching you to Voice Mail." The guy was rocking back and forth, long thighs in old chinos, scuffed desert boots, like he was hearing some music in his head.

"How'd they let you in?"

"I showed 'em a work order, set-up for a Squid Titties concert. That's a band. Whatta they know?"

He didn't look that dangerous, but you never knew. Some kind of tool belt. Could be a bomb. Be cool for Jessie's sake. She punched a button.

Eddie pulled out a stuffed envelope. "So this is the bills and my receipts—"

Pepper forced herself to hold her gaze directly into his hazel eyes as she spoke with dead calm into the mouthpiece. Speak very slow, baby, like when the Mexican kid stuck a gun in your face at the Seven-Eleven. You did it right then: he's dead and you're alive. "Security, there's an unauthorized man at my cubicle. Would you send somebody up right away?"

"Listen to me. Now here's the check I got—"

Pepper stiffened. Security was on Voice Mail. The guy was saying something about his phone bill. Maybe he was just here about his phone bill.

"Look, Eddie," Pepper said, "this is not the place for dealing with this."

"Where's the place?"

"Guess!" She heard the knife edge in her voice and wished she hadn't said it.

Eddie grinned. "Did you ever tend bar?" How'd he know that?

Fourteen lights were lit. Granny Bell cared, but not all that much. "Look," Pepper offered, "I can direct you to Accounting, Atlanta, Georgia, you want the street address?" Eddie didn't reply. He stood there grinning, playing with the snap ring of his keys, holding her eyes just that extra moment. Pepper dropped her gaze. "Okay, I'll try to do something on my break. It gets sent to Winnipeg or Bangladesh maybe. Thanks for letting us be of service. Granny cares. Eddie, I've got a bunch of calls—"

"Yeh, I'm sorry—"

"They said it's always like this after Election Day. People call to complain because nobody listens." She heard herself nattering on.

"Election?" He didn't seem to understand the word. "Oh yeh, I remember. Look, I'm sorry, I was working all night, short concert, but then we had to strike and set up for the Rumbling Slugs. Who's the picture?" He pointed at her desk.

"My daughter. Okay, receipt for the check—"

"I do audio," he said. "Lotta bands, recordings, parties, conventions."

Pepper glanced at the blinking lights. "Scuse me, does this relate to me?"

"I'd like for it to," Eddie shrugged. "I mean, could I like buy you a beer or something after work, to say thanks? You know, I got a lot of credentials as an audio engineer, but frankly I tend to get fired a lot, same thing with relationships, although there was one for quite a while, but we split up, which was a trip—"

Her eyes fell to his sharp hipbones and his stubby fingers playing with keys. "Sorry, Eddie, I've got a little girl to take care of, so that pretty much takes all my energy. It's really hard for me to go out and stuff. Thanks anyway."

Eddie stared at the floor. "Friend of mine," he mused, "we were working in a machine shop, he's trying to score with this girl in the office. So one day some guy's not looking and chops off a finger. So Jerry, my friend, picks up the finger, brings it into the office, lays it on her desk. Now they're married."

That broke the spell. This guy was a joker. Never trust a joker: either they'll slap you around or they'll hock the silverware. Stay celibate and learn to like it. "Well, so," Pepper muttered, "when you find a loose finger, try me."

Eddie rocked on his heels. "Right. Cool. Loose finger. Who knows?" He started to walk away.

"Interesting T-shirt," Pepper mumbled. Suddenly she longed to draw him back, to sink her nails into those trim muscular buttocks disappearing forever to the west.

Mr. Henry's face appeared over the divider like a pink balloon. "Pepper, I'm sorry," he whined, "you know you're not allowed visitors. I'm going to have to write you up. I'm sorry."

That's fine, sir. We do what we must. When he brings me the chopped-off finger I'll pass it right along, up yours. She watched her bank of lights flashing in perfect rhythm: *Help me! Help me! Help me!*

At dinner, Jessie tried to tell her about a new friend at school and a boy who did a bad thing, but Pepper was curt. She was worried about Jessie's after-school care. Mrs. Day's daughter, an eighth-grader, took her home, and Mrs. Day kept her till Pepper picked her up. But the errant Mr. Day was back home, stewed, and Pepper did not want Jessie in a drunk tank. If she could only find a night babysitter, she could go back to the bartending job she'd left two weeks ago. That was safer than offices, where people came in to make their complaints with more expensive weaponry.

Another day, another dollar. She knew that tomorrow on the bus she'd try to remember what had happened today and she'd draw a total blank. What had she packed for Jessie's lunch? Had she read her a story? If anything, she'd probably see only the headline she'd read at the newsstand:

MOMMY KILLS DADDY, THEN FIXES SUPPER.

What was that guy's name, with the cute butt in the chinos? Eddie, his name was. That guy Eddie had a killer grin.

Chapter 6
Balloon Help

Harold and Rosalie sat at the Action Desk awaiting their cue. Patting his hair, Harold caught himself patting his hair. Stop patting your hair, he admonished himself, it looks faggy. He remembered the days when fags were in, but now they were out. He'd always been broadminded, but in the last few years he'd begun allowing himself to use the word *fag*, just for the fun of it.

He glanced at Rosalie. Could they record the day's last segment before she broke apart? Around her eyes the cake makeup was starting to crack, and underneath he saw the drugged face, like a haunted weasel — Harold had tried to be a poet once.

One minute. He patted his hair. Rosalie stiffened and cranked up her smile. She could still manage to rev up the radiance on cue. He'd married her for her smile, he reflected, even though he'd known it was fake — a savage cartoonist's slash across the face. But it showed she was a pro.

Thirty seconds. Harold saw her sag, and a sudden bloat came into her cheeks. He patted his hair. Yesterday she'd held up production, running to the can three times. She'd managed to get through the shoot heavily sedated, and he could see in her eyes that she had no idea what she was reading. "Look at the camera!" he'd hissed. "Smile!" and she did.

Fifteen. Maybe it was the news that did it, that daily ingestion of toxic sludge. They were pros, Harold and Rosalie, and they'd been a team for twenty-five years, working up from the local traffic report to become the top-rated Beloved Couple in the nation. In fact they'd pioneered the concept of Beloved Couple on the evening news. Now every two-bit station in the sticks had its own Beloved Couple telling you the day's betrayals, but it was okay because you could see with your own eyes that, through it all, they loved each other. Lies to live by.

Harold and Rosalie knew that every Beloved Couple in America wanted to be the next Harold and Rosalie as soon as they lost their grip. Yet even as Rosalie dazzled with her smile and Harold charmed with his Action Wit, millions of viewers yearned to know if he beat her, if they were divorcing, if they held sex parties with children. They were both aware that they were also the most Hated Couple in America because of their immunity to the ravaging plagues they reported. No wonder Rosalie screamed in her sleep.

"Does this coffee taste funny?" Rosalie asked. The floor manager signaled GO, and her smile skidded into place.

TOP OF THE HOUR, ROSALIE. WHAT'S NEW?

HERE'S ONE, HAROLD. AT THE NATIONAL
ARCHIVES A TEMP WORKER HAS
BEEN ARRESTED FOR DOWNLOADING
PORNOGRAPHY. J.G. BABCOCK CLAIMS
THAT HE ACCIDENTALLY STUMBLED INTO
THE TOP-SECRET FILES OF HOMELAND
SECURITY. DHS IS INVESTIGATING.

Harold said something witty about porn in high places, and the nation chuckled.

J. G. Babcock sat at the dinner table, eating a light salad and reading *The History of Mauritania*. He looked across at his sister. She hadn't touched her food.

"Sis, it wasn't my fault. I know, everything's my fault. Life is my fault. And I have to be honest with you: I wasn't paying total attention to the job. I had this very interesting book on the history of Eighteenth Century porcelain. The Chinese influence on European culture was superficial, but superficialities compounded can be devastating." She did not reply.

"In any case, I was indeed actually working, developing a fascinating database on the demographics of Congressional districts before the Civil War. But I had this very old computer that didn't even talk. Not that I enjoy talking computers, I find it rather intimidating, actually. They always sound much too friendly." No response.

"But this one had that old system of Balloon Help. You move the cursor and a little balloon pops up to help you. And it just comes on, any time. You point to a file and it says THIS IS A FILE. You turn it off, then it comes back on. It's like if you were walking down the street, somebody comes up, says, 'This is a street you are walking down.' Do I need to be apprised of this startling revelation?"

Babcock munched his salad and turned page 128 of *Mauritania*. His sister Allegra was too insulated, too unworldly, to understand. It was nice of her, though, to allow him to multitask at dinner. She had a loving nature, but she was so very silent about it.

"So the Balloon Help popped on, and I tried to turn it off. There's a little pull-down menu, you pull it down and it says BALLOON HELP OFF and you turn it off, and it flashes BALLOON HELP ON. And it's popping up these inane messages, and I'm getting frantic, and finally I— Sis, you know I'm not a violent person. Am I really? The only time I ever had a fight as a kid was with Spud, and he hit me once and I went down and stayed down. This is not your major Action Hero." He picked a leaf of arugula off page 130.

"But I got very upset with Balloon Help, and I did a really silly thing, sitting in my little cubicle. I just suddenly smashed my fist on the keyboard. Bam. And for a moment, I have to admit, it felt really good."

His sister said nothing. Babcock flashed her a smile. His mother had told him long ago that his smile was irresistible. In fact the entire world had resisted it, so he didn't rely on it much. Still, his round chipmunk face, his twinkling eyes, his quizzical voice, his bald spot — those must count for something.

"So when I smashed the keyboard, the computer crashed, rebooted, and logged me into this other world. I guess maybe my boss's server was bugged, and the bug was from DHS, and it did a backflip, and I don't know what they do at DHS but— You know, I like that dress, Sis. I wish Mom and Dad were here, don't you?"

Babcock paused, munched his salad. He loved garbanzos and kidney beans. The one satisfaction of being an adult was that he could make salads with copious garbanzos and kidney beans.

"And so suddenly it reboots, and I have these strange images. Sis, I mean, I can't really say, but there are very fat men who are, how shall I say, seeming to be at the mercy of small children with, um, toys in their hands. This was not of my choosing."

He picked up the last garbanzo in his fingers and ate it. Life could be beautiful when it wanted to be. Sis was silent, but he knew her so well.

"And so this alarm goes off, these big guys come crashing in and put me in handcuffs, and on the screen the Balloon Help is flashing a Balloon Help saying that Balloon Help has been disabled."

He munched, turned the page. He knew it was somewhat disrespectful to read at the table, but Mauritania had its claim to attention, with the white Moors and the black Moors, the exploitation of its iron reserves, its struggle to increase rice production and cope with irregularity in the flow of the cranky Senegal River — so many absorbing complications.

"So I mean, Sis, I think our culture is a lot more enigmatic than we imagine. They arrested me, I had my book along, and they took that. They asked if it was a terrorist book, I said it's about the history of porcelain. They asked why would I read something like that? They thought it was in code. I posted bail and called the temp service, they said don't come back. Sis, I'm really sorry, but while there's life there's hope. That's from Cicero, *Ad Atticum*, I think. An extraordinary man, although he was killed, of course."

She didn't say a word.

"I'm sorry, Sis. I'll check the want ads tomorrow if I don't have to go to, well, prison, so to speak. Things just seem to get very complicated." She started to fade. "You look nice in blue."

Later he sat in the living room reading a popular history of the writing of the Constitution. During the latest campaign, President Pert had admitted he'd never actually read the sacred document but said, "I get the gist of it." Since then Babcock had found himself drawn to Constitutional history. He skimmed the chapter about Gouverneur Morris drafting the Preamble. "We, the People. . ." he mumbled.

Tonya put the final touches on the ten p.m. news. Post-election, you could pretty much coast along. Go back to the archives, better known as "the compost," and lift stuff verbatim. Everything was the same, only more so. The re-elected criminals would promise a new beginning and call on Congress to make a bipartisan commitment to approve their maddest depredations. She was thankful she wasn't an editor. She didn't decide what got said or manufacture the lie. She just gave it words.

Rosalie had started to stumble over sentences of more than five words. In fact it was no sweat to fit the news into that span, but it did change the show's rhythm. Tammy, the cute little intern, hurried past with a mop and a bucket of water. The girl idolized Rosalie, and her life's goal was to be Rosalie some day. Mopping up after Rosalie was like a sacrament.

Tonya stared at the screen. All week she'd thought about quitting. The week before, she'd written copy for Rosalie's report on a new Federal study linking dreams with rectal cancer. Again she'd had trouble writing flat lies, but at last she wrote it as satire, and of course nobody noticed. Maybe she should have Tammy's job, something hands-on and down-to-earth. At least the election was over. If voter turnout kept shrinking, maybe they'd cancel the series.

Yesterday she'd had a meeting with the Director of Genesis. He liked her style. He broached the possibility that she might transfer to Genesis at a gut-busting salary increase. Genesis was the scene of the action. Deciding what would be effective news, exciting news, news that thrilled, then helping it happen. Proactive journalism was nothing new, of course, going back at least to the Spanish-American War. But methodologies had evolved. We encouraged wars to happen that needed to happen. We induced criminals to commit newsworthy acts. We put people in bed together, then pulled off the sheets. We envisioned the news, and the Word became Flesh.

She told him she'd think about it. It was an opportunity to move into a socioeconomic class she'd always loathed and despised, and what a relief to get past all that loathing and despising. If only she could be blind to Loki's eyes.

She finished up the ten p.m. copy before mid-afternoon, so there was absolutely nothing to do until five. At one time she'd have enjoyed the challenge of downloading leather dyke porn on company time, but her heart wasn't in it now.

"Excuse me?"

Tonya looked up. A bespectacled gerbil stood before her. Yes, this smiling round-faced little man was unmistakably the resurrected spirit of Loki's long-deceased and still-mourned gerbil. Tonya drew a blank. The gerbil, in a brown polyester suit and blue necktie with polka dots, stood stock still, as if waiting for a tip. What was he smiling about?

Tonya remembered. The appointment had slipped her mind. "Oh, you're Mr. Babcock. Sorry."

"No, I'm used to it. Somebody has to be me." He smiled. "That was a joke," he explained, "although my sister warned me against making jokes at job interviews, since according to some self-help book one isn't hired to tell jokes, especially if one does it badly." He shrugged. "Or even if you do it well."

Who had we here? Polka dots. Tonya seemed to recall polka dots on some lost grandmother. "So, Mr. Babcock," she offered, rising to a quick limp handshake, "have a seat."

"Thank you," he said, "I appreciate that. You know, these days in most interviews they make you stand, which was the practice certainly in the courts of Europe until the Twentieth Century except among peers, but the concept of the peerage itself has nearly disappeared, you know."

Tonya didn't know, or if she did she hadn't thought about it lately. "So, Mr. Babcock," she began shuffling her papers, finding his resume, trying to avoid those polka dots. "You know we're hiring here on an hourly wage, no benefits? That's why they let me hire my own research assistant, instead of going through Personnel."

"That's fascinating," he marveled. "There's a definite logic to division of labor, which seems to me, really, the definition of civilization as we know it, but who would have thought it would go to this extreme? Division of labor, separation of powers, mind/body split, who would have thought?"

Tonya had no idea who. "So, Mr. Babcock, the job is this. A story breaks, we need background, so you go down to the archives, look up some old stories, bring back the salient facts that I write into the copy, and then it all gets edited out." She heard her own cynicism, and she was so sick of it. "This isn't journalism, Mr. Babcock, this is entertainment, but still there's an old tradition that truth needs to be well researched before it's ignored completely. Sort of like the Incas preparing the virgins for sacrifice."

"Actually, the interesting part of the Incan sacrificial practice was—"

"Don't tell me. Let it be a surprise." Tonya made a mental note, with this guy, never to say more than was absolutely necessary. She looked at his resume. "So, Mr. Babcock, why would you be interested in this position?"

He looked at her with the most naive eyes she'd ever seen. "I need a job," he said.

"But according to your resume you have a Princeton Ph.D. in history? Why don't you teach or write books or something?"

"I'm no good at that. I taught high school for a while, but they just kind of sat there, and I talked and they didn't really listen, and I asked them to write a paper but they didn't, so I thought I wasn't doing this very well, so I quit."

"What are you good at then?"

"Well, I learn things. I have a syncretic mind."

"Do you have any references?"

"Well, my sister, I guess maybe, although she's not highly communicative. The concept of references is—" and he spoke at some length about the concept of references as a legacy of the English class system and his wonderment at its persistence in a representative democracy.

At last Tonya interrupted. "And you've had a number of jobs for very short durations, it seems."

Babcock shrugged and his polka dots shrank. "That's true. I get fired."

"What for?"

"Not going to work."

"Why didn't you go to work?"

"It wasn't interesting."

Tonya stared at him. Here was the most honest man she'd ever met. That in itself was sufficient to make him unemployable. And J.G. Babcock had never stopped smiling. She felt a deep sudden pang for Loki's gerbil.

"And for Other Professional Experience you indicate that you are presently under indictment for felony possession of pornography?"

He kept smiling. "Well, I'm not actually guilty. That was official governmental pornography, I believe. I've never really understood the appeal, although the practice goes all the way back to the Sumerians, at least as a spiritual metaphor though not as a commercial commodity, so it definitely has a lineage in Western thought."

"And so why did you choose to put a felony charge on your resume?"

He thought a moment. "Well, it's a significant educational experience."

Tonya sighed. "Well, Mr. Babcock, it's been a pleasure talking with you. You seem like a very nice man, but on one hand you're vastly over-qualified, and on the other hand my superiors would be very upset, in fact they would shit bricks if they knew I had hired a potential sex offender. Because people really depend on the integrity of broadcast journalism—"

And as she started to hear what she was saying, her chariot horses bolted, foaming at the mouth.

"—which has been perverted to the point where nobody believes one fucking word we say, and no wonder because we make it up out of thin air and kiss every ass that's fat and white and available, and so goddammit, who gives a shit? Mr. Babcock, you're hired. You can start Monday, barring further arrests."

"Oh." Babcock smiled his resistible smile. They shook hands. And in the Chevy Chase office of DHS, a man with shaded lenses watched the monitor. "They're shaking hands," he announced.

The recording done, Harold lapsed into silence as Rosalie lurched toward the bathroom. Well sure, he wanted a divorce. Who wouldn't dump a crackpot, even after twenty-five years, when he could have his pick of nubile interns? But their contract forbade it. It even required them to sleep in the same bedroom and kiss once a day in public. Image was image. Business was business.

Something needed to happen. Something big.

Chapter 7
Phone Bills and Poppy-Snoops

When the phone beeped, Eddie had just managed to unhook Chelsie's bra. It was one of those tricky front hooks. With the incredible technological advances of the past decades, some things never changed. You could construct whole new animals, but you still fumbled those cranky hooks on a bra.

He ignored the beeps. Voicemail would pick it up. He couldn't get distracted. Chelsie was the first girl he'd had up to his room in months. He'd met her on a gig, lead singer in a lousy band. Maybe she thought he could make her sound better. She'd soon find out.

When the phone re-beeped, it unsettled him. It might be Marty with a gig. It might be his sister, who called periodically to tell him she was killing herself and ask did he care? He was about to pick it up, but what Chelsie was doing now she was doing very well.

He kneaded the muscles of her strong wide back and felt a surge of wonder as she arched over him. Like most guys, he always chased after the lookers and sometimes caught one, with subsequent regrets. Yet here was Chelsie, plain as a cantaloupe, built like a potato with little cockeyed tits, drawing him to her like a rip tide. He loved Chelsie instantly and forever.

When the phone beeped the third time, he answered it. Years after, he still wondered why. At the peak moment, amid throbbing quarter-tones and a chain-saw scream of guitars over the pounding bass of her thighs, the phone beeped and he reached to pick it up. Was it an inflated sense of potency, feeling no harm in taking a break to tend to business? Or was it that he knew who was calling?

It was Pepper. She was swearing a blue streak as Eddie struggled to disengage various limba. Chelsie stared at him, stunned by the mid-concert crash of the system. He waved feebly at the cell phone as if it had suddenly appeared there by accident. Pepper ranted on. He sat up on the edge of the bed. "It's a business thing," he stammered to Chelsie, "a phone bill." She only stared.

Pepper had emailed Eddie's bill to Central Accounting in Atlanta. It had been returned with instructions to redirect it to Data Search in Omaha. But Data Search had been outsourced to New Delhi, and when the transaction ricocheted through the Republic of Congo, something was lost in translation. Pepper had been billed for Eddie's eight thousand bucks.

"That's not my fault," Eddie mumbled.

"What's not?" Chelsie asked.

"Phone bill."

Pepper raged. Countless blind alleys, but at last she'd found that, yes, an Accounts Receivables office with living, breathing people was actually located in Washington DC. She had an address, no phone number.

"They gotta have a phone number," Eddie said, "They're the phone company."

"Who is?" Chelsie asked.

"The people this lady works for," Eddie mumbled.

"What lady?" He caught the edge.

Pepper demanded that Eddie go with her to straighten it out. She'd meet him there at nine a.m. and lose only a couple hours of work. Curtle Building, out on New York Avenue, Northeast. Eddie said he had to be up late tonight, couldn't get there that early, but Pepper was adamant. Eddie looked at Chelsie. She'd turned away. "Okay, nine o'clock."

Pepper gave him the address, directions, and assorted threats. Okay, get off the phone, back to bed, dive into the rip tide. He clicked off. Chelsie had her clothes on, heading out the door.

"Chelsie, hey, I'm—"

"Fuck you!" She slammed the door.

"Yeh," Eddie murmured, "fuck me."

Pepper hung up. She sat at the kitchen table, shoved the bills aside, swigged a beer, nibbled a piece of cheddar cheese. Why did she sound like such a bitch? She thumbed last week's newspaper. President this, President that. The guy had built his first campaign around the slogan *A Fair Shake for America*, and she'd been haunted by her memory of Mom, crazy with rage, shaking her screaming baby brother. She never followed politics, but it was scary, all those people going nuts. Two on her floor last week. Roy had come to work with a pistol, but they shot him at Reception. And Conchita, the fat old Mexican lady two cubicles down, had returned from the ladies' room stark naked, singing "Happy Birthday" and prancing up and down the aisles until Security tackled her.

Pepper flicked the vid. Who watches golf at ten at night? She flicked it off. Her limbs ached with fatigue, but her nerves were working night shift. She got up for another beer and found a leftover pizza crust. Eddie had sounded distracted. Was he with somebody else? *Somebody else?* What did she care? He was just a disgruntled customer. Pepper sat at the table, flushed.

She recognized her symptoms. She was hot for this Eddie guy and couldn't figure why. With all that hair and wisecracks he wasn't her type. She liked men who were clean-cut, well-dressed, sour-faced, bereft of all emotions but rage. The two she'd married were disasters, but that's what got the heat up.

"Mommy?" Jessie appeared in the doorway. She had almost outgrown that nightie, and Pepper knew there'd be a flood of tears when those frisky faded monkeys got sent off to Goodwill.

"Honey, what's wrong?" It couldn't be dreams again. She was doping the kid to the max. Jessie climbed into her lap. "What would you like in your lunch box?" Pepper whispered.

"Poppy-Snoops," Jessie murmured.

"No, that's just for a treat. That's just for Sunday." Then Pepper winced. Her mom's voice, clear as a bell. Ask the kid what she wants, then tell her she can't have it.

"Mommy?"

"Yeh, sweetheart?"

"When's Christmas?"

Ah, the season of nagging, denial, splurge, regret. She hated seeing Jessie morph into a rabid little consumer. "It's a while yet, hon."

"Cause then it starts to get sunny." Jessie snuggled to her. No, it wasn't the pathetic presents. Jessie was waiting for the miracle of winter dissolving.

Pepper carried her back to bed, tucked her in. On the floor were scattered photos: Jessie had been into the snapshots again. Pepper gathered them, returned to the kitchen, dumped the pile onto the table, started to sort. Forget digitals: Jessie loved those old-time photos with their heavy paper and fuzzy drugstore processing. "Who's that?" she'd ask, and Pepper would dredge up another aching memory to entertain her.

Chewing the last of the pizza crust, she shuffled through the years. Mom and Dad in Oklahoma. Herself as a redhead. Old boyfriend leaning against his Chrysler. High school girlfriends, giggling into eternity. Bowling team from the bar. She and Clint at a truck stop, driving east in the U-Haul. Clint in his uniform. Sterling with his briefcase.

She always made the dumb choices, stood in the wrong supermarket line, married the wrong sonofabitch. Clint: "Don't worry, honey, you've got the whole U.S. Army to protect you." Sterling: "We'll move to the suburbs where it's safe for you and Brian."

Brian. She'd hidden all the pictures of Brian. She didn't want to explain to Jessie that she'd had a brother. "Where is he, Mommy?" Jessie would ask. Well he isn't. He just isn't.

Mom and Dad. Every weekend Dad beat up Mom and her brothers, but he never touched Pepper till she'd stayed out all night with what's-his-name and he caught her coming in at dawn. He'd whipped her with a belt till her face, arms, and breasts were a waste of bruise and blood. She'd fought back, which enraged him more, and he might have killed her if she hadn't gone for his nuts. Except for one last face-off, years later, he never hit her again. It was the hospital bills, she thought, that gave him pause.

And these were the memories she kept in a little box on the dresser and wondered why. Now she couldn't get film for her old camera any more, and she couldn't afford the new ones. Better that way. Snapshots of kids wouldn't last, or the kids.

From the back room Jessie called out. "Mommy!"

"Go to sleep, honey!"

"I can't."

"Why not?"

"You're crying too loud."

Pepper blew her nose, shuffled the photos together in a pile, checked a paper scribble for the address of the Curtle Building, and walked over to the counter to pack Jessie's lunch. Oh what the hell, she thought, ripping open the box of Poppy-Snoops: surprise her.

Chapter 8
Bombshell

In Room 714B of the Curtle Building sat Sergei Rupp, primed to explode. He was motionless for twenty-seven minutes. He timed himself.

The Curtle Building had seen better days. Built in 1924 amid the roar of the Twenties as a department store crowned by office floors, it went bankrupt in three years through creative management. It was vacant until the Crash, then was purchased by an Englishman who felt the looming cataclysm was only a necessary market corrective. Reopened in anticipation of a major rebound, it limped along for seven years with tenants including a shoe repair shop, a Mafia-run vending machine company, rehearsal rooms for the Federal Theatre Project, and storage for the records of failed Nebraska banks.

Actors, mobsters, and bank records were evicted as prospects brightened for a major war. The economy filled the building with plaster dust and money. The Curtle Building changed owners three times amid rampant speculation, and the last owner renamed it Jefferson Plaza, for reasons unknown. After the war, the neighborhood underwent a slow decline. At various times, the building housed a modeling school, a savings & loan company, a community murals project, a number of down-at-heels lawyers, an ancient dentist, and a literary agent with a single client who'd written a self-help book for the afterlife, *If You Know You're Going to Hell*. Plus the shoe repair shop, which had weathered countless attempts at eviction and the first owner's suicide at the end of a boot lace. At any given time, the edifice could offer future entrepreneurs the availability of 35,000 sq. ft. of vacant commercial space, cheap.

Its heyday came with the War on Poverty, when it teemed with government offices and brought well-paid professionals back into the neighborhood, allowing muggers to make a decent living without commuting to work. Subsequent administrations brought in offices that couldn't be housed on their home turf, usually programs due for the ax. If you were moved to Jefferson Plaza, it was time to start sending out your resume.

Jefferson Plaza was seven stories high. From nearly a century of renovation, its floors were chopped into a labyrinth rivaling the Holy Roman Empire. During the first term of the Realist Administration, as Thomas Jefferson fell into disrepute and research revealed that the original Mr. Curtle had been a major financial backer of the Indiana KKK, the building was rechristened the Curtle Building.

Three years ago, two floors had been occupied by Granny Bell, but those departments were now in Denton, Texas. On the fifth floor, mislabeled Fourth Floor for the past nine years, were an attorney's office, a bail bondsman, the ancient dentist son of the original ancient dentist, and Snavely & Snavely — no one knew what they did, but it had something to do with a steady string of single gentlemen. On the first floor, a boarded-up coffee shop announced OPENING SOON, but the sign was rotting. The shoe repair shop still flourished as the front for a sting by the DEA, which had supplied most of the meth and crack to Northeast Washington for the past three years with no arrests in sight. The basement was leased to the Pentagon, and it was into this huge barren room that Dr. Sergei Rupp and the Office for New Age Research were moved. Furniture would follow when feasible, or never.

Rupp sat in shadow at a huge desk stacked with books, portfolios, and left-over sandwiches, surrounded by bare shelves. A ceiling fluorescent was on at the far end of the cavernous room. Carpeting that might have muffled the sepulchral echo of his breathing lay in rolls along a wall.

He blinked out of his trance, adjusted his thick glasses, and riffled the pages of a slim report. Its yellow portfolio was too frivolous, but nothing else could be found. He tapped his pencil on the edge of the desk and mumbled, in a thick stew of accents, Russian, Chinese, and Brooklynese, "My little bombshell. My sweet little bombshell. . ."

The night before, at a Washington cocktail party, Rupp had listened to a prominent news anchor cracking jokes as his co-anchor wife sat white-faced in the corner shredding her cocktail napkin. He meandered through the crowd, trying to catch the eye of a young Congresswoman newly appointed to the committee overseeing his departmental budget. At last he came to a halt before Rep. Constance Grambling.

"Sergei Rupp," he announced to her, grasping her hand and holding it in a vise. "Theoretical physicist. Paranormal research for Department of we-call-it-jokingly Death. I am vanguard of new dimensions. Offspring of Russian/Chinese/Brooklyn nobility now defunct. Come to Free World, it is no longer free, you pay through nose. I am having budgets of billions — power, carpets, secretaries — and then I do not. I am at bottom of barrel. You have beautiful breasts."

The Congresswoman excused herself, turned away to take an anchovy. He pinched her earlobe. Her American flag earring cut into the skin. "Not only breasts," he whispered.

She went rigid. His lips were close to her ear. "Clandestine use of dolphins," he whispered. "Mass hypnosis. Shamanic targeting. Kabbalistic ballistics. Military applications of Hindu Chakra system." She was wide-eyed, on the verge of impalement. "I have intimate acquaintance with energy systems," and two fingers of his left hand dug into the base of her spine. A spasm shook her.

She turned and met his pin eyes behind the coke-bottle lenses, the eyes of a rabid weasel. A short wiry black-haired man, some kind of Oriental, and she could already imagine his fingers scuttling over her naked body like a scavenging cockroach.

He walked her to the hallway. With a pang she saw her faithful constituents in Des Moines cheering her off to Washington to save their children from evil. "Realists ask more bang for buck," Rupp hissed. "It is military desire for big exploding dick. Money for bang-bang only: big exploding dick. In fact I have very big dick and they do not." His fingers were locked on her nipple.

Ten minutes later, in one of a series of dimly-lit rooms in an adjoining wing reserved for members of Congress, Dr. Sergei Rupp and The Honorable Constance Grambling were locked in heavy caucus.

The progress of their lovemaking was the deliberate motion of tectonic plates and the sudden explosive upthrust of mountain peaks never known to Iowa. Rupp barely moved, yet his thickness pulsed at her center and the merciless waves convulsed her again and again. *Who am I now?* she wondered, as she heard her distant cries.

Then they lay sprawled across the folding bed, flotsam, jetsam, drained. Images floated in Connie Grambling's eyes: her valedictorian photo, her sweet mom and dad, her hubby's Volvo dealership, her election night victory speech, her radiant Episcopal priest, Sergei's magnificent cock and his beady weasel eyes.

As she dissolved like a dream of surf, she heard him mumble his history. German/Chinese father, Siberian mother, raised in a Russian enclave in Brooklyn . . . father a brilliant painter, forced his son into science . . . doctorate at age 19, three patents before age 25 involving human neurotransmitters interfaced with missile guidance systems . . . first U.S. citizen to be classified TOP SECRET.

His other talent came by way of genes. His great-grandmother had been lover to all the major physicists of the early Twentieth Century. She had described to her tiny great-grandson, in graphic detail, their deepest intimacies. Planck came in tiny discrete bursts. Einstein shortened as acceleration increased. Heisenberg was sweet but unpredictable, always felt observed. Rupp surpassed them all.

His erotic genius was a mixed blessing in Washington, gaining him attention from females in high places, occasionally an ardent champion on the floor of the Senate or even in the Cabinet, but rarely translating into hard budget figures. His research could not be measured in megatonnage. His arena was a shadowland, a science fiction universe of warfare on astral planes. It was incomprehensible to the military mind and not remotely expensive enough.

For the Realists he was suspect by definition, and his department might have been axed immediately. But field tests of his missile guidance devices embedded in the neural systems of sheep embryos showed remarkable promise if the embryos could be brought to term and the sheep bred to attack. Nevertheless, the newest generation of thermonukes with supersized gigatonnage and Smart Fallout carried the day, and he was transferred to the Curtle Building. Soon after, the first data from the Morpheus trials appeared.

Rep. Grambling stirred from her reverie. Sergei was staring at her, his black pin eyes burning behind his heavy steamed lenses. "I am in love with you," he said.

"Don't be." She knew this type. They fell in love with anything that twitched. They were absolutely sincere for ten minutes.

Constance Grambling was among the frail but vehement minority opposing the Realist agenda. She knew she was utterly ineffective. She suspected that two of her major donors bankrolled her merely because her humanitarian bleating offered a ready target for ridicule. Only rage kept her going. Early in her term she found herself, for the first time in her life, sexually voracious. Congressmen, lobbyists, staffers, busboys, constituents, caterers — a lust as primal as a yearning for salt. Somehow she was drawn to men who were frankly loathsome. Next morning, that loathing seeped from her like chemical waste, begetting implacable rage. It was the rage that got her through the day.

At the party she had found Sergei suitably abhorrent. She had imagined him as a plucked chicken, his scrawny worm dangling, pecking her into a suitable fury for tomorrow's debate on privatizing Mars. Instead, she felt the nakedness she'd felt on her wedding night and a brimming joy she knew she'd never feel again. She took a breath, and the sobs began.

"You know what they do?" she gasped as he patted her shoulder softly, "They addict us to hating them. It's an addiction. I dream about killing them."

"You *dream* it?"

"What?" she snorted between deep gasps. "You think we pop those pills? Congress is exempt. We protect you, but we just have to tough it out." Sergei wagged his finger frantically. "No, we're not bugged. It's a deal with the Energy Lobby. They're the only ones powerful enough to provide Congress with truly private trysts. Check my voting record. I'm a Leftie, sure, but I lubricate with Big Oil."

Sergei knew the mood had shifted. She began to stiffen like death. He sat up cross-legged, untangled the boxer shorts bunched around his ankle, adjusted his glasses. Time for business. Sad.

"We're out there pumping adrenaline," she went on, "and they love it. While we chant our slogans and scream, 'How dare you!' our teeth rot, our marriages fall apart, our blood pressure sets an Olympic record while they chow down. 'How can you do that?' we screech, and they chuckle, 'It's easy.'" She rolled over, face into the pillow. "My husband moved back to Des Moines with the kids. We talk on weekends, when I remember to call. He knows what I'm doing. He tries to be nice about it."

She rose from the couch and dressed in silence. As she shut the bathroom door, Sergei thought he caught a sigh, but it might have been the hinge. He pulled up his boxer shorts, sat on the edge of the bed. She returned, unwrinkled, untouched, and sat beside him. "I believe there was something you wanted to tell me." He nodded. "Well then I believe you should tell me. I have another engagement."

So he told her of the impending catastrophe. He outlined the Morpheus evidence, the computer models, and what might remain of America. He suggested personal precautions to take and strategies for maximum political leverage. He stressed that, as with the unheeded warnings on climate change, disaster was inevitable but might be lessened by instant course reversal, fat chance though it be. He offered her his card.

She informed him she had his full dossier, including FBI interviews with his many past wives. She said that two special assistants would visit next morning to receive his documents. She told him the identity code they would use. She promised to put the documents in the appropriate hands. "It's certainly a bombshell," she said.

"My sweet bombshell," he said with a sad smile.

"Well, Dr. Rupp, thank you for an enjoyable experience. I wish you the best of luck with your research. . ." Her voice trailed off. He started to speak. She stiffened.

"I once had secretaries," he said. "They had beautiful breasts."

"I'll see what I can do."

Despite her very best intentions, Connie Grambling did nothing at all. She had a late date with a rotund lobbyist who, after inconclusive motions, cried himself to sleep. Next morning she was at her desk promptly at eight a.m., then sat there nine hours, ignoring her staff's earnest inquiries. Next day she boarded a plane for Des Moines, reconciled with her husband, resigned public office, survived the catastrophe which is the imminent subject of this narrative, and chaired a capital campaign for the First Methodist Church.

And in Room 714B of the Curtle Building, Sergei Rupp sat at his desk tapping his pencil. He gazed across the vast expanse of file cabinets, cardboard boxes, folders in disarray, toward the clouded glass door. Before him lay the thin yellow portfolio.

"My little bombshell," he whispered to the darkness, "my sweet little bombshell." Patiently awaiting delivery.

Chapter 9
Time for Show and Tell

Next morning, Pepper waited for Eddie in the cavernous lobby of the Curtle Building. Its facade was obscured by a construction scaffold, and it was no easy task to find a building that was having its face torn off. The guy was late. She'd expected that. But after twenty minutes she began to panic. It was past rush hour, and not a living soul had come through the lobby. How long was it since she'd been in a public building with no guards, no metal detectors, no UniQard slots, no vid-scans, no machine guns? It was like stepping into some Colonial America theme park. She half expected to hear chickens.

When Eddie shambled in, it took her a moment to recognize him. Shorter than she'd thought, and he wore a corduroy jacket and a blue plaid billed cap that made his shaggy hair look like something growing out of leftovers in the fridge. "Nice cap," she mumbled. Great, start a relationship with a lie. *Relationship?*

"Plaid," he replied. "I thought I should go formal."

She wanted a cigarette badly, but he didn't look like a smoker. "You're not a smoker, are you?" He shrugged. Damn, condemned to be healthy one more day.

"I heard chickens this morning," said Eddie. "Chickens outside my apartment. There aren't any chickens in Northwest DC. I mean there aren't even chickens any more, just chicken substance from these chicken-results factories that plop that pumped-up sucker onto our dinner table full of all those great chemicals to live by."

This wasn't the conversation Pepper expected at nine in the morning. What was this chicken thing in her life today? She looked at her scribbled note with the suite number of Granny Bell Receivables: 714B. "I don't eat much chicken," Eddie said. "Lotta hot dogs. That's worse. That's sorta like—"

"Look—" She cut off the onrushing metaphor. "I'm sorry we played phone tag—"

"Your kid answered. She sounds smart."

"Way too smart. Look, so I got this address, but— See, I

sent your stuff to Accounts Receivable, suddenly I get back this bill, eight thousand forty-two bucks, with my name on it—"

Eddie snickered, then stopped as he saw her lips draw thin.

"So I try to call, but there's no way to call. It's the phone company, so they don't answer the phone unless I call Granny Bell Cares, which is me. I look up Receivables, and of course Access Denied. So I hack Security and get this address—"

"Computer skills, there's money in that."

"Just think like a beer-belly drunk and you understand the computer. Listen to me! I get this address, but it's a dungeon here. Directory's blank, elevators are dead—"

"Empty buildings, yeh, take out the CEOs there's lots of space."

"We can try the stairs. Maybe they've got a note on the door."

They began to climb. Seventh floor? They climbed rapidly, focused on their mission. At least he's in good shape, Pepper thought, then caught herself. Good shape for what? Don't even think it, girl child. No time for a shaggy lover who talks about chickens on a first date. *First date?* In a stairwell?

They reached Four. They'd just passed Five. Why was Four above Five?

"Two friends of mine this happened to," Eddie said, "and they got erased. Datapop popped 'em. No records, no bank accounts, no identity. Nonexistent." They climbed past an unmarked floor. "They thought it was political, cause their band was the Sweetie-Pie Commies, but I said it's just fuck-ups."

They reached Seven. The hall was bereft of life. It dawned on Pepper that she was in a deserted building with a shaggy plaid-capped loony. She felt in her purse for her tiny spray can of Equalizer. Eddie tried a few doorknobs. Making a sharp right turn, they stopped. Sprawled flat and stiff before them was a dead dog. "Wrong floor, I guess," said Eddie, and turned back to the stairwell. "714B," he read from the scrap of paper. "Maybe B is basement." They started down the stairs. "Was that a German Shorthair?"

"Pointer. My dad had one. Shot it."

"Why'd he shoot it?"

"It looked at him funny."

They reached the basement. Directly before them stood a frosted glass door, ajar. 714B. "Persistence pays," beamed Eddie, turning his full-wattage smile toward Pepper. Their eyes met, held for that one moment longer. His smile wasn't about the open door, it was about a door opening.

"Come in," called a high thin voice. Eddie opened the door. At the far end of a low cavernous room, like a single rat in a vast empty warehouse, sat a small thick-spectacled man in a baggy beige suit.

"Scuse me, we're looking for Granny Bell," Eddie said, "about a phone bill."

Silence.

"We had this address," Pepper added, "but obviously we're not in the right—"

"*Phone bill*," the little man chortled in a thick vaudevillian accent. "Yes, yes. And I say to you, *Time for Show and Tell*."

Eddie turned to Pepper. "Is this for real?"

The little man rose from his chair. "*Is this for real?* Code verified! Sit! No chairs? I am terrible! Bang head! Yes!" He slapped his forehead repeatedly.

Eddie entered the room, Pepper followed, and they made their way across thirty yards of bare battleship linoleum. "Okay, so—" Eddie began, as the little man rubbed his reddened brow. "So what it is, name's Eddie Grabowski, and I got billed for what I'd already paid for, then suddenly I get this check, and then she processes my complaint at Customer Service—"

"So now I'm getting billed for him," Pepper finished it off.

The little man flung his arms wide. "Life!" he exclaimed, then grasped a thin yellow portfolio and offered it to them. "I am Sergei Rupp," explained Sergei Rupp. Eddie approached the desk and took the portfolio.

"What's this?"

"Data. I desire you convey how close we blunder on catastrophe. America gone kaput. I want you convey full facial expression."

Eddie shrugged. "I'm lost."

Rupp's voice rose to a rasping squeak. He charged around the desk waving his arms. "Disneyland destroyed! Consumers consumed! Horror is not in movies now. Nightmares are us!"

He clutched Eddie's jacket, and Eddie instinctively grabbed Rupp's striped necktie. "Not that I'm bored with the movie stuff," Eddie said, "but what about my phone bill?"

Rupp patted Eddie's shoulder, and his face twitched into a smile. "Yes yes, *phone bill.* I like disguise. You look like plumber. I give you coffee but have no secretary to make. I had secretaries, beautiful. Yes yes." He patted Eddie again, then stared hard at Pepper's chest.

"Maybe we're not understanding something," Pepper ventured, pulling her jacket shut.

"Explanation, yes." Rupp patted Eddie, gestured toward the portfolio in Eddie's hand, walked back to his chair. His manner had changed. In a gentle monotone, gesticulating with one forefinger, he began a calm exposition of the forthcoming destruction of America.

"Definition of sanity: functional behavior within given environment. Yes? Context is fixed, you align or do not align. If within given environment you do not align, you are defined insane. Correct?" Within the given environment of Room 714B, Pepper thought, that seemed entirely plausible.

"However! Option! That instead of context fixed and people lunatics, context aligns with lunatics. Material reality twists to align with twisted psyches. Mad psyche, sane context: insane. Mad psyche, mad context: sane. Sanity is function of alignment, madness squared, Q.E.D. America faces catastrophic sanity as Hell comes to Earth."

"So what does this have to do with my phone bill?" Pepper interjected.

"*Phone bill!* I hear you! You have said it. *Phone bill.* Code six. You are so sexual. No! Down, Rover, they say!" He slapped himself on the forehead. Pepper and Eddie glanced at each other. They were in the wrong place, for certain, but this odd wind-up toy held a strange fascination. Rupp adjusted his dense glasses, twitched another smile, continued his lecture.

As early as the 1920's, he explained, physicists had proposed the existence of multiple dimensions. String theory of the 1980's necessitated ten or eleven space/time dimensions on the sub-quantum level. Ten years back, a team of physicists, led by Gerhard Hoxhi, claimed to have personally journeyed to the core of the sub-quantum Calabi-Yau paradigm and diagrammed its characteristics in equations subsequently analyzed as an ancient Sumerian recipe for beer. The team soon began to exhibit strange behavior: migraines, bed-wetting, compulsive channel-surfing, then catatonia.

But the equations were confirmed. They provided precise prediction of E-Factor variables, and for the first time the Nobel Prize was shared by institutionalized psychotics. "They confirm E-Factor!" Rupp smiled broadly, slapped his desk in triumph, and began to weep.

Pepper took Eddie's elbow. "This is crazy. This is some kinda mad scientist movie. I've gotta get back to work. Fuck this."

Eddie looked at her, then at the yellow portfolio in his hand. "What's the E-Factor?"

The little man wiped his eyes, rose slowly, with two fingers of his left hand pointed directly at Eddie and Pepper. "Eros!" he grinned.

As a kid, Pepper had watched old sci-fi movies on the all-night movie channels. Dad didn't have money to fix the kids' teeth, but he had a front-yard dish antenna right next to the pickup truck on cinder blocks. She was enthralled by mad scientists. No family should be without one. Their thick glasses, wild hair, and mangled accents called forth a world where Oklahoma never existed, and their savage schemes for world conquest, usurping the power of God — well, if God hadn't done any better than this fucked-up world, then He oughta let somebody else have a try.

So now Pepper was torn between the pull of her rational instincts, which said to get her ass out of there fast, and her fascination with this gesticulating pin-eyed freak who, inches away, placed his forefinger on his lips, which puckered into something that resembled, to her, a cow's asshole.

"It is Eros," Rupp whispered, and Pepper heard her brother Alec whispering to her the facts of life as he fingered her hairless cleft. The last she'd heard, Alec now sold furniture and had three kids, a prolapsed hernia, and phone bills of his own. "E-Factor. Eros. Binding force of humans. Quantifiable! Tangible! Collective unconscious within vibrational fields of microcosmos. Hoxhi smart guy but very bad breath." Rupp gave a vicious snort, acknowledging a fellow genius's genius.

Pepper glanced at Eddie. Eros was having its stern implacable way.

Rupp forged on. "Dimensions exist, blocked by waking senses. Dreams are dimensions with heavy traffic between. Block dream receptors, block E-Factor. So!"

Long silence. Rupp's heavy breathing echoed through the vast empty limbo. At last Eddie sighed. "So what exactly does this involve?" Pepper tried to concentrate: something was being said here that wasn't sci-fi, it was survival. She focused on the puckered lips, which spoke these words:

"Experimental data from Morpheus. Here: Control Group A, authorized to discontinue dream suppressant dosage, so. No sweat. They dream." With a wave of his left hand, he conjured up a placid melange. "Here: Control Group B, taking their dosage. Four percent report dreams in spite of dosage. Thirty percent, psychotic symptoms, national average. Sixteen percent, severe psychosis, national average. Fifty percent, no symptoms, no dreams, no sweat." With a sweep of his right hand, he conjured up Action News.

"But Test Group C—" He grabbed himself by the lapels, whispering vehemently. "Group C maintain suppressant dosage but confined in constricted space under stress, loud music, boom boom, stress stress boom!" Pepper stepped back. Again the little man was set to explode. Rupp seemed to sense her anxiety and dialed down his biorhythm. "Results are these. Dreams flow between, like copulative fuck on subneoquantum level. River must flow. But—"

It's the obligatory sci-fi scene, Pepper thought, where the lunatic explains the scientific principle and the heroes rush into action. Suddenly she was living it, but she didn't understand a word. She only saw the terror in the little man's insect eyes.

"Blockage," continued Rupp, "breeds disruptions in field. Block dreams, then force moves to cut new channel. Test Group C does orgy, first-class, hot stuff, but reality blowout. Nothing left but dentures and flock of chickens. Deep shit."

Eddie interrupted. "So what you're saying, we create reality together and the E-thing binds us into it, yes? And wild ideas, like monsters, that stuff, don't fit with it, but they get drained off by dreams so we all stay on the same trip. Block the dreams, the toilet clogs up and the plumbing explodes."

"We are holocaust as pimple pops."

Pepper felt a rasp of rage at Eddie. Was he buying into this crap? She felt her world spinning, caroming off the bumper and thwacking the eight-ball hard toward the corner pocket.

"Scuse me," she asked, "but what about my goddamned phone bill?"

Rupp stared at her. For the first time, he seemed confused. "Phone bill?" he echoed. "*Phone bill* is password. You say *Phone bill*. I say *Time for Show and Tell*. You say *Is this for real?*"

"Is this Accounts Receivable?"

"I make mistake?" In the dim mausoleum, his face went dead white. Suddenly his necktie stiffened and he grabbed for the portfolio. "Classified. Please return."

Eddie held it back. "What's your name, Jack?" he asked.

"R-r-rupp!" exploded the little man in a vehement gargle.

"Rupp." Eddie held his eyes. "Rupp, look, hey, we're kidding. We're in disguise. We're whoever you thought we are." Rupp looked doubtful. "We were making a joke. Americans like to kid around." Rupp stood rigid, calculating all probabilities. Pepper expected his mouth to pop open and extrude a print-out. "We'll take care of it, Rupp," Eddie assured him. "We'll put it in good hands."

The little man turned his gaze to Pepper and sighed deeply. "What's up?" she asked.

His face became a child's, sweet and clear. "I am seeing your beautiful breasts."

Pepper bit her lip. Nothing was to be gained by profanity at nine in the morning. Eddie drew the little man away and spoke urgently under his breath. "Rupp, take it slow. She's a top agent, trained in martial arts. Her body parts are deadly weapons. She can kill with one tit."

They hurried out the door.

Sergei Rupp sat at his desk, gloomily tapping his pencil. "I am significant fool?" he asked the assembled file cabinets. They pondered the question.

Pepper and Eddie scurried up the basement stairs, bolted across the lobby, emerged into the chilly wet December, and hurried two blocks to the bus stop. Gasping for breath, they stood looking at each other, each waiting for the other to speak. Eddie fumbled the yellow portfolio from hand to hand. Pepper spoke at last. "So what do I do with this fucking phone bill?"

That evening, two aides from Rep. Grambling's office were machine-gunned in a men's room of the Czech Embassy. Their assailant, dressed as an Islamic fanatic, was quickly apprehended and died in FBI custody, reportedly of natural causes. Next morning, the proprietor opened his shoe repair shop in the Curtle lobby, expecting his weekly shipment of meth. Two Federal agents, disguised as Federal agents, approached. One asked him the way to Room 714B. He told them he'd never heard of it, and they left. He hated cops, and the little pin-eyed Russian guy always said hello.

Chapter 10
The Dissolution of Jimmie Larson

The proprietor of the shoe repair shop — who had never repaired a shoe — was Jimmie Larson. "Larson" was from his mother, who'd emigrated from Norway to work in a mid-scale brothel on the Upper East Side of Manhattan. "Jimmie" was the salesman father, which she knew because the baby turned out brown and she didn't usually cater to colored, but the guy had given her a very nice tip. Later she fell on hard times, and from early childhood Jimmie saw the bottom of the ladder and what the ladder was mired in.

When Jimmie was seven years old, he had a dream. He was in a funky-smelling shop, and he picked up a ring. Putting it on his finger, he found himself falling through time with flashes of movie stars screaming past. At last he plopped into a vast bed of lettuce. It was the planet of the Lettuce People, a movie he'd seen the week before, filching the price of a ticket from his mom's rent money. The Lettuce People wrapped him in a red-edged embrace, and Jimmie Larson felt himself dissolve.

He woke to find he'd peed the bed and that he no longer existed. Sure, he had to get up, make coffee, shake his mom awake, and face a long boring day as an under-age petty thief. But he knew that the soul of Jimmie Larson had been dissolved. A few years later he understood this better when his cellmate, a sociopathic Buddhist named Fritzie Fred, explained the concept of detachment. Do whatever you want, counseled Fritzie Fred, as long as it's not you doing it. Just watch it happen and dig it. That seemed to work for Fritzie Fred.

Jimmie Larson went on to do a fair number of things that he was glad to know Jimmie Larson hadn't really done. But facing the prospect of having his kneecaps smashed during a routine audit, he preferred not to be mistaken for the balding thug who wasn't Jimmie Larson. Tearfully he said goodbye to his mom, who worked at a WalMart in Queens, and moved to DC, where another ex-cellmate set him up as a distributor for the DEA. He made a good wage plus benefits and filched a bit of each shipment to provide for retirement. Occasionally someone brought in a pair of shoes to repair, but he said he was backlogged and directed them to another shop. His life went on, and he observed it all from a safe distance.

Jimmie Larson — the sluggish pot-bellied pimple-nosed dope wholesaler who had not been Jimmie Larson for many years — turned back from the counter as the Federal agents left. He opened a cigar box. On the second shelf he kept a box of Cuban cigars. He was modest in his indulgences. He ate a pint of cherry vanilla ice cream every night before bed, got a blow job every Thursday at noon, and on rare occasions he smoked a Cuban cigar.

Mumbling obscenities about FBI faggots, Jimmie Larson selected the remaining cigar on the top row and removed the paper band. Then on a whim he did what he'd loved to do at the age of seven when Mom's pimp Reggie smoked a cigar: he slipped the band onto his finger.

Jimmie Larson watched as the finger of Jimmie Larson was sucked through the paper ring, and then the hand, arm, shoulders, and pot belly of Jimmie Larson disappeared down a drain in the air like the Bab-O Cleanser ads of his youth, and Jimmie Larson was living out his hideous dream.

ONK ONK. Little Green Men again. Here is Johnny remember, hello. I send from Planet Gruk2Bic, danger oh shit you say. I be good boy. I love you. Smooch to Planet Earth.

I bring Boss data from Planet Earth fat fellow we squeeze it out. Boss now kill me maybe but not kill Earth. Earth we need for vid. I walk in hall of HAPPY DAYS old vid. Gruk2Bic go to Principal's office ha ha.

It is two of weeks only now. Then we do life but now we watch the vid. Love man with Action News. Love ladies win bucks and scream. Love family stand in room. Love men throw ball in hoop but falls out bottom. Favorite all is killing and fucking. More killing than fucking is. Same here. Fuck one or two a day but kill a shitload more. But we do not kill but the killers do.

Knock knock to the Boss who kill me maybe. I hope they do me quick not slow with bugs inside.

RICKIMORFT.

SAVOOTEBAH.

I come in room. Boss kills when eye is red but it is shut. I tell a joke. We will take measures, I say, three inches. He laughs and holds his pants at penis. Boss is baddest and that is why he is Boss, by jingo.

POOTYPOOTYGEEK.

He beats his head. He asks the news is true? Yes I tell him slow so he not kill me soon. Old man human who out of wormhole poop said what the fuck, named Jimmie.

We not know what we want but he not telling us it. Interrogations R Us, an Earth joke. I say shithead talk. On vid old cops say shithead talk. Tell stuff I say. He says what the fuck. I say talk or we squeeze till you pop. Fat human Jimmie screams. Needles are good. He miss the penis gone.

We say tell us the truth of killing and fucking. Tell how you get them do. We love so real. Then fat human Jimmie screams loud as holy shit—

THAT'S ACTING, YOU STUPID FUCK!

We stop the needles in. He tell. He spill the beans buster, by crackie. He tell all the acting. Vid is acting. Acting is fake. All we love it is fake. I say to the Boss and he says me back—

YOK?

NUK.

NORDLE?

Part time they kill or fuck is real. Part time they kill or fuck pretend. Humans pretend are actors big and rich. How humans know what is real they don't. Real is the great big thing. And us the Little Green Men is the wanting of real. Vid not real. We screwed.

Boss look me big red eye oboy. I am last day being Johnny. But big sudden light bulb blink. I say ORKABORK meaning *Eureka Boss*. Eureka meaning hot shit.

Boss say HUH. I got him now.

We go to Planet Earth I say. We do real of humans vid. Follow humans real. Find humans killing fucking all. We fire up computer Biloxi3. It is great big. Change real in bitty bits. Better than Earth vid. We know what we want. We not want sea turtles. We not want balls in baskets. We want killing and fucking. We devote our deepest minds.

Boss look to me. Am I big smarty? Will I be killing Boss?

Do I be made not Johnny? No. Boss is sold, yahoo. He shoots his hand with staples. I will be shit on shingle. Boss say we do a girl. This is big honor. We do a girl yessiree. She screams the best. I say thank you Boss that you do not kill me. He says my gun is out of squirt. We laugh ho ho. I go to the can and scream and scream.

Sorry we pop Jimmie. But I love you all. Big smooch and I am Johnny.

So this was the path by which Jimmie Larson, son of a whore, became Jimmie Larson again as he dissolved in lettuce. And Jimmie Larson might justly claim to have brought about, months later, on the Bay Bridge from Oakland to San Francisco, a bridge Jimmie Larson had never seen, the deliverance of our heroes, who did not yet know they were heroes but would start the knowing soon.

Chapter 11
Our American Stories

At recess Loki sat by the fence running his fingers over the chain link maze. Before, he'd looked through it at the high school as if to the Promised Land. Now he kept his eyes focused tight on the steel webbing. The high school lay beyond like a vast hotel of the dead where he had an advance reservation. He could see himself trudging up those steps and through the heavy one-way doors.

He listened for chickens. According to Mom, who worked for the TV news, people had reported hearing chickens. Three Unitarian congregations had been arrested by Federal agents for satanic ritual abuse when chicken bones were found in nearby dumpsters. He'd never actually met a chicken.

A sudden cry. He looked around. At the swings Artie and Dennis were fighting, and the other kids shrieked for blood. Artie landed a blow, and a geyser of rage spouted from Dennis, a mad spray blinding the sun. Loki slapped himself to shatter the vision, and Mrs. Clemson's shrill whistle cut through the children's playtime.

Officer Merck, the security guard standing by the teeter-totters, shifted his grip on his pistol, finished his candy bar, folded the wrapper, stuffed it neatly into his pocket, and scanned the playground. The rotund sentinel didn't mind if the kids slugged each other. His only job was to protect them from being shot by terrorists or other kids.

Loki tried to avoid the news about people going nuts, but still he felt invaded by stories. Stories were coagulating, skittering over the asphalt, running up his ankles, and they were real. Billy was real, the sterile halls of the high school were real, the bursts of blood were real, and even the imaginary chickens. Was this how it happened? Suddenly, one day, would he find himself with no skin to shield him, no eyelids to shut out the seeing? How many days could he stand to live without skin?

In the corner where the tree used to be, he saw the little girl. Jessie, he remembered her name was. She'd been scared when they'd played together, so she must know about things.

She must know how, when they played being trees, they really were trees. And she must know that they'd be married and have babies and grow very old. But how that would happen, how they would find their way from the playground to the caves of great mysteries, he couldn't see. He could only imagine a long long walk, like when Mom had a flat tire and they had to walk miles on a highway in Delaware.

The little girl scraped in the dirt and looked sad. He started toward her, then thought better of it. He hated being teased for talking to little kids. Artie had seen him playing with Jessie and jabbed him with a pencil, but he didn't think he'd have more trouble from Artie since he made Artie's teeth stick shut all day. Artie must know it was him.

The bell rang, and they lined up at the door. He walked in beside Artie, who glared at him but said nothing. Dennis, with his swollen lip, walked behind them, planning how to smuggle his dad's gun past Officer Merck. They trooped down the hall past the class bulletin board and into Room 103, Mrs. Clemson's room. Mrs. Clemson asked them to take out *Our American Stories* and turn to "Young Abe Lincoln."

Loki realized he hadn't brought anything to read. Since they'd gotten their new readers last week he'd gone cover to cover six times, but he couldn't stand one more trip through "Young Abe Lincoln." Sandburg's bio of Lincoln he'd liked, though Gore Vidal's novel seemed more realistic. But he couldn't say for sure because he knew he couldn't read.

The one good thing about Mrs. Clemson was that she knew Loki was retarded, so she didn't call on him. He could sit in back and bring a couple of books, maybe Dickens or Stephen King, and usually finish them by the end of the day. He'd really liked *The Idiot* and *David Copperfield* and *The Shining*, even though they had lots of sad parts. Molly Pzatryzoszyki teased him for pretending to read big fat books by turning the pages fast, but other kids teased Molly for not being able to spell her own name. So it went.

Mrs. Clemson started to talk about Young Abe Lincoln, how special he was, and Loki wondered if he was retarded too. His gaze wandered around the room. The flags, the pictures of American Presidents and famous billionaires, the Pepsi machine, the FBI warnings, the Ten Commandments in lettering you couldn't read. And the big vid where every morning they watched the happy news and the hit commercials. Mrs. Clemson was telling about Young Abe Lincoln reading by candlelight, but nobody was listening except Ariella, the fat girl, who raised her hand and asked, "Mrs. Clemson, did Young Abe Lincoln watch vid?" There were snickers because Ariella was fat. Loki would have felt sorry for her except that she was always pinching and shoving little kids in the hallway.

"Sorry, Ariella," Mrs. Clemson smiled. "No questions, remember? We need to listen to the lesson and not waste our time with questions, even if they're well intended."

Loki recalled the first day Mrs. Clemson had tried to explain the new policy. Studies showed that children who asked questions in school tended to ask questions in later life and develop dissatisfaction with the answers. So the school board agreed to comply with the new Federal policy that school was for the purpose of learning the answers. The lesson plan contained the answers the children needed for the tests. If they wanted more answers, their parents could take them to the zoo.

When Mrs. Clemson hated whatever she was saying she always said it with a big pinched smile. She believed in Right and Wrong, and Right was doing what you were told to do even if it was horribly wrong. Suddenly, the squawker squawked:

MRS. CLEMSON TO THE PRINCIPAL'S OFFICE.

She stopped abruptly, smiled, said, "Excuse me, children," and stepped out of the room. Officer Merck appeared at the door, cradling his automatic as he picked bubble gum from his upper lip. Since the shooting at Gates Elementary, many teachers were armed, and the guards were at the ready, waiting for someone to snap. Loki wondered if Mrs. Clemson had a gun and if she'd use it on a girl.

Mrs. Clemson's departure provoked a riot of screaming, hair pulling, and hurling small projectiles at the ugly girls or at Darryl the smart boy. Loki, in the back, felt fairly safe. He started to doodle in his notebook. He drew a series of squat overlapping ovals: that was Mom. A set of thin neat rectangles: that was Mrs. Clemson. The question had nagged him as long as he could remember: why were people so different? The Little Green Men he saw in his mind were all alike, and so were ducks and gerbils as far as he could tell. Yet every morning he saw

Mom and then Mrs. Clemson. How did they get that way?

It wasn't just their looks. Mrs. Clemson was white American, the way you were supposed to be, while Mom gleefully called herself an Afro-Cauca-Pino. Mom let him do anything, say anything, no boundaries, while with Mrs. Clemson there was Good and Bad and no wiggle room. Mom flopped around the house in old T-shirts and work pants, while Mrs. Clemson was tucked into her blue suit like a birthday present too neat to open.

He loved Mom, but she was like no other mom he'd ever read about. She had said he could call her "Tonya," but he called her Mom and she didn't hassle him, just said, "Whatever." He knew she blamed her acid trips for his being retarded, but he thought it was because he didn't have a dad. She'd tried to explain about his being conceived from a donor, not a dad, but it fogged his mind. If his father had no face, then where did he get his own? It was one of those monstrous paradoxes that lurked in the mist like a Moebius strip, and some day he knew he'd have to confront the dragon.

Mom would ramble off into stories of what she'd done and who she'd done it with. Loki tried to pretend he understood, but he couldn't keep it straight. He knew he had two half-sisters and they were living with some grandma and maybe he'd met them, but he couldn't remember. Mom said she'd been real young. Then there was Joy. Joy was Loki's daddy except she was a mommy, and Mom had Loki because they wanted a baby. But Joy had died, and Loki got born and tried to understand the precise anatomy of it all.

And then there was Benny. Benny was sort of like a dad, and when Benny visited Mom they'd make lots of noise behind the door. Loki liked when he played his guitar and sang funny songs, especially the one about dead cat soup. But Benny was gone weeks at a time, gigs he called it. Mom had other friends who'd come over and make noise behind the door — Miklos, Betsy and Homer, Woodie, Starflower — but Loki knew Benny was special.

The only thing he didn't like was when he heard Mom crying alone at night, even though he'd read lots of novels about moms crying alone at night, so maybe that's just what they did. Plus, she was a really bad cook.

But he knew Mom loved him, and she'd been proud of his work on the bulletin board for Parents' Night. She taught him a lot about the news, so he'd dug up lots of news, lettered headlines, and helped Sherry Pilaster pin stuff all over her map of the United States between the dancing rabbits. Rabbits didn't have much to do with the Presidential election, but Sherry liked to draw rabbits. Both Mom and Mrs. Clemson said they did a good job. Sherry got inspired and drew extra ears on her rabbits.

Now Mrs. Clemson returned to the room. She was pale and her hands were shaking. Officer Merck shambled out. She stood for a moment staring at the floor. Then she raised a face etched with an agonized smile. "Boys and girls," she chirped, "you know sometimes we do something we think is good, but then we find out it's not? Have you ever done that, where you thought you did what your daddy told you, but your daddy said it was bad? Well, that's not your fault or your daddy's fault, it's just a mistake."

Loki knew that it was very hard for Mrs. Clemson to lie. It wasn't natural to her. She always grinned frantically when she had to do it. It must have taken her many years of practice.

"So you know the Current Events board that you worked on so hard? And your parents thought it was a very grown-up thing, and everyone who worked on it — Loki, Sherry, Todd — should feel very positive. . ." She trailed off. For a moment she seemed to be crying, she was smiling so violently.

"But so, children, we need to take it down. Because it's just about people's opinions and not about what's real. Because no one really thinks our President is bad, and we don't want them thinking we think so. Not when we're right in the middle of 'Young Abe Lincoln.'" She squeezed out a giggle. "Because, Loki, maybe you'll be President some day—"

The class erupted in laughter. Loki shrank. Mrs. Clemson hushed them, said that anyone could be President and that if one of them was President they wouldn't want people saying bad things about them. "Because, children," she concluded, "in America we have free speech, but we won't have it for long if we use it all up."

She assigned Ariella and Barb to go out and take down the bulletin board display, then sat at her desk looking blankly at her lesson plan. Later, as they were reading the assignment, she came down the aisle to Loki and whispered to him that it was a very good job and that he wasn't to blame because he didn't realize what he was doing.

All he'd done was put up news that showed the President was a psychotic fascist crook, but didn't everyone know that already? Two hours to go. Loki decided to count the occurrence of each letter in *Our American Stories*, starting backward from the Z's.

He wished something big would happen.

Chapter 12
Green Tea and Decaf

Eddie and Pepper sat staring at the portfolio. They were in Bob's Diner. They had no way of knowing that there was no Bob, that there had never been a Bob, that Bob was actually a pot-bellied holding company in Houston. They had other worries. The yellow portfolio lay in the center of the pink Formica table, staring back.

"So," said Eddie.

"So?" On the subway, Pepper had pulled the report just far enough out of the portfolio to skim its right-hand two inches. Intermingled with mathematical formulae were words like *irreversible* and *devastation* and *end*. She knew her nightmares would begin right on schedule. She'd better take an extra tab of NoNarx.

"I don't like the way it's looking at me," Eddie quipped, shrugging to indicate it was a joke even though it wasn't. "Pink and yellow don't go good together."

The waitress came with coffee. "Anything else?" the pale creature asked. Her paper hat bore a smiling cartoon Bob.

"I ordered tea," Eddie said.

"I ordered decaf."

"Oh, sorry. Okay, decaf," said the waitress, as if taking their orders for the first time, "and what kinda tea?"

"Green tea."

"Green tea and decaf. Got it." The waitress raised two fingers and shambled off.

Eddie watched her go. "You suppose they're right about microwaves? They're rotting people's brains?"

"They just put that stuff out to sell newspapers," Pepper said in an undertone. "If somebody really proved it, we'd never hear about it." Feeling Eddie's gaze on her, she stared at the portfolio.

"So we sit here waiting for it to have babies?"

"Whatta we do, Eddie?" Pepper asked, instantly regretting her words. Survival depended on letting no one — not even yourself — see your naked fear.

"Well, we make some copies and pass'em out on the street? Or sell it to the movies? Hey, why do we assume it's true? Scrawny little maniac in a basement, maybe writing a novel. Does that guy look like a perpetrator of mass destruction?"

Pepper thought a moment. "Well yeh, he does."

Eddie drummed his fingers, then stopped. "I'm surprised," he said cheerily, "I'd mark you to be a heavy caffeine person."

Pepper looked at him. "I got too short a fuse. What's with the green tea?"

"I like green tea. My mom used to drink it. It was a big thing for a while, but they never have it now. I just order for the hell of it."

Again, the waitress brought their coffee. Again, Eddie explained that he hadn't ordered coffee, he'd ordered tea, and decaf for Pepper. The waitress looked at her fingers.

"Oh yeh, I know how I made the mistake. You said decaf and I remembered on one finger, then you said green tea and I remembered on the other finger, but that was two fingers then, and when I got to the kitchen I saw the two fingers I thought two green teas, but we don't have green tea so I brought coffee."

Eddie was silent, then smiled at her. "Yeh, well just gimme regular tea. You got a way you can remember it this time? Why don't you write it down?"

"I can't read my handwriting," she whined, adjusting her Bob hat, whose jollity seemed unperturbed, "but I'll remember." She trotted back to the kitchen.

Pepper met Eddie's gaze. "I better keep in mind that when you grin it means you want to kill somebody."

"Not always." He grinned.

Pepper looked away. Why did she look away? She never made eye contact that wasn't a staring contest, and she never lost. Even when the scrawny Mexican kid came into the store with his ancient .38, she'd held his eyes as she made her slow underwater move to the cash register, gentled open the drawer, handed him the bills. The kid was transfixed. She could have shot him any time with the 9mm under the counter, but it was Tommy's money, not hers, and Tommy was an asshole. Eyes glazed, the kid ran out the door directly into an oncoming garbage truck. Pepper, the winner and still champ.

This was different. Eddie's eyes invited her in, and she

knew a trap when she saw it. "Last week," she murmured, "I was complaining that my life was totally boring." She tapped the portfolio. "So where we going with this?"

"How about dinner?"

She jerked back. Did he think he could reel in the catch before he'd hooked it? "Eddie, I didn't think of this as a date, actually. I'm not sure I know you well enough to star in the same horror movie."

He grinned. Damn that grin. "Okay, we can fix that," he said. "Eddie Grabowski, thirty-four. Work on sound crews. Actually I'm an audio engineer but I get fired a lot. Married once for about ten minutes. Had a girlfriend for like five years, but she went thataway. It wasn't personal, we just had this political problem."

Pepper looked toward the kitchen. This dialogue could only end in orgasm and all the debris that followed. "Thought you said you weren't political," she heard herself say.

"Yeh, but Dottie was. She got into work on the campaign. She's real smart, brilliant even, but she gets inspired by these hyperthyroid morons. Being a Realist means don't let reality stand in your way. New ideas! Action! Actually, she got me some gigs setting up for speeches, but she knew I thought it was crap. Plus I'm not real easy to live with. So she split."

He looked up at Pepper. She was staring a hole through the portfolio.

"And let's see," he added, "when I was a kid I had this thing for sticking cats into mailboxes, so they'd pop out at people. When people still had mailboxes. But I haven't done that since second grade. What else you wanna know?"

"Who said I wanted to know?"

"I thought you kinda liked me."

"I kinda like you, Eddie, and maybe we oughta keep it that way. I'm looking at this little package while you're running off at the mouth, and I'm feeling very creepy. I'm sorry, Eddie, right now I'm just thinking what to do."

"I vote for dinner."

"Listen, dammit! I'm not in the market for boyfriends. Try me in about ten years when Jessie's out roaring around, if I haven't forgot how to fuck by then."

Eddie chuckled. "Wow." Pepper stared at the portfolio.

It seemed to be breathing a measured rhythm. *Que sera sera.* It was an old song her mom used to hum around the house, the worst song Pepper ever heard. This twit kept asking would she be rich and famous? Would she get laid? Would she get cut across the face with some guy's leather belt? So everybody was all full of wisdom, and they sang, *Que sera sera,* which meant basically, *Don't bother me, bitch.*

"My first husband was real hot into politics," Pepper mumbled.

"First husband?"

"Career Army, if you need to know. And the second, he sold plumbing supplies. They don't last a long time with me."

"So how'd you get to DC?"

"Space aliens dropped me. Look, Eddie, we're not—"

"You got other kids?"

"I got Jessie. Shut up with that."

The waitress came out of the kitchen red-eyed and empty-handed. She'd been crying, her frizzy brown hair was in disarray, and Bob was gone. She approached the table, lifting her hands in surrender.

"I'm sorry, could you— Cause I'm confused, I'm— Sometimes I— There's a mental block, kinda—"

Nothing new. Pepper saw it at work every day. In the two weeks she'd been there, besides the other incidents, one guy had sprayed the vending machines with a fire extinguisher, and a supervisor had brought a teddy-bear to work and carried it under his arm until mid-afternoon when he jumped out the window. Every week or so, Francine told her, Security had to drag out some woman who'd barricaded herself in the toilet. Pepper had friends who couldn't remember their maiden names — even guys, who didn't have one.

Eddie spoke very slowly. "What we wanted was, we wanted one cup of decaf coffee and one cup of tea."

"You wanted green tea," the waitress gasped.

"Yeh, but you don't have green tea," Eddie reassured her, "so I just wanted tea."

The waitress held up two fingers. "So say that again?"

"Decaf and tea. Any kind of tea."

The waitress stood there, tears welling up. "I'm trying to understand," she whimpered. "It's like there's bugs in my head." Pepper looked around. There was an old couple at the next table eating apple pie. How did they ever get apple pie? Maybe they brought their own.

"Okay, try this," Eddie offered. "Go to the door of the kitchen and I'll order the one thing. Okay?" The waitress sobbed quietly but went to the kitchen entryway. "One decaf!" Eddie called. "Tell me when that's ready. Just yell it out." The waitress smiled wanly and disappeared.

He turned to Pepper. "See, I don't expect that much. If two people can make each other feel better, have some fun, that's good, that's something we can do for each other. It's no big deal, it's just the way people do."

"You got a one-track mind," Pepper snapped.

"No, I multi-track. I just mix with the rhythm out front. It's not all in the lyrics. Although if the lyrics are good, maybe we get closer and then we're not alone. Cause otherwise we just sit around and tell each other how scared we are. If we're gonna wait till all the monsters turn into kittycats, we're gonna miss a lot."

The waitress appeared at the entryway. "I've got the decaf," she said, blurred but hopeful.

"Great," Eddie called. "Now set it right there where you can see it and then make a cup of tea. Any kind. Tea." She disappeared.

Pepper pressed her fist to her forehead. "These bastards," she muttered. "I guess we oughta be grateful to the newscasters, cause they really go out of their way to keep us dumb. There's stuff out there we do not want to know about. Does Jessie grow up in this madhouse? I mean if I could take a bomb and stick it far enough up the right guy—"

"Well, we got it right here in front of us. Who do we stick it up?"

Suddenly Pepper knew. She grabbed the portfolio, stood up, and jammed it into her shoulder bag. "Saturday!"

Eddie started to speak, but from the kitchen the waitress called, "I got it!"

"Great," Eddie said, "so bring the two cups out here. One in your left hand, one in your right."

The waitress lunged out of the kitchen, carrying both cups, banged into a table, spilling the cups over the elderly couple eating deep-dish apple pie. "Spiders!" the old woman gasped, throwing her fork at her husband as she screamed, "Forks! Pie!"

The waitress recoiled against another table, landing in the lap of a freckled-faced woman with two little boys. Hamburgers and fries flew like shrapnel. One boy grabbed the ketchup bottle, flung it against the window blinds shouting, "Atomic bomb!" The mother heaved the waitress off her lap and slapped both boys hard in the face. The waitress slipped on a pickle slice and went sprawling, wracked with sobs.

Eddie and Pepper rose to help the waitress, but she was wadded into a blue polyester ball of despair. Eddie kneeled and spoke softly to her, "Hey, it's okay. Happens all the time. Some days are like that." Pepper saw his gentleness and felt a sharp cramp of longing.

They quickly left Bob's Diner. Curled under a table, the waitress screamed after them, "Where's my tip?"

(No one could have imagined that this waitress, Tina Butterbaugh, would, by a strange twist of fate, go on to success as lead singer for the Onion Rings. Her song *Some Days Are Like That* went platinum.)

Eddie and Pepper walked with rapid strides toward the subway. At the steps she stopped, reached out and touched Eddie. They stood silently for a moment, neither knowing what words might be said or who would say them.

It was Pepper's voice. The noise of the traffic died away, a thin tremor filled the air, and her voice stood out full and clear. Eddie never figured out how that effect could have been engineered.

I wouldn't mind if you just held me. Would you do that, Eddie? Could we get together, maybe, sometime soon, and you just hold me?

I could do that. I sure could. Yes I could.

Had they spoken out loud?

Chapter 13
Animals

Saturday, Tonya sat on the single unrotted bench in the dilapidated little neighborhood park, shading her eyes as she scanned the want ads on her Pad. Most of the listings weren't real, she knew, but only posted to give the illusion — boosting the stock value — that the companies were expanding. She admitted to a nostalgia for the old days when they listed jobs in newspapers. Nowadays the only reason people bought papers was for their dogs to dump on. A memory from the past, but the past was the only certainty she could hold onto.

Today was almost like summer. Freaky weather. Loki stood by the swings twisting two dangling chains together then clanging them against the steel uprights. Tonya couldn't recall when the swings had ever had seats. Liability issues, probably.

As scroungy as the park was, Tonya was grateful for it. A few years back there were plans to pave it over, as they'd done with most other parks and half the Mall, to discourage the homeless encampments. But the Administration had solved the homeless problem by making "Premeditated Poverty" a Class 2 felony. To their credit the Realists had fulfilled their campaign pledge to put vast new sums into public housing: prisons. Now the parks were clear.

She scanned the ads: dermatologist, dietitian, director of development. She could do any job that didn't actually kill someone. You just concocted a resume, surfed the Web to learn the jargon, and spent the first two days on the job faking it while picking up the basics. Sailing instructor, sales, seismic research— No, she needed a sit-down job.

If only her body weren't betraying her. She liked her body — a squat muscled eggplant — when it behaved. She'd pushed all limits, explored the crags, clefts, and caverns of every gender passionately, furiously, joyously, full wattage, non-stop. But now the machinery was failing — her lower back, her arthritis, her knees.

Loki clanged the chains. "Enough with the noise!" she shouted. He gave her a cockeyed glance through his dense spectacles, then pulled a wad of string from his pocket and started untangling it. How would he look at sixteen? Already at nine her son was a gawky beanpole, thin face, thick glasses, baseball cap, delicate fingers so easily snapped. Of course he looked nothing like her, not remotely. When people asked about that, she always made up something. Actually he's adopted. Actually his dad had really hyper genes. Actually he looks like my grandfather, who was white. Actually it's none of your fucking business.

Yes, he looked like Joy. Her paleness, her fragility, her wonderment. And a little bit like Moondog, their friend and sperm donor — that broad mouth, those big ears. Now Moondog was dead and so was Joy and so were their dreams. And Joy's egg, fertilized in vitro, implanted in Tonya and born from her womb, was weaving an intricate cat's cradle between his fingers. In the sun his face was Joy's, but his shadow was her own.

She focused back on the want ads. Technical writer: she bookmarked the ad. To write what was actually true? She could do that, though she'd need a little practice. These days she didn't even believe her own grocery list. She checked her watch: just past noon. They should go back to the house for lunch.

She looked over at Loki and saw a tiny girl standing beside him. Both were staring at the cat's cradle web in his fingers. Near them, a wiry blonde woman. Tonya recognized her as someone with whom she'd exchanged chit-chat at Parents' Night and maybe once at the park. Some spicy name, Ginger, Cinnamon, something.

"Hi there," the woman called. "Jessie, I'll be over here." The little girl paid no attention. Tonya's lips tightened. She didn't do mom-chat easily, and especially with some lady whose taut butt Tonya could feel thirty feet away but who was probably as straight as a pool cue. The woman approached Tonya. Down, girl, Tonya told herself. Every vanilla lady you've made it with, you've been crucified.

"Yeh," Tonya stammered, "We met at Parents' Night? School? I was trying to think—"

"Pepper McBride." Tonya saw that she had a slight gap between her front teeth. That always meant loud cries. Suddenly she felt she was fifteen again and Bix, the stud athlete, had her pants down and knew he could do any damn thing he wanted to do. Which, bless him, he did.

"Pepper," Tonya heard herself saying, "Yeh, I knew it was something hot." Stop it. You don't get involved with straight women, remember?

"Garlic, maybe," Pepper smiled. "Aren't they cute?" She nodded toward the kids, who had seated themselves on the cold asphalt. Loki was weaving Jessie's hands into the webwork.

"Aren't we all?" Stop it, you idiot, you're flirting. "I'm Tonya."

"I noticed you here on Saturday sometimes."

"Well, he's nine. He's a handful. One way to get him out of the house."

"Jessie's six," Pepper said, then shouted, "Jessie, keep your shoes on!" She gestured toward the children. "They seem to be getting along."

"Loki has a problem making friends. They put him in Special Ed, he's either really dumb or really smart, I don't know which, but he's got a pretty active imagination." She heard herself chatting away like a junior high girl who needed to pee. "He amazes me. He was two and a half, he walked into the lake like it's solid ground. Course he sank and I jumped in, but he said, 'Mommy, let me try again.' Want a cookie?"

Pepper took a ginger snap, and Tonya realized suddenly that she'd been talking about Loki. She never talked about Loki, even to lovers. He was her own mystery, undiscovered. Yes, Joy, he's what we made together. He's what's left.

Pepper was asking something. Tonya saw lips moving, tasted the lips, and braced herself against the pang. Then for a moment she saw herself reflected in Pepper's eyes: this little brown butterball, multiracial pumpkin, prurient freak, tattooed fireplug, phantasmagoric lump. She'd had dozens of lovers, but right at this moment in time she couldn't imagine she could attract flies. Snap out of it, sister!

"You said you worked for, what, the TV news?" Pepper's voice cut through the fog.

"Copy writer. Yep. Things are getting kinda creepy there. I was just checking the want ads. I'd like to find something where I could let my hair go back to its natural color."

"What's that?"

"Green."

Pepper offered another ginger snap. "My mom loved ginger snaps," said Pepper. "Only thing we had in common besides hating my dad." She stood up. "Jessie, get your fingers out of your mouth!"

The kids paid no attention. Loki had the stringwork back onto his hands, and Jessie was sucking her fingers that had been woven into dreams, trying to keep the taste. The little girl stared at the web, and as Loki turned his hands outward it shifted its working. Jessie saw the air change color.

Pepper sat back on the bench. "Do I remember your husband was a musician?"

Husband? Tonya drew a blank. Then she remembered she'd said something at Parents' Night about Benny. *Got to get back to my man*, or some such crap. Benny had been visiting that week, and she'd taken a few hours to get up from the sack and go to Parents' Night.

"Oh yeh, that's Benny, but he's not— Yeh, I guess he is sorta husbandlike. He travels, musician, we have good times when he's around. Why get married?" She refrained from saying that Benny might be clinically insane. Who could say? He'd never been to a clinic.

"Yeh," Pepper nodded, "I'm between episodes myself. I was always attracted to the bad boys but married the good ones. To my regret." They sat in silence watching the kids, who were now sitting under the single dogged evergreen. Pepper clutched her shoulder bag. Her lips were flint. For Tonya the thrill of sitting beside this hot-wired fox was wearing thin.

"So on TV, on the news, I always wondered," Pepper asked, "do they make up that stuff or is it all real?"

"I don't ask," Tonya said after a moment. "I get stuff off the wire, boil it down, add some jokes, try to make it entertaining. They tell me if they want it sunny side up or fried like leather, and I oblige."

"You don't sound too positive."

Tonya was silent. The very fact that right now she was soaked in humid lust was a sure sign this lady was bad news. She sounded like Texas or Oklahoma, was probably born-again and loved President Bud. "Time for lunch!" she called out to Loki. He gave no sign of hearing.

Jessie looked up from the tangle of tree roots to see Loki, behind his glasses, staring cross-eyed at her nose. He was strange, but he didn't act mean like the other boys. "What are you looking at?"

"Your third eye." Yesterday he'd read a book about India, where people had a third eye. The third eye saw what the other eyes didn't see. The gods had one and so did people. But in people it was closed, like the eyes of baby birds. You had to think it open, and if your third eye was open then you didn't have to raise your hand and ask Mrs. Clemson the truth, and she didn't have to lie. You both knew.

"People don't have three eyes. They only have two." He glanced away. She was sorry she'd said it. "Don't they?"

"No."

Loki's mother called him again. Jessie didn't want him to go. She remembered a story Mommy had read her long ago, where the children made up a world and then lived in it. She'd tried to tell the story at school, but the teacher said it was bad because it wasn't real. She had to go sit in the Bad Girls' Seat, and she'd cried and cried.

She remembered the first time she'd met Loki. *Want to play animals?* But he meant *be* animals. That was very scary, but she'd thought about it every day since. Maybe he really knew how to be animals. Maybe they could be animals with three eyes.

"How do you be animals?" she asked.

Loki turned to her, looking funny. She couldn't tell if he was happy or about to sneeze. "You want to?" he asked wide-eyed.

"Maybe."

His mother was calling again. She sounded mad.

"Animals, okay. We just— We're on all fours, but kinda feel like your spine is a snake and kinda make your nose long, and you're not you, there's somebody else inside. . ." He started barking and prancing about on his hands and knees. Jessie laughed. It was all just a game. Loki beat his chest like a gorilla with huge bug eyes. "Animals! Animals!" they shouted.

On the bench Tonya started to rise, then gave it up. "He gets pretty rambunctious," she said, then lapsed into silence.

Under the tree the children cavorted, barking, meowing,

growling, cackling like crows. Then suddenly they found themselves crouched face to face, and they froze, deep in each other's vision. Jessie felt her eyes glaze. Her breathing slowed to an alien rhythm. She felt a power flow into her small hands and haunches, the savage grace of a cat. They gasped, and their third eyes blinked open.

Just for an instant. The eyes that reflected each other were ageless eyes, older than rivers. Death and deathlessness shook them, and they heard an echoed laughter. And then they blinked shut. Years later, making love, they sometimes caught that ancient glimmer of eyes startled open.

The moment was gone. The game trailed off. Scarcely breathing, they stared at the gnarled tree root between them. Jessie glanced up at Loki. His cheeks were wet. Was he happy or sad or grit in his eyes?

"What were we?" she whispered.

"Just animals," he said in an odd thin voice. Jessie dug at the root. She wanted to cry for the joy of it all, but Loki was sitting totally still, so she did too.

Tonya rose. "I think I'm gonna have to drag Loki home by the ankle." Pepper was still staring straight ahead. "Sorry, I never asked like, what do you do, that stuff—"

"Phone company, customer service. I tell people to fuck off." Pepper clipped her words like fingernails.

Tonya mumbled a vague apology about not being very good company right now. Just get out of here, she thought, there's something funny going on, and you don't need to know what. "So I'll be seeing you." She started toward Loki.

Pepper rose. "Actually, I remembered you," she blurted. Tonya stopped. "I wanted to talk." Tonya waited for her to speak, expecting what? A confession of lust? Evangelism? She was jolted by the burning eyes meeting hers, but the voice was distant, quavering. "How would somebody, like, get something on the news?"

Tonya shrugged, forced a laugh. "What, like if you're doing a cookie sale?"

"No," Pepper continued in a slow treble sing-song as if someone had a gun to her head forcing her to speak. "I mean like if there was gonna be a major disaster that might destroy the country, and you just happened to find out?"

The thought hit Tonya that maybe this lady was nuts.

"Like if somebody thought you were a secret agent and gave you a top-secret package, and you thought what the hell is gonna happen to my kid so you had to do something about it but you didn't know what to do?"

Tonya tried to pull away from those fierce eyes, but she couldn't. Tell her to write a screenplay and make a bundle. Tell her to get laid. Tell her to stop reading junk fiction. Tell her to get real.

"Well, I dunno," said Tonya, shaken, "I guess you'd find somebody who worked on the news and give'em the— this top-secret package. If you wanted it on the news."

Pepper reached into her shoulder bag and drew out a yellow portfolio. She handed it to Tonya.

"What's this?"

Pepper looked at her. The fear was past. "News," she said.

And by the tree, which was theirs now, Loki stood up. "See you," he said.

"Okay," said Jessie. "I will too."

Chapter 14
Something Big

Five days later, bundled against the chill, Loki sat with Jessie in the corner of the schoolyard, holding two pine cones.

"So what they're saying is, the Flunky says SNURF. That means, *Okay, Boss, all systems go. The Galactic Improbability Generator is fired up. All the Earth people for the reality show are going to start next week on Channel One.* And the Boss says NORMATAZOT GOBATOPAT BOOMBOOM OCONOMOWOC!"

He paused. Jessie knew he wanted her to ask him what that meant. "What's that mean?"

"It means *Great!*"

He tossed the pine cones over the fence. Jessie asked him if there were really Little Green Men. He said that he would tell her when he knew. The bell rang.

Harold & Rosalie sat at the Action News desk, facing their ruination. After a resonant pause, Harold forced his lips open to say:

> AND THIS: THE PERT ADMINISTRATION
> REACTED SHARPLY TODAY TO OUR ACTION
> NEWS EXCLUSIVE ON THE ALLEGED
> DANGERS OF NONARX. SPOKESMEN CALLED
> THE REPORT "ALARMIST" AND VOWED A
> PROBE. ACTION NEWS WILL OF COURSE
> COOPERATE FULLY.

Theme music kicked in, a commercial blared, and Harold deflated to half his volume. Rosalie tried to peel off her smile, but it clung like a hysterical tick. "Or else, baby," she whispered.

They sat through their two-minute break saying nothing. Harold adjusted his undershorts. Rosalie knew what he was suffering. Ten seconds before GO he'd discovered a dark stain on his shirt. He spat on it, which enlarged it, then finally pulled his tie diagonally to cover the blotch. To compensate he leaned ten degrees off perpendicular. Now he'd strained his back.

Rosalie thumbed the three blank pages in front of her. One, two, three. Three sheets, as always. Blank, as always. Yellowish beige. These sheets, to millions of viewers, contained the latest, hottest Action News. She glanced at them once at the top of each broadcast to indicate that the news she reported was documented in black on yellowish beige. Then she read it off the prompt. Whose idea was it, years ago? Why did she thumb them to assure herself that they were there?

She waited for GO. Don't panic. It was Harold's turn to carry the ball. They needed sincerity now, and he could turn on the spigot. She was no good at sincerity. The public loved her smile, but they knew it was fake. She glanced at Harold, whose brow furrowed up, getting a running start on his sincerity. Five seconds to GO, and suddenly Rosalie felt her face falling off.

She touched it with her fingertips so as not to muss her makeup. It had started to crack in the dressing room, and now she felt hairline fissures weaving their jagged paths across the skin. She'd caked it over and that seemed to hold it in place, but now the fabric was giving way. She knew it was hallucination. For weeks now her face had been cracking, her fingers elongating and squirming about the news desk, her breasts hardening into hairy coconuts. Grotesque, but she'd got used to it and pretty much conquered the panic if not the vomiting.

The floor manager signaled GO. Rosalie fastened her smile in place and ground her teeth. She felt the left rear molars crumble like granola. It was all illusion, but it felt so realistic. She gagged, and Harold said her line without missing a beat.

NOW, SOMETHING ON THE LIGHTER SIDE—

But Harold's mike was dead. A voice like a cranky blender filled their ears.

CHANNEL SIX NEWS, THIS IS MABEL
MCCLAFFERTY! AGAIN!

It was the viewer response line going out live. As the camera zoomed in on Harold, Rosalie pinched her nose back into place.

LISTEN, THIS REPORT THING, WHATTA YOU
APOLOGIZING FOR? IT'S A KNOWN FACT. MY
NEPHEW WAS IN THE MARINES—

The floor manager was signaling them, patting the top of his head. Rosalie had no idea what that meant. The voice squawked on.

—HIS SQUAD, THEY'RE OUT ON PATROL, START
HEARING EACH OTHER CROAK, AND THEY

TURN INTO BULLFROGS. WITH NAME TAGS.
MY SISTER, SHE BROUGHT HIM HOME AND
PUT HIM IN THE FISH TANK. HE CAN CROAK
YES OR NO.

Harold grinned into the camera. It's that charm, Rosalie thought. Smiling like that, he could cut out your heart and you'd swear it wasn't his fault. And he was a matchless improviser.

THAT WASN'T US, WAS IT, ROSALIE? THAT WAS
CRAZY HENRY, UP IN THE BOOTH, TRYING
TO LIVEN US UP. BUT NOW FOR SOMETHING
ON THE REALLY LIGHTER SIDE...

Rosalie touched her face. There was always a numbness after the hallucinations. She felt a gentle breeze through her eye sockets. Her face was stable, but she'd lost her eyes. She heard her cue, looked at the prompt, but she had no eyes to see with. "Oh Christ," she stammered, and then it all came up.

Tonya was clearing out her desk. The Administration's reaction to the release of Sergei Rupp's report had been savage. In fact, she'd been surprised that the report ever saw light. She'd simply handed it to the news director, knowing there was no way to corroborate its validity. But it was station policy never to question what appeared to be an official government press release, so came the avalanche. The Press Secretary called it a terrorist act and announced investigations by the FCC, FBI, DHS, and EPA. Harold's on-air assurances of cooperation were followed instantly by an abject disavowal of the report. But the station needed a scapegoat, and that was Tonya. If they hadn't targeted her she'd have volunteered. With severance pay she'd be fine for a couple of months. Her superiors' pusillanimous capitulation left her vastly relieved.

J.G. Babcock stood by her desk as she emptied folder after folder into the shredder. "What about me?" he asked.

"I dunno, J.G.," she said, "I wish I could tell you. You might just hang around and not get noticed, and as long as there's a credit to your balance every month, you might cash in for quite a while."

"Would that be honest?"

"J.G., what's the purpose of history if not to rationalize stuff? Just ask yourself," Tonya went on, shaking the shavings out of the antique pencil sharpener she'd insisted on keeping, "do you think human beings, once they're born, have any inherent right to exist? I'm asking what you think, not the entire history of Humanism."

"Well," Babcock ventured, "I suppose I do."

"Okay, so this is the means by which the universe offers you personally a right to exist. Don't question it."

Harold appeared at the cubicle. "Tonya! Hey, what's happening!" He grinned.

Startled, she looked up. "Well, Harold, you must be out of the loop. The official motive for my dismissal was, I believe, high treason, bad breath, something like that."

"Tonya, it's all a screw-up. You're okay."

"I'm okay? Right, yes, I know. You're okay too, Harold. I'm okay, you're okay. Isn't that in the Bible?" She tossed a bent paper clip into the shredder.

"False alarm, babe," grinned Harold. "We're all home free."

Tonya stared at him.

"Tonya, I always admit it when I'm wrong. We're cool, we're flying high. Journalistic integrity is back in the saddle. Who woulda thunk it?" Harold babbled on. The higher-ups had ordered blood sacrifice to stave off reprisals and braced to ride out the debacle, so they were ill-prepared for hitting the jackpot. Two days after the story broke, the ratings were astronomical. Now all media conglomerates, though vigorous supporters of President Bud, were headlining the revelations. Faced with the ballooning integrity of American journalism and a couple of private calls from billionaires, the President appointed a blue-ribbon panel. Terror swept America and skyrocketed his approval ratings to nearly 20%.

"Tonya, the public is scared shitless," Harold exulted. "We did it. You did it. We can ride this story like a rubber duckie. This'll play longer than— Who was that lady that boiled her kids? You're hot stuff, babe." Harold could almost taste the tang of dark meat now, and he was on the verge of inviting her out for a drink to see what might transpire. But he caught the faintest glint of murder in her eye and desisted.

Tonya just stared. Harold's smile held, then began to sag. Babcock's stomach growled, and Tonya turned to meet his silent plea. In her heart she wanted to pinch Harold's smile into a scribble across his face. To spit in his eye. To jam his necktie into the shredder and flip the switch to espresso grind.

Instead, she gazed into Babcock's gentle dog eyes and said, "Fine, Harold. Thanks. Glad it worked out."

At the kitchen counter of his Georgetown condominium, Sergei Rupp pared a thick slice from a chunk of kefalotiri, refilled his water glass with vodka, flicked on the vid embedded in the door of the fridge. His luxury apartment was utterly bare except for the wall-to-wall carpets, an air mattress in the living room, and four bedrooms so clogged with stacks of books, files, and storage boxes that he could no longer enter them. Despite the clutter it was spotlessly clean. He nibbled his cheese, took a swig of vodka, and tuned into Action News.

> MORE BIZARRE EVENTS, ROSALIE, IN THE
> RISING CONTROVERSY OVER NARCOFLIX.
>
> HAROLD, WE HAVE ON-THE-SCENE FOOTAGE
> OF THAT STRANGE REPORT FROM NEW
> YORK. WHAT ARE WE SEEING HERE?
>
> WHAT WE'RE SEEING, ROSALIE: IN LOWER
> MANHATTAN, PASSENGERS EMERGED FROM
> THE WALL STREET SUBWAY IN RAGS AND
> SHACKLES, BELIEVING THEMSELVES TO BE
> THE CARGO OF A PORTUGUESE SLAVE SHIP.

The train doors slid open, and a thin woman in an Italian-cut linen suit, shredded and stained, staggered off the train. A hand grasped her ankle and she fell to her knees. Through the door, gasping for air, stumbled a frantic throng in tattered business attire, battering each other with briefcases — bloody, haggard, some with open sores, stripped to the waist or entirely naked except for a necktie. Somehow the viewer could catch the overwhelming stench of excrement. A pudgy face scarred by the lash. An executive secretary clutching a dead baby to her sagging breast. A child dressed for day school, its face half eaten by rats. Lunatics all, impelled by their hellish illusions. The camera zoomed in on the manacles.

Sergei wrote an equation on his steno pad, chugged vodka, giggled as he wept. Harold's brow furrowed with his trademarked concern.

> THE SLAVES INCLUDED A SENIOR VICE
> PRESIDENT OF MERRILL LYNCH. THEY WERE
> TREATED FOR SCURVY AND RELEASED.
>
> HAROLD, THE PRESIDENT BLAMED THE
> INCIDENT ON LIBERAL TEXTBOOK BIAS
> AGAINST THE FREE-MARKET ECONOMY.
>
> HERE'S MORE, ROSALIE. A GROUP OF
> JAPANESE TOURISTS ON ALCATRAZ
> ISLAND HAVE BARRICADED THEMSELVES
> IN SOLITARY. THEY ARE REPORTED TO BE
> HEAVILY ARMED AND SPEAKING WITH
> CHICAGO ACCENTS. NEGOTIATIONS ARE
> UNDER WAY.

The camera scanned the face of the Rock. No signs of life. Suddenly a fedora appeared in a dark window slit, and the glow of a cigar. Sergei scribbled his equation, poured another glass. "Berger/Luckmann hypothesis," he mumbled. "Here and now. Shazam." Rosalie flashed her fiercest smile.

> ON A LIGHTER NOTE, HAROLD: THE RESIDENTS
> OF THE CODGERS AND CRONES NURSING
> HOME IN LINCOLN, NEBRASKA, WERE
> WATCHING MONDAY NIGHT FOOTBALL,
> AND GUESS WHAT? THEY STARTED PLAYING
> FOOTBALL THEMSELVES.

Squad cars pulled up screaming. A team of blue-rubbered firemen prepared a water cannon. A nurse scurried down the flagstone walk. Cheers were heard. Close-up of an old lady's toothless maw crying, "Go, team, go!"

> THE CODGERS BEAT THE CRONES 39 TO 6 BUT
> SUFFERED TEN FRACTURES AND THREE
> DEATHS FROM EMPHYSEMA.

Sergei screamed at his refrigerator door. "You see? Is real! Is real!" He refilled his glass and toasted the proof of his predictions, laughing, screaming, sobbing in triumph.

Harold burbled on about the President's claim that the flood of hallucinations was clear proof that the Realist policy was working to bring the kooks out of the woodwork. "They are not hallucinations!" howled Sergei Rupp. "Not hallucinations! They are reality! They are hundred fires blooming, and center will not hold!"

> MORE NEWS AT TEN.

Rosalie's china face crazed into a thousand shards that floated down, as weightless as cherry blossoms. Harold sauntered off with his latest intern — sour-faced wide-butted Katrina — while his wife sat sobbing like a muddy rag doll. As a woman, she wanted to die. As a pro, she knew they were onto something big.

Chapter 15
The Omelet of Consummation

After dreamless sleep, Pepper woke facing a hairy back. As her life flashed before her eyes, she puzzled on the hairy back's identity. Not as woolly as Clint, and Sterling was bare and pimply. Then it hit her: Eddie. She braced for a rush of panic but was startled to feel contentment. She drowsed back to sleep.

When she woke again, the other side of the bed was empty. She threw on her bathrobe, stumbled to the kitchen. Eddie was cracking eggs into a bowl, while Jessie was convulsed in giggles. "Morning," Eddie said, "take your time. Coffee's on."

Pepper went to the bathroom. For the past week Eddie had been persistent, and at last she'd arranged for the neighbor's kid to babysit while they went out to dinner. Eddie talked a blue streak — electronics, bands, politics, old girl friends — but he was different from the jerks who went through their two-bit routines. He talked to her. He looked at her. It seemed as if he saw her.

And he was funny, give him that. No, she didn't trust jokers, but he didn't tell jokes, he told life, and life on his tongue was an acrid, endlessly comic dance. She thirsted for that. Still, she'd said very little through dinner, only her one silent mantra over and over again: don't get involved!

They'd returned early to find Tina, a rotund seventh-grader, sprawled on the sofa amid her collection of monster comics reading aloud, in a high sing-song voice to a saucer-eyed trembling Jessie, the saga of Argasmo the Human Squid. "She wanted a bedtime story," Tina explained, glugging one last glug of her third Pepsi. Pepper took Jessie off to bed, steeling herself for a marathon of *Don't leave me, Mommy!* though relieved that at least she wouldn't have to make excuses to get Eddie out the door. But Eddie followed her into Jessie's room, put his hand on the spooked child's forehead, and said, "Jessie, you know what?"

And then he'd told Jessie that he used to work with Argasmo the Human Squid, who played lead guitar with the

Sucker Puppies and had truly reformed since the days when he slurped out people's brains. Jessie whined angrily for him to stop — she knew she was being cajoled — and Pepper tried to hush him.

But Eddie went on to tell of Argasmo's family, his long-suffering wife and their five little squidlets, and how he liked to eat little boys but little girls were too sweet, and he forgot to brush his teeth and got a toothache in his tentacle. And Eddie fell into Tina's sing-song treble and told of Argasmo's search for love when his wife left him because his whiskers sprouted all over his body, until he met a lady lobster who combed him out with her pincers and he felt a lot better after that—

And when Jessie whimpered Eddie whimpered, not in mockery but in whimper-speak, the sound of *Yes, I know*, the language of children and baby birds. Argasmo had whimpered too when he read the comic book that told all the bad things he'd done but didn't say how he helped old ladies raise their geraniums, and one old lady was Baba Yaga, a magical witch who turned him into a duck—

And Jessie was asleep.

Pepper and Eddie had risen from the edge of Jessie's bed without a word, walked hand and hand into the bedroom, made love, and Pepper wept with the joyous impossibility of it all.

Now, shuffling back to the kitchen, she filled Jessie's cereal bowl, poured coffee as Eddie set an omelet and toast in her place at the table. "You never asked me if I liked omelets," she murmured.

"You like omelets?"

"Yes."

"Then you got one."

She sat down, irritated and gratified. Jessie dawdled over her cereal as usual. "You know what Loki said?"

"Jessie, Loki's a nice boy, and I'm sure he said neat stuff, but right now, honey, I'd like it if what Loki told you was to eat your cereal."

"That's not what he said."

"Okay, honey, hurry up."

"He said there's a big boy who hurt a girl bad."

"Bad-ly."

"Bad-ly."

Pepper knew what Billy Sturgis had done. Every parent in America knew it. And every parent remembered having a similar urge to let it all go and smear the classroom with blood — an AK-47 if you had one or a No. 2 pencil if you didn't. Once there'd been a radio guy who asked people things like, "Did you ever stick your finger up your ass?" The pundits hated him, maybe because they'd all stuck their fingers up their ass, but people loved him because he was asking questions they couldn't. Had the President ever stuck his finger up his ass? That guy would have asked it. People didn't ask things now.

Jessie looked up at Eddie. "Are you going to sleep here?"

Eddie hesitated, grinned at Pepper. "Well, maybe. If I'm invited."

Pepper took a deep breath. How did she get into these things? "That okay, Jessie?" she asked. "Once in a while?"

"Sure."

"Hey, Jessie, eggs coming up."

"Jessie doesn't like eggs."

"You want eggs?" Eddie asked Jessie.

"Yes, please."

"Okay, you can have an egg," Pepper said, "but you have to finish your Huggle."

Eddie placed a small omelet in front of Jessie, who dug in eagerly, ignoring her cereal bowl. Eddie stroked Pepper's hair as he asked her softly, sweetly, why she was feeding her kid such vile crap.

"I beg your pardon?"

"Huggle is crap. Why do you feed her that shit?"

"That's not your concern, Eddie—"

"There's nothing to it. It's not food."

"She likes it."

"Because it's all sweetener and salt."

"And vitamins—"

"And Styrofoam. Huggle is crap."

Eddie had worked the sound crew recording the first Huggle commercials four years ago. Worst job he'd ever had. He normally liked these gigs because they'd have a great lunch buffet for the crew. There, everything was Huggle. Fifty-six varieties of Huggle. All sweet salty slippery slimy plastic.

Think Hamburger Helper meets Bubble Wrap. It had started as a weight-loss supplement: tiny polymer granules that cohered until the digestive fluids dissolved their bond, at which point they were fast-track legislation out the other end. You had the sense of being stuffed to the gills, then the rampant trots. Sales were low until some whiz kids developed a constipant that reassembled the rioting mob in the upper intestinal tract. "Makes'em all hug together," a lab technician joked. Marketing ears pricked up, and Huggle was born. The promo theme was Family Reunions.

It wasn't easy. They had to create tastes and textures to prevent people from gagging. Tofu Technoids did a good job on the textures — fibrous Huggle, fruity Huggle, flaky Huggle, more — but the plastic stench penetrated the strongest flavor. Finally they solved it the old-fashioned way: heavy sweetener and tons of salt.

Despite an award-winning ad campaign, sales lagged. People didn't lose weight. The sweetener induced sharp cravings for carbohydrates, and folks just got fatter. The target market was wrong. It was Sissy Winker, a newly-hired college grad in the ad agency, who said, "Why don't we just call it *food*?"

Simultaneously, the newly-installed Pert Administration faced a PR crisis. The poverty level stood at 32% and worsening. The clamor was muffled by raising the poverty threshold, but it remained a thorny issue. Then lobbyists floated an idea on a surf of hard cash, and President Pert announced an unprecedented humanitarian initiative to abolish hunger in the United States of America. The War on Terror, he proclaimed, must include a War on Hunger, Want, and Injustice. His speech writers lifted whole passages from Kennedy, Johnson, and Martin Luther King, and the Feds funded a massive food distribution comprised entirely of Huggle. It supplanted the school lunch program and other discredited federal giveaways like Social Security and promoted a uniquely American way of banishing hunger from the face of the Earth: indigestible food. Eddie could rant about Huggle for hours.

Pepper spun around to confront him. "Look! Don't tell me how to raise my kid. That's off limits. Being right doesn't make it right. That better be understood or this is going to be one damn short relationship." Her eyes were needles.

Eddie shrugged. You didn't argue with those eyes. "Okay. Cool. Sorry."

"Sorry, Eddie, you just hit a nerve." She sipped her coffee and took a bite of the omelet. Good, he liked onions.

Jessie finished her omelet, drank her milk, and left her Huggle untouched for the rest of her long eventful life. "Mommy," she ventured, "last night did you make a real loud sound?"

Pepper stopped chewing. She looked at Eddie, then replied matter-of-factly through the last morsel, "Yeh. I was just happy." She began clearing the table. Jessie hopped down from her chair and began walking in circles around the table, making a low droning sound. She seemed to be happy that Mommy was starting the day happy.

"She's a sixty-cycle hum," Eddie said.

"Jessie, look," Pepper said, rinsing the plates, "today's a school holiday, but it's not for Mommy, so I had to call in sick cause I've got some business. So we've gotta go downtown, but then maybe we can go see the dinosaurs."

The tiny girl's arms extended to a span of thirty feet, and she flapped her leathery struts. Her beak shot out and clattered its glittery teeth, and colorful fern-like scales bejeweled her brow. A wee blonde archaeopteryx bounded around the kitchen emitting banshee squeaks. It was a good day for chomping those pesky mammals.

"Okay, Jessie, that's enough now—" Pepper caught herself. The voice of her mother, that same bitter mouth in the presence of joy. "So, hon, okay, now get your coat and your dolly if you want. Now hurry." Jessie bounded out of the room with a thin squeal that inside her head was a thunderous roar. Pepper watched her bantam reptile flutter away, felt Eddie take her hand. "I guess I'm kinda noisy," she said with a shrug.

"I'll bring my VU meter. We don't want to bend the needle."

"Better not pursue that one." She was amused, then irritated at her amusement. She felt a sudden tidal surge — whether to grab Eddie and kiss him hard or fling the skillet at him, she didn't know — but she simply let the wave break on the shore. Eddie held her gently at the waist, a shy boy after the prom. She ran a finger over his unshaven chin and looked him in the eye like a shopper at the meat counter scanning what might cook up for dinner without too much fuss.

"I like you a lot, Eddie," she said with a faint smile. "I don't want a big slobbering relationship, but you might get invited some. You might."

They were unfamiliar with each other's gentleness. The night before had been the rush of need, and they were perfect partners in tumult, mustangs in the storm wind matching stride for stride. Now their touch was fragile, inept. She raised her lips to meet his and missed. He grinned. So did she.

Pepper moved to the counter and picked up an envelope from a stack of sorted mail. Eddie suggested going out for dinner, bringing Jessie along, maybe Tofuttiville. "They've got like for kids this big plastic tube they can crawl through, twists all around like a gut. Makes it seem really fun to get digested."

Somehow she sensed he was going to jump from plastic guts to politics. Too early in the morning. He'd said he was totally non-political, but once he got started he couldn't shut up. "Crazy thing," she waved the envelope to stop him, "I get this thing from the IRS two days ago. I'm getting a refund, imagine that? Civic Compliance Benefit, whatever the hell that is. Only why can't they just send it? I gotta go down to their office, drag Jessie along, miss work. Maybe they're going to give it to me in pennies."

"That's kinda funny."

"What?"

"That's where I'm going." He reached into his jacket, took out an identical envelope.

"That's freaky," she said.

"What you expect? It's the Feds."

"Look: Hensworth Federal Building, ten a.m. Penalty for non-appearance. They give you two days' notice."

"So maybe that's to scare you so you'll flee to Canada and they can keep the loot." Eddie skimmed the fine print.

Daily, Pepper had been looking over her shoulder. Last week's adventure with the mad scientist, the portfolio, its delivery, and the wildfire explosion on Action News was like a dream. When she was very small she'd got mad at her big brother and hit him in the leg. He paid no attention, so she whacked him again and kept pounding him till he punched her in the face. That taught her a vital lesson: hit where it counts or don't hit at all.

But a knee to the crotch of a shambling drunk wasn't as risky as kerosene up the ass of a grizzly bear. What the Feds could do to you was pretty special, and they had thousands of people paid good money to do it. This past week she'd found that the bullshit they'd taught her in civics class, that every citizen can make a difference, was in fact true, that one mad bomber could make a very big bang. But she'd dreamed that same moment again: early morning up the stairs, meeting her bare-bellied dad, his snorty breath, his leather belt with the buffalo buckle, the first swack.

"Jessie!" Pepper called, stuffing the envelope in her coat pocket. "Well, no big deal. I can use the money."

"I could give you a lift," Eddie offered, "and invite myself along to the dinosaurs. I got a load-in starts at three."

"Great." She flushed with pleasure and annoyance. Jessie bounded out of her room and into the coat Pepper held for her. Eddie opened the door as Pepper helped Jessie button up. "God, all week I been looking around behind me," she muttered. "What a roller-coaster."

"Well see," he said, "like everything we record is within about a thirty-decibel spread, rock'n'roll maybe twenty to thirty. Not absolute volume, but the dynamic range, which for a symphony, that's maybe eighty, that's a challenge. But if it's just nothing but loud then it's pretty easy." Eddie paused as if he'd said something comprehensible.

"Did I miss something?" Pepper asked, taking Jessie's hand.

"I'm talking about life."

As they climbed into Eddie's battered Volvo they had two observers. From an unmarked sedan across the street a federal agent named Thad — whose rank offered an excellent benefits package that would soon comfort his widow — reported their location and trajectory, mumbling into his necktie. And through the plastic mesh of a public trash receptacle a Little Green Man grokked a signal from Gruk2Bic:

GLORTZ.

Which translates roughly as *Follow the Pepper Eddie.*

Get them fuck more. We like the Pepper on top and Eddie jokes. It is big hit.

The Little Green Man scrambled out of the trash receptacle, brushing ketchup out of his stubble, straddled an object resembling a can of beans, and shot down the street in pursuit of the Pepper Eddie, who were headed, with a small ecstatic dinosaur, toward certain doom.

Chapter 16
The Sting

They tromped through the December sludge to reap the rewards of the American Century. Two citizens, their bond newly consummated, entered the monumental portals of the Hensworth Federal Building shortly before ten a.m. with a fledgling sauropod in tow. They slid their UniQards through the slot, passed through the metal detector, the iris scannner, the effluent sniffer and the sonic frisker, and crossed the lobby. Above loomed a vast photobill of President Bud with his patented grin of compassionate wrath.

"These buildings," Pepper groused. "Are all the buildings in DC like tombs?" She checked the directory.

"Where's the dinosaurs?" asked Jessie.

"Dinosaurs after we're done," Pepper told her.

"Remember being a kid two weeks before Christmas?" Eddie mused. "The sense of eternity? And then summer vacation would last about two days."

Pepper looked around for the elevators. Christmas, hell, she wanted to say. Bunch of cheap crap in big wrappings, and Dad knew he couldn't pay for it so you'd better look real enthused or you'd get your shitter kicked. And then it all fell apart, so by February all that was left were the bills. Plus the wrappings, which Mom folded away on the shelf till it was time to haul them out again to wrap the same lies. They found the elevators. "Thirteenth floor?" she asked.

"I want the dinosaurs," Jessie whined.

Eddie squatted down to her. "You remember the names of 'em? There's the streptococcus and the orthodontist and the gallywompus—"

"Eddie! What is with you?" The night's magic had worn off and Pepper could only think of the snarls ahead. She'd known sensitive guys like Eddie. They were all respect and comfort and talk talk talk, but they were harder to shake than crab lice. One fuck meant a long-term lease on your twat. "Just stop getting Jessie all worked up," she growled, "I'm the one that has to deal with it."

"Just making conversation," Eddie replied. "Hey, Jessie, seriously, you know the theory is that dinosaurs are still alive? That they turned into birds?" Jessie was transfixed. "So the big tyrannosaurus with the teeth, we already saw him outside. He was that pigeon."

"No!" Jessie whacked him on the leg, then giggled. Pepper jabbed the button again. How was she going to ditch this guy? Now she would spend the day looking at bones and teeth, seething while he cracked jokes, and then it'd be, "Mommy, when's Eddie coming to dinner? Can Eddie come see us, Mommy?" She ground her thumb into the button.

The door slid open. Alone in the compartment stood a Little Green Man holding a small vid-cam, staring with lidless yellow eyes as if into headlights — caught flat-footed. Like most urbanites, though, Eddie and Pepper rarely noticed fellow creatures in public, and they shuffled onto the elevator, mindless of their singular tourist. Jessie stared at the trembling creature. "Mommy? There's a Little Green Man."

Pepper pulled Jessie around to face the door. "Honey, it's not polite to stare."

The elevator made a grinding sound, then began to climb. "Elevators always freak me," Eddie said. "In the movies they get stuck or they crash or you open the door and the monster's there, or maybe these two guys wearing gangster sunglasses and they grab onto your elbows while the elevator heads for the basement, and that's entertainment."

"My impression was you didn't talk much," Pepper said, tight-lipped. She was still puzzling why she was getting a tax refund. People in her bracket always got screwed. The elevator stopped grinding and began a soft whine. Eddie punched a button.

"Hell, we're going back to One."

"Maybe somebody pushed it in the lobby," she ventured.

"Some kinda glitch. Maybe it's the Little Green Men."

"Stop it, Eddie!"

"Or the bogeyman."

"What's a bogeyman?" Jessie piped up. New worlds were unfolding to her.

The elevator ground to a halt and the door slid open. An elderly couple with faces like pale melted candles stood at the entrance. "We've got an appointment," said the woman. "Quackenbush."

"This is the elevator," Eddie told them.

"No problem, we got insurance," said Mr. Quackenbush. The couple shuffled in and others followed. Suddenly Jessie squealed like a pig in ecstasy. She was standing face to face with Loki.

"We're going to the IRS," said Loki. "Are you coming too?"

Pepper and Tonya stared at each other. "Is this kinda freaky?" Pepper asked. "Hey, it's great seeing you, but what's going on?" Loki tugged at Tonya's coat. He'd seen the Little Green Man. Tonya ignored him.

"We need Seven. We're going to the doctor," said Mrs. Quackenbush.

"Seven," echoed Mr. Quackenbush.

"Got it," said Eddie, punching the button. Tonya stepped into the elevator as the door began to close. Years later she thought about that moment. What would have happened, she wondered, if she'd taken one step back?

"Can Loki see the dinosaurs?" Jessie asked.

"We're going to the museum after we finish here," Pepper said. "I had to take off work. You want to come along?"

The elevator commenced its slow grumble upward. The assembled citizens of the Republic stared in dumb wonder at one another. "This is Eddie," Pepper told Tonya.

"Hi. Sure, I took the day off too," said Tonya. "I'll get shuffled to a dozen different offices, never fails. So what are you doing here?"

"Going up to the IRS," Pepper said. "Can you believe I'm getting a refund?"

"So am I."

Tonya pulled out an envelope. Pepper and Eddie pulled out theirs. They looked from envelope to envelope. "Did you get a refund notice?" Tonya asked the Quackenbushes.

"We got an appointment," said Mrs. Quackenbush.

"For the doctor," said Mr. Quackenbush.

"He's getting a checkup."

"It's for her." It had been twenty-two years since they'd looked each other straight in the eye. Suddenly they did. He's got blue eyes, thought Mrs. Quackenbush. Who the hell is she? thought Mr. Quackenbush. They looked away.

"Mama, there's a Little Green Man," Loki reported to his mother. She made a distracted remark about respecting people's differences. Which Mrs. Clemson often said but which didn't quite apply, Loki felt, to the Little Green Man at his elbow.

The elevator squeaked, clucked, gave out a low whine. Eddie looked up at the numbers. "We're going back down. Thirteen!" He punched the button fiercely then gave up. Elevators had voice recognition systems, of course, but nobody ever used them since they rarely worked. The obsolesced push-button backups were often in disrepair, so in many buildings the elevators sat dormant in the lobby or wandered randomly up and down their shafts, delivering people wherever they pleased, resulting in frequent marriages or murders.

"It really pisses me when stuff doesn't work," Eddie muttered. He nodded to Tonya. "Eddie, by the way."

"So I heard. I'm Tonya. Hi." The squat brown woman turned to Pepper, stage-whispering over the elevator's moans. "I've been meaning to call you. Things are getting kinda heavy. Actually things are getting very heavy—"

"Is it the dinosaurs yet?" Jessie asked.

Mrs. Quackenbush felt she was being addressed but couldn't locate the source. "We got an appointment," she responded.

"We called last month," said Mr. Quackenbush.

"He's having spells."

"She's on the decline."

The elevator settled with a sigh. Ground floor. Loki ran his fingers over the metal bumps by the numbers, Braille for blind people. Then he felt it again. It wasn't Braille. It was just metal bumps.

The door slid open. The surveillance camera confirmed that the retinal images of those who waited matched the terrorist conspiracy data. The suspects were identified as J.G. Babcock, Mrs. Irma Jean Clemson, and Mabel McClafferty. Their digital files were downloaded to the appropriate quarters. Pepper and Eddie recognized Mabel. Loki recognized Mrs. Clemson. Mrs. Clemson recognized Tonya. Tonya recognized Babcock.

"J.G.—"

"Yes. Well."

"Hello, Mrs. Clemson."

"Why hello, Loki. And you're Loki's mother."

Tonya stared. "Is this my birthday or something?"

Suddenly, Pepper was seized with an overwhelming urge to flee. She grabbed Jessie's hand. "This is nuts! Excuse me! Eddie, hold the door!" She started to push her way out, but Mabel shoved in, her wide load of packages blocking escape.

Eddie was preoccupied, pushing Thirteen. "I could fix it if I had my tools."

Mabel greeted Pepper. "I met you on the bus."

"Scuse me, we're getting off—" But Jessie had squirmed out of her grasp to grab onto Loki. The door slid shut and the elevator started its climb to deliver its huddled masses. Pepper gave up, stood for a moment just breathing, then asked Mabel distractedly, "More packages?"

"Oh yeh," Mabel said, "Never done with." And seeing Eddie: "Hey, this guy, the noise boy!" Mabel never forgot a face.

"I'm getting a tax refund," Babcock announced to Tonya, holding up a brown envelope. The others held up identical envelopes, glanced about, then looked at the Quackenbushes.

"Punch Seven," said Mr. Quackenbush.

"Mommy," Jessie whined, "can I have an envelope?"

Eddie glanced up at the numbers. "This time we'll make it. That's Three."

Squeezed into the corner of the crowded elevator, the quivering green alien slipped his toe into a wad of bubble gum on the floor, located the wormhole, and shot at hyperphotonic speed home to his planet. Loki and Jessie waved him goodbye. And below in the lobby an undercover agent of the DHS, in trench coat and shades, spoke into his thumbnail:

ALL ABOARD OPERATION CHICKEN COOP.
ROLL OUT BIG MAMA.

The elevator made its slow ascent. "Four," announced Eddie. Pepper, chilled to the bone, closed her eyes and tried to remember a prayer. Any fucking prayer.

Shoved tightly together, Tonya and Mrs. Clemson smiled at each other, groping for a topic of conversation. Tonya had had some testy sessions with Mrs. Clemson, who had once flunked

Loki for an essay using words too advanced for his age group. Once she had lectured him on the evils of plagiarism because he was a C- student and his "Plague of Frogs" was obviously an A+ poem. Once Loki had been chastised for not mumbling the Pledge of Allegiance with enough feeling. All this in three months. Tonya had given up on it. Let the kid cope.

"I loved the bulletin board the kids did," Tonya said, "about the election."

"Oh I'm so sorry about that—"

"It was amazing."

"Five."

Mrs. Clemson, with downcast eyes, shook her head. "I just didn't provide proper supervision, because children are so creative, but—"

"But they really caught all the crapola."

"The principal suggested I should have exercised more control."

Fuck the principal, Tonya wanted to say, but kept her mouth shut. Why torment the lady?

"I received a reprimand," Mrs. Clemson said. "I've never received a reprimand."

"Six."

"Well, it was great," said Tonya. "I'm glad Loki was part of it."

"Well, yes indeed," Mrs. Clemson nodded eagerly, "it was very artistic." She smiled a smile that reminded Tonya of an earthworm shriveling on the sidewalk. Both turned their eyes to the numbers.

"Punch Seven," said Mr. Quackenbush.

"Seven," Eddie announced.

The elevator crawled past Seven.

"What'd he say?"

"It went past Seven."

"We've got an appointment!" cried Mrs. Quackenbush.

"Eight," announced Eddie.

Babcock's voice rose. "You know, an amazing thing: in 1857 the first steam-powered passenger elevator was introduced, and five years later, 1862, Congress enacted the first income tax—"

"Eddie!" Pepper whispered. "We gotta go back down!"

"Then five years later," Babcock went on, "the tax was eliminated, but the first hydraulic elevator was built exactly the same year. Doesn't that seem like a strange coincidence?"

"We waited three months! We want Seven!"

NINE.

Jessie asked for the dinosaurs. Tonya said that the circumstances were freaky indeed. Pepper mumbled something so strangled she couldn't tell what she said. Mrs. Clemson scanned the elevator license and penalties for non-compliance as Mabel McClafferty mumbled, "Let's move it! Who runs this thing, the Post Office?"

Eddie jabbed the buttons. The elevator continued its climb. All watched the numbers.

TEN.

Pepper grabbed Tonya by the elbow. She was the only person who seemed sane enough to look scared shitless. "My uncle raised pigs. This is like getting set to de-ball the pigs."

ELEVEN.

Tonya shrugged. "So what are we supposed to do, babe? Let's just entertain the possibility that this is not a nightmare or some crazy plot to bring people who barely know each other into a cage for extermination, but just purely and simply your stupid Federal Government in their lovable fucked-up way giving you and all your friends a tax refund."

TWELVE.

For the first time in her life, enclosed in the elevator's plastic wood-grain veneer, Pepper felt utterly helpless. Either she was acting like an idiot or she was delivering her daughter, her second try at herself, her precious golden egg, into a cauldron of demons. Even strapped down on the table birthing Brian, legs splayed, split open, heaving, she knew the work she had to do, but now— She heard Jessie call out, "Mommy?"

"Punch Seven!"

The elevator stopped. "Thirteen," Eddie announced. "No problem, friends." The door slid open.

A moment of catastrophe induces an altered state. The motorcycle blows a tire, skids across the freeway, and time extends its gentle tentacles around the rider in an odd equilibrium. *Ah, I'm going to die, that's interesting. How slowly the fence posts pass before my skin smears the concrete.* Three seconds of peace before the crash.

Flashing lights. Alarm gongs. The little bug-eyed Russian rushes down the hall toward them, arms waving, braying like a beagle, "Is trap! Shut door! Begone!" He lunges into the elevator. "No tax refunds! They are men with major guns!" The door slides shut. Someone pokes a button. The cage descends in frantic jerks. Pepper hears screams. *Is that me?* Will her nightmare end if the alarm clock rings?

"Punch Seven!" the old couple rasp in unison. They lurch to a stop. Open the door. Can't.

FBI.

"We're here for the doctor," the old couple whine. "Ten a.m."

COME OUT.

Mrs. Clemson raises her hands in surrender. She's always taught her third-graders how to do that. The speaker booms:

FBI.

A tiny voice says, "It's God." Pepper knows that voice.

COME OUT.

Between floors?

SURRENDER WEAPONS.

"There aren't any weapons here!" Tonya shrieks. "There are children here!"

"Quackenbush! We called last month!"

Pepper pounds her fists on the door. A burst of distant popcorn. Shots? Explosions? The clustered humans push like cattle in pens, going nowhere. "I am on the staff of Action News! This is being covered by Action News!" "Punch Seven!" "Put the kids in the middle." "If he doesn't like the waffle iron he can send it back!" Pepper clutches Jessie's hand, kneels, embraces her daughter fiercely.

THIRTY SECONDS.

Silence falls. They listen. "Thirty seconds for what?" Eddie asks the wall.

"It wasn't my idea," Mrs. Clemson explains, "it was the children's idea." No reply.

TWENTY SECONDS.

"Okay, so you got a speaker in the ceiling," Eddie tells the ceiling. "You need to roll off your highs and boost your bass. You got headphones? Can you hear me?" No reply.

Jessie struggles against her mother's embrace. Overhead she hears a calm voice: "Just typical, historically, of official unresponsiveness, the France of Louis XVI—" And above Babcock's warble the rasping bark of the bug-eyed man: "I explain phenomena! We postulate a quantum world, eleven dimensions—" She catches Loki's eye. He too is held in a mother's furious grip. "What is it?" Jessie whispers.

"I think it's terrorists," Loki says, "so maybe we're gonna die. But that doesn't hurt, that's just like losing a baby tooth." He'd read that somewhere.

"But I want to see the dinosaurs." Her face crinkles toward tears as she knows suddenly that her life is going to be very different from here on in.

TEAR GAS.

Gas jets hiss. The passengers huddle, choking. Sergei Rupp beats on the walls. Mabel beats on Sergei, for no apparent reason.

HANDS IN AIR.

Tonya raises her thick arms, bares her teeth, and shrieks through the blistering fumes, "You fucking assholes, listen! We don't have weapons! We cannot come out! We are between floors! We are stuck! There are children here! There are old people here!"

"We got an appointment—"

FIRE.

Bursts of machine gun fire. A silly *Woop!* from Federal Agent Thad, with the excellent benefits package, as he is sliced in half by a volley from Federal Agent Smetzer.

WE'RE UNDER FIRE. THEY'RE HOLDING
CHILDREN AS HOSTAGES. CUT THE CABLE.

The gas hisses off. The gaping silence before the hurricane. The tremulous breath of the dragon. The stink of fear. One thought fills the minds of those who cough, choke, and weep from the fumes of their own tax dollars: *Hold your breath.*

They feel the distant thud of a tired heavy fist and then free-fall. "We're going down," Eddie mumbles.

"Punch Up," offers Mabel.

No more. They lose their grip on the meaning of Now. They move into time dilation, the slowing of duration, glimpsed by Einstein but known only to the dying. They hear themselves scream, a comic book scream, a scream with scribbly lettering and exclamation marks across a full page, a scream as distant as an owl. Blackness drenches them. They plunge, held tight like a mash of souls in an infant god's fist. They feel a burst of shattered light, and then the screaming is done.

Chapter 17
The Blue Terrapin

In the center of the westbound lanes of Interstate 90 south of Rochester, NY, stood a deer with her single fawn. Around the curve headlights loomed. The next moments flashed in the archetypal night: deer in headlights, her frozen stare, the oncoming hulk, the sickening thud, the bloody smear of meat.

Instead, the deer saw, *Oh, that's a bus,* and ambled to the shoulder. The bus rumbled past. Her fawn nibbled a milkweed. *Times were a-changing.*

At the wheel of the bus a leathery gray-haired man, late sixties, squinted to see the deer and waved benignly. He reached backward and tugged his ponytail as if flushing an English loo. It was a habit he suppressed when people were about, but at eleven p.m., with the passengers drowsing, he did what he damn well pleased. He flicked the windowglass vid.

He would never get used to vehicular TV. Way back, he'd been the last of his buddies to get a cell phone. Those microwaves were sure to fry your brain. Yet even as the science rolled in to confirm it and the corporate juggernaut rolled out to suppress it, he got a cell phone. Same with these watery images swimming on his windshield. With imbedded diffractionated crystals you could see the road through a transparent layer of cheer — the porn star's tits and the oil tanker rushing at you — and try to decide which was death and which was whoopie. When they came out five years ago, he'd predicted that fatalities would double. Wrong: they quadrupled. So all vid sex was banned except for the religious channels that showed hard-core porn with hellfire voice-overs. Never would he have one of those gizmos, he'd thundered. Now he did. *Times were a-changing.*

A burst of static, and the news flickered on. Strange to see these faces as vivid as mirror reflection yet filmy as daydream. No limit to what technology could achieve so long as it raped your brain. He turned up the sound.

ROSALIE, HERE'S THE LATEST FOOTAGE
FROM THAT TERRORIST ATTACK AT THE
HENSWORTH FEDERAL BUILDING. THREE

AGENTS KILLED, SIX WOUNDED IN HEAVY CROSSFIRE. NO WORD YET ON MORE THAN FOUR HUNDRED PEOPLE WHO WORKED AT THE HENSWORTH BUILDING.

MAKES YOU WONDER. ANY WORD ON THE TERRORISTS, HAROLD?

NOT A PEEP, ROSALIE. THE FBI CONFIRMED THAT THE MILITANTS WERE HEAVILY ARMED AND EQUIPPED WITH INCENDIARY DEVICES.

NEXT: ALL THE LATEST SCORES.

He flicked off the vid. Hadn't he heard something like that back in December? Maybe they just waited six months and said the same stuff over again. That was the toughest thing about getting old: all the news was re-runs. Once, he'd tried to fight it, fight the whole thing — globalization, militarism, climate change, fast food, designer genes. Now, he drove a rickety bus that carried the last faint echo of a twinkling dream. *Times were a-changing,* but not all that much.

"Hey, Smoky." The second driver slid into the bench seat directly behind him. The kid was on his first cross-country trip. "You want to switch over? It's early but I can't sleep."

"Say a mantra. OM FUCKIT FUCKIT. Works for me." Tim, that was his name, or Timothy or Ted or Tad — all a blur. Faces were vivid, and smells, but names leaked away like water. Last year Smoky had lost two molars, this year he couldn't remember names. A Tarot reader had once told him he'd live to be a hundred. At this rate they'll have trouble distinguishing him from a turnip.

"Lotta stars out," the kid said.

"Enjoy 'em while you can," Smoky replied, "they're getting bought up."

"You don't want to switch?"

"Not till we stop to do the bunks."

"How long you been driving Blue Terrapin?"

Damn, the kid was a chatterbox, but maybe it'd wear off. "Let's see, I guess about thirty-five years off and on. I quit three, four times, drifted back into it. Used to keep track the number of trips, but I lost count." He glanced in the mirror at the lights racing across the young man's face. The kid looked very lost.

"How do they keep these buses running? How old is this thing?"

Smoky grinned. This bus would run till Hell went on vacation. He'd rebuilt the engine with jerry-rigged fuel cells, put in a new driveshaft and suspension. In fact it was mostly a new bus, like a human body completely renewing itself, every cell changed, still feeling old but still chugging. Somehow it managed to be as wobbly and shambling as when he'd started driving it, but it was a mean machine. "Scotch tape," Smoky replied.

He glanced at Tim. His second son would be about this age. Those two sons, so different. One gets a sex change, the other joins the Marines.

They rode a while in silence, glancing at each other's face in the mirror. Tim clearly wanted to talk, and at last Smoky obliged him. "So what's your story?" he asked, hoping it might not be too depressing. Tim talked in little disconnected bursts. He'd gone to art school, in love with cartooning, graphic novels, the mad stretches of fantasy worlds, then graduated into a job as a commercial illustrator. He'd burned out fast: no stomach for cramming chocolate-covered plastic into the guts of little kids.

So he'd rambled through a series of jobs and wound up as an emergency medical technician. Do something for people, he thought, save lives. But he got tired of seeing people die on the highway with their dead eyes still glued to the Disney Channel. He saw an ad for a bus driving school, got his license, drove a school bus for two months and then got hired by the Blue Terrapin.

Smoky took it all in, forgot it. These kids had a vision, but they saw no highways open, no maps. A ravenous urge for the taste of the avocado, but no clue that avocados might really exist, no hope on the tongue for that buttery green. His own road had been as jagged, sure, but he'd always had the scent of some vague destination. He felt Tim's need like a phantom limb, an itch that could never get scratched.

The bus rumbled on through the night. The drivers were silent. Then at the back of the bus they heard life stirring. First the rustle of coats against upholstery, then a shuffle of limbs, a cough, a whimper, then words.

"What happened?"

“What the fuck?”

“Are we dead?”

Smoky glanced into the mirror. “What’d they say?”

Tim sat up. “Somebody asked if they were dead.”

“I don’t make value judgments.”

Tim looked into the darkness. He saw faint movements. The voices rose.

“Jessie, honey?”

“Mommy, I think I peed.”

“Our appointment’s at ten.”

Tim leaned forward to Smoky. “We’re riding a lot lighter,” he said. Smoky had the urge to say something curmudgeonly but couldn’t think of a thing. The bus was riding lighter.

A dim figure worked its way down the aisle. Tim looked up. The figure halted. “Scuse me? Are we on a bus?” mumbled Eddie Grabowski.

A moment of silence. Tim turned to Smoky. “He wants to know if we’re on a bus.”

Smoky gave the question serious consideration. Never regard any question as frivolous, he thought, because that’s the inevitable reaction when someone questions your assumptions. At last he replied, “Yes, we’re on a bus.”

“Are you FBI?” the figure asked.

Smoky had once seen a play they called “theatre of the absurd.” He didn’t like it. Why pay good money for what you see every day? So he responded in a slightly sharp tone. “These days I don’t know whether to ask’em if they’re on drugs or if they’re not on drugs. My friend, if you bought your ticket for the Blue Terrapin tour bus, Boston to San Francisco, fourteen days, and you got on and you didn’t get off, then that’s where you are. Five hours to Lake Erie, we’ll stop there for breakfast.”

There was a long span of dead air. At last, the dark figure stammered, “Holy shit.”

“Sleep it off, my friend,” Smoky advised. Eddie went back up the aisle.

“What’d the guy say?” a strident voice cut through the darkness.

“He says we’re alive.”

“I mighta known,” moanedMabel McClafferty.

The dim figures looked around at one another. One started

to get up, then sat back down. A woman who remembered being named Pepper in a previous life murmured, "Oh my God, oh my God. . ." as she clasped a small bundle she hoped might be her daughter.

Smoky caught a glimpse of movement in the sky. "What's that? Up there? Lights moving?" Tim strained to see out the windshield.

"Helicopters."

Part Two: Fantasies

Chapter 1
Hello Smoky

Smoky knew there was a plan behind the Universe. Spirituality had never been at the heart of his life except as a way of chasing women, but it flickered around the edges. He'd been raised Presbyterian, left the church in his teens, but he still valued that faith for having given him no coherent beliefs whatever. The best foundation you could have.

He'd sampled various religious paths and felt some affinity with the Native American stuff, where the chicks were a lot foxier than at Quaker meeting. But he never could buy that business about Earth being a big turtle. Maybe he was just too literal-minded. He remembered flunking a high school quiz about the difference between a simile, a metaphor, and whatever the other damn thing was. To Smoky a turtle was a turtle and Earth was a big wet rock.

This had been a source of strife between himself and Shadow, the love of his life. They'd had a long sumptuous night of peyote erotics, and in a mellow hour of early dawn he'd asked, "Why do you believe that shit?" It was a joke, but she didn't laugh. He'd driven the pickup into town, and when he got back, his bags, his guitar, and a fifth of Wild Turkey were in the driveway. His last parting shout at the figure in the doorway was, "It ain't a fucking turtle!"

Since then he'd spent years on cross-country drives, staring ahead to the rolling plains, the crested mountains, the cloud ballets, classical and modern. His thinking had evolved. He no longer felt that the Universe was meaningless. There was a Plan, divinely guided. The rocks, the trees, the rivers, the delicious women — everything was suffused with this Plan. The Plan, in the inscrutable mind of the Divine Presence, was to create this amazing planet, to set it in motion, to endow us with a sacred soul, a divine essence and freedom of will — and then to sit back and see what kind of shit we pull.

Smoky drove on, dismissing the pot-head passenger's meandering and the helicopter, which had passed in a flash. His mind wandered back over a life of missed rondy-voos with destiny. He'd been just a kid in Scranton, PA, when he saw a news blurb about Woodstock on TV. His sex drive shifted up from neutral, and that pretty much eroded his interest in church or school. He would run away and be a hippie as soon as he could grow some fur on his face. He'd live in perpetual tickle.

Over the next years he looked for his cue to run away from Miss Ketter's Algebra II, Mr. Stuelke's American Civ, Mrs. Collingwood's English Lit, but it never came. His parents didn't mistreat him, so he didn't have that excuse. The few long-hairs at Scranton High were as image-conscious as the jocks and disdained his short-clipped locks. He'd gone to a couple of sparse political rallies in town to see if he could get laid, but all the girls were either too old for him or looked very grim.

He longed for graduation, when he could either dodge the draft or join the army — he didn't care which, as long as it meant a change. Sure, he was against the war but figured that if he could bring the same capabilities to military service as he brought to Algebra II he might serve the cause of peace. Instead, he graduated, got a job at the post office, and watched TV a lot.

Looking back, he realized how passive he'd been. He'd married Estelle because she asked him to, left when she told him to, agreed he'd been a bastard, yes, but a quiescent one. Once a month he'd find some reason to go to New York and pay to get laid. He stopped looking in the mirror, even to shave.

After Estelle kicked him out he started to grow his hair long. He thought they might fire him. He had no good excuse to quit the post office, but if they fired him he'd be free. They were too damn tolerant. His mother said, "Don't come into this house with that long hair," but relented. She kept telling him he looked like his Aunt Halimah. He started to get drunk a lot.

Smoky shook his head to scatter the memories, but they kept settling like the snow in that Christmas paperweight — the only thing he remembered from visits to Aunt Halimah. Why dredge up all that misery? Reminiscing was something you did when you had somebody with you in bed, and you could cuddle up and she'd say "Poor baby" and pet your balls. Not behind the wheel. Not tonight. Not alone.

Alone? The new driver Tim was huddled against the window, zonked. Where was Bailey? Hadn't seen him the last hour. Had the little beast slipped out the door looking for lady ferrets? He glanced in the rear-view mirror. The befuddled passengers had calmed down.

What had saved Smoky from a slow death in Scranton was an ad in *The Village Voice*. Ride the Blue Terrapin, it said, fourteen days, Boston to San Francisco. You'd bunk on the bus, you'd all pitch in to cook, you'd meet girls with long hair and full lips and gaps between their teeth. He sent for a brochure, put it in his top drawer, forgot about it, except in his dreams.

Three years later he had his first streak of good luck. His dad died, his mom went nuts and put her head in the oven, and he was fired for being drunk. Dad left him some money, and the day after he was canned he called the Blue Terrapin to see if it still existed. It did. He made a reservation, bought a guitar that he couldn't play, and stepped aboard his future.

The first day out from New York he sat on the U-shaped bench at the back of the bus beside a black-haired olive-skinned girl who was talking with a thin perk-breasted albino woman, early thirties, in some foreign language. They turned to him and the olive sizzler asked him in a heavy accent, "Vat's you name?"

"Smoky," replied Arnold Lunz.

Why Smoky? He didn't smoke. Maybe it sounded Wild West. But he knew he'd never get to first base with either girl as Arnold Lunz. It worked. Within three days he'd made love with both the slurry-hipped olive beauty and the spasmodic red-eyed albino. Ecstatically. Repeatedly. All for free.

And then he'd gone right on through the passenger list.

It wasn't really the name that did it, he knew. It was the countryside, the freeway, the trees, rivers, and the distant glistening towns in the night. For the first time he was mad with the liquor of freedom, and his face was radiant. At each stop Arnold whispered into the burnished steel restroom mirror, "Hello, Smoky."

Three years later, after two more trips, he became a driver for the Blue Terrapin. It wasn't easy. You had to be a good mechanic for these decrepit beasts. You had to be a master chef to manage the communal cook-outs. And you needed a license to drive the thing. He worked at it, faked it, and finally landed a job. Now it was thirty-some years.

He whistled through his teeth for his pet ferret Bailey, who gave him no end of trouble but kept the bus free from any threat of rationality. Bailey never responded to whistling, but Smoky did it anyway. Once on acid he'd commanded the sun to rise and it did. Very slowly.

Over the years Smoky had taken a couple of breaks for marriages and other mishaps. He'd had trips where he didn't remember what happened after Chicago. Trips where faces glowed with that surge of wonder he'd seen in his own reflection. And he'd watched his own face change. He'd known riches and loss. Roads that used to be there. Women disappearing out from under him.

He'd spent a night with Angie under the desert stars. She blew up her air mattress and they tried to make love. But Angie was over two hundred pounds and took up most of the mattress. He climbed aboard, but she wiggled like crazy so he kept rolling off her and flopping over the edge of the mattress. They laughed and laughed and he never managed an erection, but he suddenly realized that sex was supposed to be like this. It was supposed to be fun.

The minute his mind turned to sex he was interrupted. It never failed. "Where's your ferret?" Tim asked. The road was getting foggy.

"How they doing back there?" Smoky mumbled. If they were passing hallucinogens around he had no problem with that, but he liked to be aware of things.

"I think they've settled down," Tim said. "False alarm."

Suddenly the bus erupted. The clutch of passengers seemed to wake out of their daze with a collective roar and rise into the aisle. Their U-turn from death threw them headlong into an uncontrollable skid.

"We never got on this bus!"

"We're innocent!"

"Are we dead, Mommy?"

Somebody seemed to be shrieking just for the hell of it. Smoky hoped Bailey hadn't skittered up somebody's pants. He nodded to Tim, and Tim lurched up the aisle to confront the churning throng.

"Hello! Hello, people!" he called out. "What seems to be the problem?"

He found himself face to face with a chunky red-headed young woman, freckles rampant, screaming, "Who are these people? Where are my friends? This bus was full!"

"I know you. You're Jodi, right? You got on in Boston?" She stared past him, sightless, whimpering. He turned to the others. "Do you people have tickets?" No one heard him. They were tumbling aimlessly in a clothes dryer, with a whine, a grumble, a whimpered "Mommy!" Tim heard himself shouting, "Could somebody tell me what's going on?"

Another swell of braying, baying, barking as Tim backed away murmuring, "Sorry, this is my first trip as a driver—" He retreated, crouched beside Smoky, grasping the handrail as the bus lurched and the ferret shot under him. "These aren't the same people," he stammered. "These are different people. We had eight Swedes, an old Chinese couple, some really obnoxious guys from Boston U., and all that bunch with the campfire songs, and a fuzzy-haired lady in a striped jumpsuit. The kinda chunky redhead, she's the same, but the others— Like did you stop some place while I was asleep?"

Smoky said nothing. He was long past questioning the irrational. Let the kids work out the world's kinks and spasms, he didn't have the energy. Tim rambled on. "There's only like a dozen people. And kids. We didn't have kids on here. One of the kids said the dinosaurs did it." Tim looked back toward the passengers. They were petrified now, whispering into the darkness. The rumble of the bus seemed louder. Tim heard a small boy's voice, "I need to use the bathroom," and a woman called out, "Where's the bathroom?"

Smoky was silent. "There's no bathroom," Tim replied. Dead silence, then another storm of protest. He watched helplessly as the phalanx of passengers pressed forward in the aisle led by a rumpled little man flapping his arms.

"We are passengers in distress!"

"It was ten o'clock in the morning—"

"Our appointment's at ten!"

"Now it's night!"

"We haven't peed since morning!"

They loomed over Tim, but he was beyond fear, frozen in certainty of nothing except that once again he'd chosen the wrong profession. Bladder pressure spurring adrenalin, the crowd was on the verge of rolling over him and crashing into the windshield when they were stopped by a piercing "EEEP!" The ferret had run up Tim's back and sat quivering on his head.

Smoky scooped Bailey from his perch and downshifted with the hand that held the ferret. "Majority rules," he announced. "You're lucky. We got a rest stop right here. No vending machines, but there's comfort facilities. Remember to use the buddy system. Wait'll we're stopped, okay?"

The bus rolled to a bumpy halt, gave a deep expiration, and the front door opened. The passengers streamed off the bus and made for the cement block structures. A man hobbled with one shoe off. A woman walked in brisk dignity.

Smoky stood outside the door petting the slithery wad of fur in his hand as Tim looked to the rear of the bus at the heavy-set young woman in a down vest, visibly shaken. An elderly couple sat beside her, arm in arm, etched by the sharp sodium light, staring straight ahead.

"How you doing?" Tim called out. No response. He made his way up the aisle through clutter that had been scattered in the melee. "Well hey, I'm glad you stuck around," he said to the young woman. She had smiled at him when boarding in Boston.

"I'm Jodi," she said, glancing out the window.

"Tim. Hi."

"I have this history," she said to his reflection in the glass. "People flake off."

He turned to the elderly couple. "You guys okay?"

The old woman leaned forward. "We don't belong here," she announced in a loud whisper. "We're different ones. We're not the killers or somebody."

"Like Bonnie and Clyde," the old man blurted. "They were old-time robbers. They were in a movie."

"He already knows that," the old woman hissed. "Don't make us look like fools." She looked to Tim. "He was going to see the doctor."

"It's her," said the man. "Ten o'clock. Quackenbush."

Tim stood watching Jodi's reflection in the window, then looked away as he realized she might be seeing his. From the front of the bus he heard Smoky flick the vid. The cheery voices of doom drifted back:

THE FBI REPORTS THOSE TERRORISTS MAY
HAVE ESCAPED AFTER SETTING THE BOMBS
THAT LEFT OVER FOUR HUNDRED DEAD.

ALL HAD RECORDS OF PROTEST, HAROLD.
WHAT WERE THEY PROTESTING?

WHO KNOWS, ROSALIE? POVERTY, GUNS,
POLLUTION — THE AMERICAN WAY OF LIFE.

POLICE IN FIVE STATES ARE ON ALERT, AND
ROADBLOCKS ARE UP.

Smoky flicked it off. The passengers were coming back to the bus. Who were these people? Some kinda funny business, which wouldn't be the first time. He looked behind him. Tim had pulled out his sketch pad and was flipping through it for Jodi. Neat way to pick up chicks. Smoky had thought the kid was shy, maybe gay, but clearly he was smarter than he looked. Wait for daylight. It always looks different by daylight. Easier to find whatever explanation suits your purpose.

No, this trip was going to be different. He could feel it. Every trip was unique, though over the years and the decades their features blended into the sameness of an ocean, one day choppy, next day calm, same currents deep under. He prided himself that he could cope with the unexpected, even the near-disasters, but could no longer be surprised by any doings, no matter how strange. His gateways were all past him, and the challenge of crossroads.

Still, he felt the stirring of something new. Not because most of his passengers had vanished into the night. Not because others had taken their place and screamed for the restroom. Not because Bailey was twitching like a barometer before a hurricane. But because, for the first time in many years, he'd seen in the darkness the face of Shadow, and she'd said very clearly, *Yes*.

Chapter 2
The Science Behind It

Mrs. Irma Jean Clemson lived by the rules. Her earliest memories were of learning the rules. Hold your fork in your right hand. Finish your peas. Look right and left before you cross the street. Don't touch yourself in bad places. Don't tell Grandma. She learned her lessons well.

Now, waiting breathlessly to wake from the dream, she found herself in the grasp of a reality where the rules were in disarray. Somehow on the elevator she had defied authority by not surrendering, not throwing down her weapons, not dying. She had violated the laws of physics in the company of total strangers. She had failed to control herself.

As she washed her hands she glanced at the steel mirror catching her reflection. Don't stare, she heard her mother saying. She had to use the mirror every morning to put on her face, but she pretended it wasn't her, it was just a face she'd checked out from the library. Now suddenly she saw herself. So much older than her forty-one years.

Mrs. Clemson dried her hands and walked out of the toilet block pretending nothing had occurred. Toilets were God's way of keeping us humble. That she hadn't believed in God since the age of seven when her hamster died was a thick guilt she held tightly in her heart, and she frequently apologized to God for His nonexistence. She walked back to the bus, climbed the steps, and came face to face with the old driver petting a slinky rodent. The man looked like one of those hippies they'd studied in college, with long gray hair and a headband, who would possibly say things like "groovy" and flout the rules of hygiene. He looked at her with knowing eyes. She shuddered.

"Excuse me," she said. "I wonder if you— It wasn't my— I mean— What are the rules?"

"Rules?" He grinned. "Who are you?"

"Ah . . . Mrs. Walter Clemson. Irma Jean Clemson."

"Irm, how you doing? I'm Smoky." He chuckled softly. "Rules, lessee. Well, Irm, don't smoke weed in the front of the bus, cause one sniff and it gets my loins up."

She tensed. "There are illegal substances here?"

"Well, I mean there's just not rules. As long as you don't get me involved you can do what you want. And at night, like, don't step on people or get so frisky in the sack that you're really screeching a lot. Is that enough rules for you?" She was silent. "And if there's an accident," he suggested, "don't die."

Did he know about the bulletin board? The shame of the reprimand still seared. It had all been to give the children an experience in creativity, which promoted positive self-image and thereby increased math scores. They had gotten carried away and criticized the President, she understood that, but she hadn't known how to let them do creativity without being too creative.

A wild-haired woman in a stocking cap ascended the steps and pushed past her, then turned. "Oh, sorry," said Mabel McClafferty, "I thought I was on the subway." She tugged the collar of her heavy gray coat, then added, "My whole life passed before my eyes, and it was not a pretty sight."

Irma Jean Clemson stood in the aisle, a little girl lost. Loki Zell got on the bus with his mother, whose last name she couldn't remember but it was different than his, she recalled. Loki held tightly to his mother's hand as if still bound to some slowly disintegrating nightmare.

"Loki, are you all right?" Mrs. Clemson said automatically. The boy stared at his feet and shuffled on. She followed them up the aisle through a section of booths with tables like a diner to an open space at the rear of the bus flanked by padded bench seats. She sat beside them. "Are these friends of yours?"

Tonya looked at her quizzically. "These are the people from the elevator."

"I meant is there anyone in charge?"

"I don't have any idea what you're talking about."

At the age of seven Irma Jean had been told, "Don't ask so many questions," and for the next thirty-four years she had dutifully complied. Throughout her education she had carefully avoided curiosity. She asked her students questions, but only those in the lesson plan. Now the stress was too great. "Well, is this a regular bus?" she asked, dreading to hear the answer.

"Freaky," Tonya responded as if the lady weren't there. "We were all crushed together, and I thought about when I took the Blue Terrapin to Mexico, I had this huge claustrophobia, crammed onto the bus with total strangers—"

"So is this a regular—"

"Yes, it's a regular bus!" Tonya barked. Mrs. Clemson flinched. She was shocked at her own rudeness in asking a question twice. Tonya turned to her. "Sorry, I'm jumpy. No, it's not exactly a— It's a Blue Terrapin. It's got its own flavor." Mrs. Clemson did not pursue it. Questions buzzed in her head like mosquitoes: Where were they going? Did they have to have tickets? Would people start taking off their clothes?

The bus door hissed shut, and the old driver stood facing the passengers. "Everybody on? Okay, I'm Smoky, this is Tim, we're your drivers, and this is the Blue Terrapin experience, like it or not. Whatever happened here I don't know—"

"We been raptured up onto a bus!" cried Mabel.

"So the deal is this," he went on. "We sleep on the bus, mostly, and stop now and then, places you probably never heard of. We cook all our meals together, damn good if you ask me, and everybody pitches in unless you're a loafer. Questions?"

Eddie spoke up. "Well, cut to the chase, chief. We're kinda scared shitless, you know? Not entirely clear about reality, so to speak, so—"

"It's the bus to Hell," Mabel muttered, "and I just sent my December rent." No, they couldn't be going to Hell, Mrs. Clemson thought. But then with a stab of guilt she remembered that bulletin board.

Loki tugged at his mother's arm. "Mama, I don't think we're dead, cause I used the toilet." Mrs. Clemson was about to admonish him for speaking of inappropriate subjects, then realized she wasn't in class. Her mouth went bone dry.

A little baggy-suited man leapt into the center aisle, and the old driver sat down to let chaos take its course. "I explain in layman's terms," announced Sergei Rupp. "Dream deprivation, we have first precondition, yes? Close proximity: squeeze in elevator, second precondition. Anxiety of machine-guns blasting, third precondition. So in nexus of potentiality—"

"Is he a mad scientist, Mommy?" Jessie whispered. Pepper shushed her.

"In primed condition," Sergei went on, "one spark strikes. Flash, thought, memory of bus—"

"My God, I did! In the elevator we were all huddled, I thought about the Blue Terrapin, when I was on the Blue Terrapin—" Tonya crackled with high voltage. Mrs. Clemson squirmed away.

"Which ruptures space-time but gratefully not body parts. We are not become fish. But space in fabric opens—"

"And the other passengers," Jodi cried out, "they were all singing some stupid campfire song and they were so off-pitch it was fucking awful. Except me—"

"—And so passengers are extracted, perhaps to be campers at camporee, and flash, whoosh, vacuum-suck, we are here!"

The bus idled, clearing its throat at times. The passengers sat silent, trying to absorb the sci-fi premise that seemed to be guiding their lives. They had no capacity for belief or disbelief. Sergei might as well have said that the Uncertainty Principle had been ratified as a Constitutional amendment or that they were all starring in a TV series on a distant planet. The little man straightened his suit coat and sat down. Mrs. Clemson opened her purse, took out a small notebook, and began making notes to share with her third-graders.

The driver stood up. "Well, whatever happened, we've already collected the tickets, so whoever's got a seat belongs here, I guess. You can figure out how you got here. My job is to get you where you're going."

"Well, speaking of which," Eddie spoke up, "where are we going?"

"San Francisco."

The passengers exploded again.

"The hell we are!"

"I can't afford a fucking vacation!"

"What about my third-graders?"

"I need to call my sister."

"He needs his prescription!"

"You don't find San Francisco in the Bible and there's a good reason for that," said Mabel McClafferty.

Smoky let the tumult peak and die like the din of a chicken house. "Well, friends," he said at last, "if you want to get off, I suggest you wait till morning. This particular reality cooks breakfast at Lake Erie. There's a ranger station there, you can figure out what you want. Meantime we gotta make up the bunks, so get outa the seats there and give us a hand. Usually we get everybody off, but there's not that many here now so just jam up and we'll move you around as we need to." Mrs. Clemson wrote in her notebook: *San Francisco.*

Smoky and Tim began rearranging the interior, and Eddie and Babcock rose to help. "Oh," added Smoky, "if you feel something furry walk over you, that's my ferret Bailey. He kinda likes to crawl into pockets. He's not a rat." *Pet ferret*, wrote Mrs. Clemson, *not a rat*.

In the front they slid out boards from under the bench seats to raise the floor level, then unfolded seat cushions to make a wide floor mattress. In the center section the recruited crew raised the seat boards of the table booths to table level and unfolded more cushions, creating three sets of tiered bunks — a double on the floor, a double at window level, and a single bunk where the luggage rack had been. They moved to the back, converting it, like the front, to a wide floor mattress that could accommodate as many as eight sleepers arranged sardine fashion. Mrs. Clemson and the Quackenbushes sat rigid, raising their feet as the floorboards were shifted.

"Mommy?" whispered Jessie.

"Yes, honey?"

"I'm not scared."

"We normally lay out thirty-eight bodies in here, so it looks like you all got spacious accommodations," Smoky said. He slid behind the wheel and put the bus in gear. They rolled onward.

The passengers distributed themselves. Sergei climbed to the top luggage-rack bunk toward the front, while Jodi burrowed into the lowest level beneath him. Babcock looked utterly lost. "Good night, J.G.," said Tonya. He gave a tiny wave as she moved with Loki toward the rear of the bus. Finally he squeezed into a low-ceilinged window bunk. For a moment he couldn't breathe. Then he found that his necktie was strangling him, so he took it off.

Mabel McClafferty took one look at the layered bunks and lay dead center face down on the mattress at the front of the bus. An array of possessions had been left by the previous occupants — sleeping bags, bedrolls, and a large teddy bear.

Mabel grabbed the teddy bear and covered her head with it.

Mrs. Clemson continued her notes. *Many bunks. Spacious accommodations. A diversity of races, colors and creeds.* She considered adding *lifestyles* but thought better of it.

Smoky pulled onto the freeway. "How you doing?" he asked Tim, who sat down behind him on the bench seat.

"I remember my first day of kindergarten."

Pepper chose a low bunk and pulled Jessie toward her. The little girl resisted. "I want to sleep by Loki." Loki and Tonya were rolling out a couple of salvaged sleeping bags on the rear mattress. Pepper hesitated, then let her go bounding across the mattress. The mothers exchanged a glance, then Pepper crawled into the bunk.

Mrs. Clemson closed her notebook and looked around for a sleeping place at least five yards from any other human being. At last she clambered up into a single bunk directly across the aisle from the strange little scientist or whatever he was. It felt odd to be lying fully clothed in what had been a luggage rack, but after yanking her clothing into place she felt a sudden delight. A blurred memory crossed her mind of being squeezed between two mattresses by her older sister — panicked at first, then filled with a surge of relief at the prospect of death. Tomorrow she would talk with the driver, arrange to be left off at a good motel, call Walter to pick her up, and prepare next week's lesson plans.

She had nearly drifted off to sleep when she heard voices in the bunk below. A man and a woman. Mrs. Clemson flushed as she strained to listen.

"You awake? Hello?" said the man.

"Hello, Eddie." It was the woman named Pepper, or at least that's what she called herself.

"You want to be by yourself, or would you like some company?" Eddie asked. Some hesitation, then Mrs. Clemson heard the sound of hands and knees fumbling their way into a sleeping bag. "So how you doin'?"

"How am I doing? That's a brilliant question, Eddie."

"Actually I'm feeling pretty good," he said. "There's a high probability that we're still alive. So I'm thinking we oughta stay on this bus or whatever it is, then head down to Mexico, cause I got a feeling this phone bill is more complicated than we thought. But we get along pretty good, and you could tend bar, and I can always find work. Jessie'd love it there."

"Mexico? For the love of Mike, Eddie, we been to bed together once and we're going to Mexico?" Mrs. Clemson caught her breath. "Eddie, give me some space, okay?"

"You kinda remind me of Marti. Serious girlfriend. We fought like crazy. Talk about multiple realities."

"Why'd you stay together?"

"Good sex."

"Why'd you split up?"

"Bad sex."

"For me it's not that simple."

"The best system is the simplest. Basic principle. I say stay together. Mexico."

"Eddie—" Pepper explained wearily that she wasn't ready for something permanent in the midst of Noah's Flood, that the most important thing in her life was Jessie and nothing else mattered, that she always got involved with pushy people like Eddie and always regretted it. He grunted assent to everything she said. At last she whispered fiercely, "You're not required to be so fucking agreeable!"

Silence. Hearing what she'd just said, she stifled a laugh, then sighed. "Look, I like you. I like you a lot, okay? You know that, don't you? Didn't you kinda guess it?" Above, Mrs. Clemson heard every word. She felt a tingling on the back of her neck and glanced at the dark form of, what was his name, Sergei or something, on the opposite luggage rack. And then in the darkness she felt her face contort with dry tears.

She knew she was a caricature. Rarely did a day go by without the phrase going through her mind: *broomstick up her ass*. She was sexually stifled, intellectually stoppered, and even her third-graders were aware of the bovine stupidity that her pencil-thin smile tried vainly to conceal. She could hardly stand being touched. She knew that when Walter made love to her now he could only do it by imagining she was somebody else. And she could tolerate his aerobics only by imagining that she herself was somebody else. Anyone but that brainy buck-toothed boobless Irma Jean.

Eddie and Pepper were making quiet movements. Mrs. Clemson felt her dark blush deepen. She was filled with images of what she was hearing and seized by a terrible fear. The fear was more than the fear of reprimand. It was a fear of what she hadn't felt for years. Delight.

Suddenly Pepper let out an unrestrained moan. Mrs. Clemson felt a withering heat in her spine, then bitter cold. But somewhere in the back of her mind — that cluttered utility closet she hadn't sorted for years — she thought, *Oh, other women do that.* Walter had shushed her.

"You're welcome!" Smoky called out. The bus slowed. Flashing lights played across the windows. Roadblock.

Chapter 3
Roadblock

Cpl. Wayne Hapletz of the New York State National Guard saw the bus approaching. Bert was watching the vid in the Jeep and Freddie was taking a crap, but it was his turn anyway. He heaved his butt up from the kerosene heater, slung his rifle over his shoulder, and walked out to the roadblock. There hadn't been westbound traffic for nearly an hour. Seemed like people were scared. They'd better be.

Normally Wayne liked Guard call-ups. They were like vacations, freed for days or even a couple of weeks from the Roto-Rooter. Wayne was a Roto-Rooter man. He hated it, though he had to admit that it got the job done. They'd tried to upgrade the technology, tested ultra-sound, lasers, genetically engineered sludge-eaters: nothing matched the good old Roto-Rooter. But he was sick of the stench and the jerks who clogged their toilets with rags or dead pets and the wisecracks when he told people what he did. He wanted to run the Roto-Rooter straight up the customers.

So whenever they called up the Guard he breathed a sigh. He could be with buddies. He could be a hero, more or less. He could imagine shooting people. But here they were in the middle of nowhere freezing their asses off, for what? The terrorists were going to drive down the freeway? He knew that right now Roy the insurance agent was humping his wife Charlene. They always did that when he went on duty. He'd found a strange necktie in bed and she'd admitted the affair without a blush. Enraged, he'd asked her why she'd been unfaithful, and she said it was because Roy wasn't fat, didn't still have acne at the age of twenty-nine, and didn't stink.

He appreciated her honesty, but honesty had its drawbacks. It made him want to kill. Not her or Roy: he'd get in trouble for that. But he longed for an excuse to blow off heads in the line of duty. Wayne served out his days with death in his heart.

He waved the bus to a stop. What kinda junk heap was this? Bright blue, with a big cartoon turtle painted on the front. He walked to the driver's window. Funny-looking old guy:

long gray hair in a ponytail, sunglasses at midnight. Rock band, maybe?

The driver cracked the window. Wayne mumbled his questions. Where you come from? See anything strange?

"Just when I look in the mirror," the driver joked.

Wayne gave him a hard stare. He flashed his flashlight into the bus, hoping for some twitch he could mistake for a threat and spurt hot lead. Everything was quiet. If they were terrorists they'd stay quiet, just like this: maybe that was evidence enough. He squinted to see the sleeping figures. Suddenly there was a flash of headlights, eastbound. He blinked, and in his dreamless eyes he saw the figures awake, dancing to drums. He'd read a book once about witches, not old green crones but young bare-breasted witches, lean young bucks, and stringy old goats with eyes blazing in the bonfire's glare. Maddened with lust, the drummers pressed them faster and faster, and Wayne had a sharp uncontrollable urge to kill them all.

But he had lived his life controlling his uncontrollable urges. So instead of a burst from his M26 tearing trumpet holes in the sleepers, Wayne blinked, belched, and cursed himself for a coward. "Checking all passengers. They'll have to get out."

"Hey, you know, we're a tour bus outa Boston. They're all asleep."

"We got orders." Wayne prided himself on being a guy who had orders. You could always find somebody glad to give you an order.

"So are you guys Monsanto?" the driver asked. Fuck you asking me questions, Wayne thought. But his pride overcame his irritation.

"Monsanto doesn't operate National Guard. They do state police. We're not state, we're nationalized, asshole." Wayne thought *asshole* would end the conversation. But the driver didn't seem to hear it.

"Then you're Disney."

"Yeh, we're Disney," Wayne said with a sullen pride. "What about it?"

"Hey, we are too. Check out the turtle, bro."

Wayne glanced at the happy galloping turtle painted on the hood. What did he mean by *bro*? Wayne remembered cop movies where niggers called each other *bro*. Was this old fart calling him a nigger? He started to raise his weapon.

"Hey, they give you neat uniforms. You look great. Bet you score with the chicks. They cream for guys with guns." Wayne's face went slack. He'd never thought of that possibility. "Look what I gotta wear," the driver indicated his headband. "We're like, man, the Old Hippie Theme Trip. Like way back in the Sixties?"

"We read about that in school," Wayne mumbled, mesmerized by the creaming chick.

"Yeh, they give us the costume and we gotta learn all the slang like *groovy* and *pigs,* and say *fuck* a lot." But Wayne saw only the chick — a hippie chick in a crash pad like he'd seen in a movie, with long copper hair, and her lips were open, whispering *Wayne*— He jerked his head sharply to fend off the dream.

"Hey, got any acid?" the driver asked.

"Huh?" Wayne heard himself grunt. He was supposed to be a fearsome bastard, but the driver kept asking questions. Once he'd had a job as a phone solicitor, and they were taught that people who were asked a question couldn't help responding. One day some lady had turned the tables and started asking him questions. He'd thought she was interested in him, and then she'd said, "You're pathetic." He'd sat in his cubicle motionless until his supervisor came up and fired him. He jerked his head.

"That's what we're sposed to say," the old guy said, "like to cops and stuff. Like the cop is really a pusher, cause like, man, the System sucks, dig? Gives a thrill to the tourists. They're all like squares — librarians, cashiers, insurance agents." Wayne saw Roy's butt plowing deep. "Got any acid?" the driver repeated, gesturing for Wayne to play along.

"No," replied Wayne helplessly.

"Hey, you're cool," the old driver smiled. "You ever do acting?" Wayne shook his head. In fact he'd been in a high school play, but he'd forgotten his lines and stood there burning with shame while the other actors ad libbed until he walked into the wings and just kept walking. "Well, so help me out here. They'll all piss their pants. Drug bust, okay? I mean we're all working for the same dudes."

Wayne knew he was losing control, but he felt the hippie chick's lips on his as the old satyr loomed over them leering.

Wayne knew what he had to do: step back two paces, raise his M26, scream out orders for instant obedience, motherfucker. But the driver was telling him his lines. It was a drug bust and he was a narc but he was really a head himself and a head was a hippie or a hippie was a head— Wayne was confused. "Don't sweat it," the driver said, "I'll feed you your lines."

Before he could respond the old guy turned toward the back of the bus, his voice a shouted whisper, "Hey, folks, we got trouble! Drug bust! The pigs are all over! Anything illegal, ditch it!" He prompted Wayne.

"Hey, got any acid?" Wayne mumbled.

"How much you want?" the driver asked, then whispered to Wayne, "A dozen tabs. See, it's a pay-off."

"A dozen tabs." And now he was back in high school, and he did remember his lines, and Linda Stitts the class slut was looking at him hard as her copper hair fell over her pointy inexcusable breasts.

Smoky reached over on the dashboard, picked up a bus schedule, ripped off a strip, then tore it into confetti. "Okay, Wayne," the driver said, "you take these on an empty stomach, and man, are you gonna trip, it's so far out, and Morningstar gives these wild blow jobs, man, she's lickin' her lips for that cannon you got there. You better be loaded cause she takes it deep!" Wayne took the tabs in his quivering hand. "Swallow it, Wayne. Have a nice trip." Wayne obeyed, the driver waved, and the bus rolled away. The confetti was nothing more than a bus schedule, but now it exuded the sweet funk of Morningstar.

Smoky looked over his shoulder toward Tim, but Tim was asleep. "Best thing about this fascist state," he mused, "it's really fucked up." He too had once been a phone solicitor, and that's where he'd learned his people skills. He'd had that special gift for holding a prospect like a deep-sea fisherman playing a marlin too big for the test line, weaving a conversation that had no punctuation marks. When he was named for the third straight month as the record-breaking salesman of Quadramatic Adjustable Beds, relieving elderly couples of sizable amounts of their incomes, he quit cold turkey. He realized that he was too dangerous.

Something else gave him that uncanny capacity to talk himself out of edgy situations. Shadow had taught him peyote, and though he hadn't made that voyage for many years he could tune in when he needed to. He'd never met anyone else for whom peyote had the effect it had on him. Shadow had said that LSD was like calling God and getting a phone machine, while peyote was a living soul telling you what you'd damned well better hear. But he saw no totem animals, felt no polymorphous oneness with the wallpaper. For him it had produced an uncanny knack for being inside other people, whether surfing on Shadow's tumultuous ecstasy or wandering in Wayne's pathetic Walmart aisles. It led him into the alleyways of the other's heart, and Wayne's alleyways were very dark. He had been inside Wayne so deeply that he had to run for the exit as the bus pulled out. How did he even know the kid's name was Wayne?

From the back of the bus, the voices of the elderly couple sitting bolt upright on the rear bench cut through the silence. "They think we're Bonnie and Clyde. Bonnie and Clyde, the robbers," said Mr. Quackenbush.

"Hear that?" said Mrs. Quackenbush. "He's nuts."

"Bank robbers. I wasn't even born. My mother talked about'em. They were famous. They didn't need an appointment, they'd just walk in and kill you."

Smoky drove on, accelerating with a mighty wheeze of the engine to outdistance his karma. This was a lot heavier than he'd expected. Toward morning he flicked the windowglass vid. Two imbeciles, male and female, in perfect synchronicity:

> CRAZY NEWS, ROSALIE. A NEW YORK
> NATIONAL GUARDSMAN WAS
> APPREHENDED WHILE SITTING ON AN I-90
> OVERPASS URINATING ON PASSING TRUCKS.
> HE CLAIMED TO BE SAVING AMERICA.
> HAROLD, ARE WE MAKING ALL THIS UP?

As Wayne popped the confetti into his mouth and began to chew, he saw the bus pull out. At once he knew he'd been conned. He was about to spit out the paper and blast away, but Freddie came out of the porta-potty, so he swallowed it.

Half an hour later he began to feel lightheaded. He thought about going to the porta-potty, but it seemed further away than it had been before, shimmering with an inner light. Its door gaped wide like a mouth.

Wayne squinted as the porta-potty's face flushed with an opulent iridescence. Its vent grill caught a glitter from the blinking hazard light and stared back at him, a hungry black eye fixed on its prey. The blinks became a heartbeat, and the wind rose up with the shriek of a gap-toothed giant. Wayne saw a tiny figure running westward into the freeway's blackness, arms waving, flapping, trying to fly, and realized that distant panicked dwarf was himself.

He was fleeing the ravening maw of the toothy devouring crapper. And suddenly he felt a surge of strength like what they say you get from that energy drink. The heartbeat was his own, his legs extended like tree trunks, and he was some ancient stilt-walking arthropod loping across the plain, miles at a stride. This wasn't real tripping, he knew in the Wayne-speck of his mind, because then the copper-haired hippie chick would be down upon him, bold-breasted and succulent.

In the distance he saw a freeway sign, a verdant green field against the blackness, illumined by the high beams of his frantic eyes. JUNCTION HWY 21 SOUTH, it declared in the voice of a hollow god. Wayne was there at its foot. He felt his hands and the soles of his feet turn viscous, sluggish, and with slow sucking progress he inched his way up the steel pole, then out to the furthest reach of the crossbeam.

As he stared eastward into the dim beginnings of dawn, he could see the aperture between sky and earth, a sliver of blue, a blazing rainbow bridge, and the distant figure of Morningstar.

Below, a convoy of big rigs on their dark night journey approached his perch, bearing sealed containers of death for entombment in that subterranean Nevada treasure house holding all of America's toxins. In an instant he knew what must be done. A hero doesn't stop to think, he just knows. As the convoy rolled underneath ignoring the puny roadblock, Wayne pissed down on the monstrous eighteen-wheelers.

This was no common urination. It came in torrents, unstoppable, inexhaustible. The trucks moved into a monsoon and swerved drunkenly as the yellow tsunami struck. For a moment Wayne feared that he might drain, dehydrate, but now he felt plugged into a primal aquifer sluicing down to scrub the concrete arteries clean with its antiseptic reek.

Within minutes, troopers arrived in squad cars, tanks

and helicopters to protect the plutonium convoy from terrorist onslaught. After repeated megaphone warnings, interpreted by Wayne as praise of his heroism, Sgt. Dickie Rodriguez of the NY State Special Forces put one armor-piercing slug perfectly between the eyes of Cpl. Wayne Hapletz. He died at his moment of highest bliss, in the hippie chick's fierce embrace.

Chapter 4
Bonnie and Clyde

The bus bucked and jostled through the night. The passengers slept on the edge of sleep. Cramped into the bunks or sprawled on the floor mats, they tossed, turned, snored, snuffled, and fumbled through fragments of dreams like ancient clay tablets excavated from rubble, a cuneiform as indecipherable as the claw prints of chickens dancing in mud.

The gray dawn sidled alongside the lumbering bus. The travelers grumbled awake, grim with residue. All except the elderly misplaced Quackenbushes. All night they had sat bug-eyed, bolt upright. They'd missed their doctor's appointment. That could be fatal.

Their senses were honed to a razor's edge. They couldn't tell which of them saw the slight jerk of the head visible in the lower bunk to the left as Pepper startled awake. But they felt her confusion, waking on what must be a bus, again facing a hairy back that must be a man. They saw a fly land on the eyelid of J.G. Babcock and a smile form on his lip, stark evidence of a forbidden dream.

As the passengers faltered into upright postures, Myra and Fritz Quackenbush looked at each other as if into a mirror after four shots of bourbon. *Who am I now?* All night they had fought sleep, strangled each hallucination as it rose from the womb. Now they stared in suspended disbelief. Who was Myra and who was Fritz? From that moment their minds were fused.

The bus bumped along a rutted road into a park and pulled to a stop by a cluster of picnic tables overlooking the flat wide sheen of Lake Erie. The door hissed open. A voice announced the presence of restrooms. A little man climbed down from an upper bunk and stumbled over littered shoes. A driver emerged from the tiny sleeping loft above the rear bench and made his way forward, stepping over the huddled lumps still drowsing on the mattress. The Quackenbushes felt an urge to cry out for the doctor, but they already knew the diagnosis.

Eddie rose into the aisle and pulled on his pants. He gave Pepper's back a tentative scratch. She arched to meet his hand as she buttoned her rumpled blouse. "One thing we could do today," he offered in a subdued voice under the Quackenbushes' lidless glare, "is lemme fix your watch band."

"What's that supposed to mean?"

"I mean fix your watch band. It's loose. I fix stuff."

"I sure know how to pick'em." Pepper pulled on her shoes. The Quackenbushes focused their melded eyes into her bleach-blonde hair and the wadded confusion beneath it.

The old driver stood at the front of the bus addressing whomever might listen. "So check your shoes cause Bailey likes to curl up in shoes or else he shits in'em." At the back he saw the elderly couple watching him like over-caffeinated zombies with golf-ball eyes. "So we got an hour for breakfast," he continued. "This is communal cooking, so once I get some help we'll get coffee on. Variety of selections, just about anything you want except crap. We're low on crap."

Mr. Quackenbush leaned toward Mrs. Quackenbush. "Bonnie and Clyde were shot right after breakfast," he said, "but before lunch."

"Can you see your watch?" she whispered.

He held his breath. "When the coast is clear."

Outside, a rag-tag crew assembled, hauling down folding tables from the overhead rack and a gas cylinder for the burner. Someone tossed cantaloupes from the rooftop into Smoky's practiced hands. The lower chambers of the bus disgorged an ice chest, assorted boxes, and a repast fit for a ravenous king.

"They're laying the ambush," said Mr. Quackenbush. A dark shudder passed through the pair.

Tonya stood at a table slicing fruit as Pepper set out pots of yogurt. "Hang in there, baby."

Pepper looked up with a tight-lipped smile. "Well, for once I don't have to rush breakfast."

"You like French toast?"

"I guess so. It's been a while."

"Never neglect French toast."

"They lay on a spread, don't they? When's the execution?" Pepper began to shake and her face contorted. Tonya grabbed her with powerful hands.

"Honey, your little girl's here. Don't freak out. Think of your little girl."

Pepper froze. After a moment she took a deep breath and disengaged from Tonya's grip. "Thanks."

"Those two there were grabbing each other," reported Myra Quackenbush, "like animals." She saw her world go a pallid yellow as if staring through her urine sample. "Did you take your pills?" she asked, then answered, "Yes, dear." Fritz mumbled in unison.

Suddenly they sensed they were on TV. They had never been on TV before. Once they'd been asked by an on-the-street reporter how they felt about the war. They didn't remember which war, though they knew they ought to be for it. But they watched the news that night and they weren't there: they hadn't guessed the right answer. Now, senses sharpened, they felt the patter of electrons, heard alien voices, knew that they were prime-time material.

      ROGAROTZ. (RATINGS ARE DOWN.)

      PLUGIT. (WE WANTED BLOOD.)

      ZORPNOI. (WE GET FRENCH TOAST.)

"Do we smile?" Mrs. Quackenbush asked, then responded, "Quick!" Both mouths tilted into thin dry lines of pain. Their Sunday best.

Outside, an extravagant breakfast blessed the weary-and-heavily-laden. Fresh fruit, yogurt, French toast, maple syrup, the hot lick of caffeine in company of fellow passengers who appeared to be still alive — all this put yesterday's screams at bay, some far-distant horror movie where you sat by the TV in your PJs and laughed at the monster's rubber seams. The ferret nibbled a stub of bacon.

The Quackenbushes were on their own journey. The light had shifted sharply. The bus was parked in the long shadows of early morning, but the Quackenbush sun was high to the west. They'd faithfully swallowed their suppressant dosage, yet the road seemed narrower now as their '31 Ford coupe bounced through the ruts of back-country Louisiana. A long hard ride over the years, and it might have been so different. They might have gotten married, raised a family, gone to church. They might have had doctor's appointments and voted for strong firm men with rabid smiles. But when you kill your first man something happens. *You know what I mean, babe? Sure do, hon. It's all boogie-woogie.*

The shadows swung back to the west, then east again as their minds see-sawed between worlds. Myra Quackenbush rubbed the wrinkled backs of her hands. "So cramped in here. That first apartment, remember the steam pipes?"

"Banging my head," said her unblinking husband of forty-six years.

"Incinerating the pot roast?"

"Me and the sink trap?"

"And that state trooper? They give guns to boys."

"Like Bonnie and Clyde."

"You got them on the brain."

"My granddad talked about Bonnie and Clyde, so they put'em in a movie." Fritz sucked out the juice from each word.

"One movie too many." They couldn't tell whose lips were talking. It hardly mattered. They could hear the tremulous orchestra swelling to climax.

Mrs. Quackenbush tugged at the thin cotton dress that clung to her hot young thighs like a smear of honey. Trickles of sweat ran down her neck the way those ravenous red ants swarmed out of her dog Buddy's corpse so many years ago. She felt the raw rasp of Clyde's hungry tongue upon her, and she moaned. Ahead, scrub trees overhung the road, underbrush pressing down like the straits of Hell. Trapped in a steamy novel, Bonnie Quackenbush froze in dread.

"It's a trap, honey!" she screamed as Clyde saw the battered pickup blocking the road and screeched to a halt. A dozen men with leveled shotguns popped out of the shadows as Mrs. Clemson appeared at the front of the bus with a plate of French toast. "I thought you might like some French toast," she chirped. "It really hits the spot."

Clyde's hands groped for the pistols stashed under the floorboard to rise up with barrels blazing. But the projector threw a hole off its sprocket and Reality hiccuped. "We're not them!" cried Myra Quackenbush, and Fritz, waving his frail fingers, piped up, "Clyde is a whole lot younger!" Mrs. Clemson held out the plate of French toast.

"Bonnie smokes cigars!"

"Bank robbers don't make appointments!"

"We go to the Presbyterian—"

And then they began to dance in the air.

Mrs. Clemson hated violence in films, even more when it was made beautiful — deaths in slow motion, blood spurting like lacy fountains, screams blending with bird song. For a few seconds she thought she was seeing a movie with the sound track off. Then came the roar of the shotguns, and she saw two human beings, twenty feet away, turn into raspberry jam. Irma Jean's shriek launched her platter of French toast into the stratosphere. She heard hollow whoops of triumph, then suddenly all was dead silent, except for some hysterical woman howling like a wind-up toy. She realized it was herself, and she couldn't stop.

Her unerring instinct for time, based on the thirty-six-minute slices of her classroom day, told her that her raving lunacy lasted twelve minutes on the dot. At last, staring at an alien landscape she finally recognized as the ceiling of the bus, she came to her senses. The young driver knelt beside her taking her pulse. Eighteen years she had taught the third-grade version of history, but she had never seen history's raw imperative: people getting killed.

Such a clutter. The old driver came up the aisle and the unshaven man kept everyone else back, shouting, "It's all right," even though it wasn't. Mrs. Clemson heard the wild foreign man and the quiet historical man outside the bus, it seemed, in earnest colloquy. She lay flat on her back staring at clouds of words that swarmed up, black flies in the morning sun.

"Bonnie and Clyde, they were only twenty-four, twenty-five. Ambushed on a back road in Louisiana, 1934. The six officers used automatic rifles, then shotguns, then pistols, until they ran out of ammunition."

"This is fact of it. Reality is collapse of potentials. Quantum particles cancel each other's options, less and less. We eat French toast, collapse to reality agreed upon by teeth and toast. But if no collapse? At back of bus all options eruct."

And the cackle of the mentally challenged lady, "Oh shut up, you guys!"

Then the voice of Loki — she knew Loki's voice so well, the child she would never have — pleading, "Stop crying. Why are you crying?" And the little girl whimpered, "Because you're afraid!"

Mrs. Clemson had an impulse to threaten calling the principal but checked herself in time. She rose up on her elbows and forced herself to look toward the back of the bus. The old couple had disappeared. No trace. But how? Sucked out in the ebb tide before the eyes of the beholders, dissolved in sunlight. Like millions of people in her pageant of third-grade history, they were not even names on the chalkboard.

"Let's get going," Smoky said. "There's no bullet holes nor nothing."

"Should we call the police?"

"Let'em catch the movie."

Outside, the passengers milled about in their private blurs, as Mrs. Clemson had seen her class at those times when the world's spasms intruded into the day's routine. The World Trade Towers long ago had been a shock, but the Rose Bowl was worse because it took so long to watch the players die. The annual riots and the bridges going down — the children became so confused. Of course they were always happy when America struck back, but Mrs. Clemson felt privately that these incidents left scars. Now she yearned to speak, as she did to her pupils, of everything happening for a reason, everything under control with lots of soldiers trained to protect us, and also God. But how do you spout this drivel to mature adults unless you're the President?

Something felt wrong about pretending that the old couple had never existed except perhaps somewhere in an appointment book. But then lots of things feel wrong and one learns to accept it. She was greatly relieved when Smoky stood on the first step of the bus and called for attention. She rose to her feet, edged past him, and joined the loose circle outside, keeping a distance lest they be drawn into some communal hell.

"So I don't know what's going on," Smoky said, brushing away a mosquito, "but we're gonna have to do this by democracy because the king is clueless."

Eddie spoke up again. "Well, chief, could you give us the options? At least as a starting point?"

The debate was long and nonlinear. Smoky summarized what he'd gleaned from the news regarding rampant terrorists, Sergei expounded on the physics of impossibility, and Babcock interjected a commentary on Western fantasy literature. At intervals Pepper swore a blue streak, Tonya calmed her, and Mabel mumbled to a nearby tree.

Finally Smoky waved his hand. "Well, okay. Only thing I can think is business as usual. So this bus is headed to the Indiana Dunes, then Chicago, across the Badlands of South Dakota, cut south to Zion, Bryce, past L.A., then San Francisco in fourteen days. Whoever wants to jump ship before you turn into Hitler or Mickey Mouse, fine, there's park rangers down the road there, they'll either help you out or they'll kill you."

Mabel swatted a mosquito. "I'm gettin' outa here fast," she announced. "They got mosquitoes in December."

" December?" Smoky grinned. "It's June."

The passengers stared at him. "June? Which June?" Eddie asked.

"This one, buddy. This is the first Blue Terrapin of the season." Smoky climbed into the bus. Tim followed. Silence, then some people turned to go down the road.

Tonya took Loki's hand, but he pulled against her and his voice rose like a bird cry, "No!" Dead silence. "We have to stay on the bus," he whispered. He didn't know why. He knew the old couple had been all alone. He knew that he and Jessie had been almost trees. "I liked breakfast," he said.

Tonya started to pull him, then stopped as she caught his stare. Behind the thick lenses were Joy's deep eyes.

Loki climbed the steps. Tonya followed. Without quite willing it, Jodi, Mabel, and Babcock climbed the steps, followed by the little scientist who turned around to Mrs. Clemson, grinned and beckoned her to follow. She reddened, hesitated. Suddenly the bus hissed its intention, and she scurried up the steps. She was terrified to be alone.

Eddie and Pepper looked at each other as Jessie tugged on Pepper's hand. "Oh Christ, Eddie," Pepper murmured, "I don't know." She waited for him to decide so that she could run the other way, but dammit, she knew that he knew it and was waiting for her to make a move. At last she let herself be tugged up the steps by Jessie, who squealed and ran up the aisle to join Loki. Eddie followed.

The door closed. Smoky stood at the front of the bus. "So as far as rules go, there's only two. Work together and have some fun. This is personal opinion in terms of trips I have known." He swung into the driver's seat, and Bailey scuttled onto his knee. The bus shuddered, jerked, and rumbled forth.

From watching war movies Smoky knew enough to conceal his own doubts. Between acid trips and Shadow, he'd seen enough magic to take stuff in stride. But if time was shifting — June? December? — what about the roadways? Who could say that I-90 would actually take them west? Or that they might not arrive full speed at an intersection where all the signals were red? At his age he wasn't prepared for a trip that shifted his status from grizzled guru to clueless dope. He'd seen his hair graying and thinning, sure, but he'd never before felt the truth penetrate right down to his prostate that he might not be immortal. Maybe he'd better dig out the leather hat he used to wear until its brim went limp. He'd always felt tough in that hat.

At the back of the bus the children bounced on a bench they pretended was bouncy. They were besotted with discovery, unwittingly bouncing on the spot where the Quackenbushes had achieved their terrible oneness. And they were in love.

"We can be animals," Loki said, "but we have to just pretend."

"What's in the sack?"

"Donuts. Want one?"

"Animals don't eat donuts."

"Gorillas do," he whispered.

Jessie grabbed a coconut donut, Loki a chocolate. They took huge bites and beat their chests. "Are you friendly gorillas?" asked J.R. Babcock.

Jessie looked at him, dead serious. "How did you know we're gorillas?"

"You're eating a donut."

"Gorillas!" Loki exulted, and Jessie echoed, "Gorillas!"

Through the squeaks of police radio and the crowing of children, the bus rolled westward.

Chapter 5
Action Figures

America lay spread out before them like a sprawled epileptic.

Once you hit the road, Pepper thought, there's a lift of spirits. The fence posts whiz past, the white dashes on the roadway are swallowed under your chassis, and you think, wow, we're rid of all that, what's next? It's out of your control. It's that point in childbirth just past transition: now it's going to happen, it's more certain than anything you've known in life, and the only thing you can do is push.

A silence hung over the bus. Now and then someone sobbed or moaned, but it passed. Once, she drifted back into the plummeting elevator and jerked awake, but she looked around and no one had noticed. Late morning, Smoky turned over the driving to the younger man and stood leaning on the dashboard to tell the passengers they'd be traveling back roads to keep out of the way of civilization. Somehow Pepper trusted him, even though she saw his eyes scanning the potentials of everything female. Lechers weren't a problem to her. At least they had some reason to stay alive and keep ladies alive.

They stopped for lunch, sandwiches tossed together and lots of juice, then they divvied up the luggage of people who'd been blown off the bus into Disney World or some other state of mind. Pepper managed to find basic necessities for herself and Jessie, even a nice pair of jeans that fit. It was harder to dress a six-year-old, but she came across a small sewing kit and a couple of T-shirts that might be altered into dresses. They'd have to hit a shopping center sometime.

Eddie had scored a pod with a good blues library, so he was out of her hair for a while. Pepper caught a faint whisper from his earplugs, some lady yowling in musical heat. She couldn't believe she was getting more involved with him at every new episode of Armageddon. Long ago she'd learned to rely on herself and nobody else, and she didn't need one more lesson in getting screwed.

Last night they'd made muffled love, and she had even

encouraged it, curling up to him with her knee over his thigh. He was a fine lay — considerate, strong, expressive — but right now she couldn't fathom why she should have the least interest in a fine lay. She felt about as horny as snot.

It wasn't the danger. Before kids, danger had been a turn-on. She could still feel the hot shivers of sitting impaled on her boyfriend's lap between him and the steering wheel, the highway screaming under them as he gunned it up to ninety then let go the wheel as she came apart in waves. She took a sharp breath, snuffing the memory.

No, it wasn't the danger. It was that you couldn't see the danger — the deep rivers running underground, the spiders' webwork laced across your path. Before Jessie was born, the doctor told her that her own blood type was — what was the silly word he used? — anomalous, that her own cells might attack her child. She cried for weeks, and then no sweat, the baby was healthy. But again Pepper felt she was pregnant with something, and the demons swam deep in the blood.

She jerked awake. A debate was in full blast. She couldn't link the words in a pattern that meant more than a random flurry of honks, barks, quacks, squeaks, but at last she remembered that, yes, she did speak English and they were yelling about NoNarx.

"Drug is poison to head!"

"But it's the law."

"I wouldn't be able to teach."

"It is to swallow insanity!"

"Who knows what happens if you stop?"

"We know what happens if we take it."

"We turn into frogs."

"We're a very scattered bunch of assholes," Eddie muttered.

Mrs. Clemson gasped. "There are children present!"

"And people too!" declared Mabel McClafferty.

"It's okay, Mrs. Clemson," Loki said, "we say stuff like that."

"Asshole!" crowed Jessie.

The wrangling continued. Some felt that they should stop dosages on the spot, but once astride the tiger could you safely get off? Mrs. Clemson declared faith in the President, Mabel cursed the Postal Service, while Sergei Rupp expounded the physics of annihilation. Pepper listened the way she listened to politicians, as if they were running their mouths to exercise their dentures. Jessie tugged at Mommy's sweater, as Pepper mumbled a silent prayer to no particular god that Jessie wouldn't revert to bed-wetting.

"Mommy," Jessie faltered, "if we all got here cause we took our pills, then if we don't. . ."

"What?"

"Then are we back on the elevator?"

Jessie was afraid to die.

Tonya saw the flicker of horror in Pepper's face. "Guys, this is serious stuff," she called out, starting to rise on rickety knees. "Can we focus a minute?"

"I doubt it," said Smoky, stumbling up the aisle. "I'm sacking out. Lemme know if we get killed." Halfway back, he stopped, leaned over to Jodi, the lumpy young woman who sat muffled in two sweaters and the sullen funk of suicide. "Hey, cutie pie," he whispered, "you're a lot sweeter than you think." Jodi pulled into her blankness.

Tonya leaned across to Pepper. "Listen, I've got my cell phone if you need to get hold of anyone."

"You were trying to call somebody. Did you get'em?"

"Not yet. Benny, he's a friend. And yeh, my mom, she's got my older kids, but they're in South Carolina. Nothing ever happens in South Carolina."

Sergei Rupp twisted around in his seat. "Cell phone is risk. Electronic detectors."

Pepper bristled. "She's calling her guy and her other kids. Lay off."

"High risk of serious death!" Rupp stared like a sunlit lizard, black eyes burning.

"Oh God, why did I get back on this bus?" Pepper sighed. Jessie snuggled into her lap, and Eddie, from the seat behind, placed his hand on her hair. She shrugged it away, then instantly reached back over her shoulder inviting his touch, leaning her head into his caress.

Tonya gazed at Pepper's thin sharp lips and imagined them opening, softening. *No, forget it, bitch. You know better.* She watched Jodi lumber down the aisle and sit on the bench seat behind the young driver. Tonya couldn't help but see the girl's groping need like a blurred video of her own smelly youth, feeling as attractive as a wad of Kleenex. Jodi paged through Tim's sketch pad, droning on. The young driver nodded obligatory nods.

"So I finish college and get a job in Boston. But I hate the job, I hate Boston. Start seeing this guy, pretty soon I hate this guy. I think, okay, go west, and I'm on this bus fulla people, they're having a great time, and I can't stand'em."

"You got on in Boston, yeh."

"Yeh. So I start reading this Stephen King book, it's nine hundred pages and I really hate it but I can't put it down. And this girl on the bus grabs it: 'Hey, whatta you reading?' And she's hanging onto this book while everybody's singing some Hebrew campfire song. Then she's singing the fucking song and she vanishes. Zip. With my book. I'm stuck on page 402. It's a spiritual crisis."

He was obliged to fill the grim silence. "Yeh, that's something."

"Well, I can do what I always do. Eat."

"I slouch a lot," Tim smiled. "I was a gifted child."

"Your stuff's okay." She riffled the sketch pad. "You catch the characters. Do me a favor. Don't draw me."

Tonya knew she should keep her mouth shut, but she leaned forward to Jodi. "Listen, I don't mean to be rude, but you really sound—"

Jodi stiffened. "You weren't in our conversation."

"I know—"

Her voice broke as she blurted, "I get this all my life! 'You're so negative, yada yada fucking yada!' What business is it—?"

Tim spoke up. "You guys maybe oughta back off—"

Jodi rose, shouting at Tonya through tears. "You don't just wake up and say 'La-de-dah, I think I'll be happy today.'"

"No," Tonya said, "it took me about thirty years."

"Do I look like I care?"

"No, you just look miserable, you look—"

"What?" Jodi challenged.

"You look like I did ten years ago." Tonya turned abruptly, staring out the window. There were jet trails high in the sky, hundreds, heading north. The thought ran through everyone's mind. Were we attacking Canada?

The heavy girl sat down trembling. After a moment Tim spoke. "Well, so—"

Jodi turned on him. "You're not really required to talk to me!" She stormed up the aisle and threw herself into a seat. Tim drove on.

Tonya took a deep breath. You'd think a state of abject terror would give us a little perspective, but we just dig deeper into our soap operas. We might be wiping Canada right now, for all it matters. Well, fuck Canada. She glanced back at Pepper, considering the possibilities.

Pepper stared out the window as the bus strained on, a blind sperm dog-paddling westward. Flat farmland. Vapor trails. Death needles. She hated disaster movies. All the starlet ever did was stand around while the hero jumped chasms and connected wires to zap the dinosaur or blow up the asteroid or whatever special effects they'd bought at the yard sale. And the lady hung there screaming as the giant cockroach took her parking place. Or else it was this very tough babe who was like one of the guys. Blouse was ripped pretty low but she had six-pack abs and she knew she'd survive: it was in her contract. Plus a cut from the sales of the action figures.

Pepper had been an action figure. There was a time she could give the bum's rush to a muscle-bound drunk and never think twice. But times had changed for this babe. She was a mommy. Sure, she'd kill for her kid if she could figure out who to kill, but now all she could do was sit on the bus and watch the movie. It wasn't much different from the ones she'd seen before. You surf across sit-coms, thrillers, quiz shows and weather reports thinking, Hey, where's my life? What channel am I on? Am I in re-runs yet? Tune in the cartoon series.

Eddie leaned forward and asked what she was thinking. What business was it of his? "Nothing," she said.

"I'm glad you stayed on the bus."

Why was she so angry at him? Poor guy, he was just trying to be supportive, sensitive, protective, and invade her life totally. Now he was breathing on her and she desperately longed to surrender, to curl up in his arms for an hour, then wake up and kill him.

"I had another kid," she said. Eddie gave a questioning grunt. "You asked if I had other kids. I had a little boy. Five years old. He was out in the front yard, I was on the phone. That was the last I ever saw him." She longed for Eddie to touch her, and if he did she'd break his head wide open.

"Wow. Sorry."

Brian. She was younger then, fighting day and night with Brian's dad, and Brian was a little devil. But she'd loved the little devil, and the grief hit her like the hammer-bolt that stunned the cattle when she'd worked at the meat-packing plant. She'd been sodden with grief, stupid with grief, bloated with grief, and at last she was hung by the heels, slit open, and the grief gushed into the troughs. There had been no fear, only numbness. Now there was fear. For Jessie.

"Jessie's going to have a hard time. I'm getting to be such an over-protective bitch," she said. He didn't contradict her on that. "But I have to. This is the real world."

"Real world?"

"This is the real world, Eddie." She felt him draw back. Thank God.

But she wasn't rid of him. "Real world," he repeated. "I heard that term too much. My dad talked about the real world, and my mom, girlfriends, politicians, same crap. It's just another word for *we're all scared shitless*."

Don't answer him, lady, don't give him the satisfaction. She looked out the window. In the distance there appeared to be a line of National Guardsmen advancing slowly across a meadow toward a flock of sheep. "Reality is reality," she growled.

Eddie's voice was sharp. "Is that what you tell your kid? Think she needs that? 'Yeh, Real World, honey, the big people are dangerous, so don't color outside the lines.'"

"That's not what I'm saying—"

"And make sure you tell her that in the Real World you don't have a right to live. You gotta earn that by grabbing when nobody's looking or giving guys their jollies. I mean there's no real happiness, there's just jollies. And don't forget to teach her to lie. Lie so well you believe it yourself."

Don't answer him, she told herself. She'd heard him run his mouth like this before. "I teach her to take care of herself," Pepper snapped.

"Great," Eddie said, "And teach her that love is like money, right? There's only so much to go around, so dole it out in little dribbles. Cause it's a commodity, something that's owned. In the Real World everything is owned. That mountain is owned, and that river, that woman. Course the moon and the stars are free and you sing songs about'em, but the songs are owned, and the singers, and the photographs of the moon and the stars."

"You can stop any time you want."

But he couldn't stop. He ranted on about school grades and guns and lies and the government and how she was teaching her kid the wrong things. All she'd heard all her life was how it was all her fault and she didn't need to hear it again—

The shock was in his anger. She had never seen him angry. She had been startled, then repelled, then attracted by his gentleness, his humor, his calm in the face of insanity. Now it all fell away like with the other men she'd known, and the rage came vomiting out. His words were fists.

"But the funny thing is," Eddie worked up to his punch line, "in the Real World nothing's real. It's numbers on a screen. It's a print-out. It's the spin. It's the plastic flower. And we teach our kids what the Real World is—"

"Jesus Christ, Eddie, shut up!"

"—And the little fuckers don't even say thanks."

Silence. A sinkhole opened between them. They didn't know where to look, where to park their eyes. Jessie came down the aisle and climbed onto Pepper's lap.

At last Eddie spoke quietly. "So you asked me if I ever talked. Well, I get wound up sometimes and that gets me fired. But you want to get noise out of a system I'm your man."

"Eddie?" Jessie said.

"What, sweetheart?"

"Are you mad?"

"Yeh. But not at you or your mom."

"You're talking too loud."

"Sorry." Eddie looked out the window. A white disk hung low in the afternoon sky. "Hey, look," he said to Jessie, "the moon's in the daytime." She looked, then hopped down from her mother's lap and ran up the aisle to tell Loki. Eddie leaned close to Pepper's ear. "Look, I'm saying something simple.

They say you create your own reality, and basically I always thought that was bullshit. But now we do it together and we need to agree on what it is."

"Gee, Eddie, I think you nailed it," she snarled.

"I mean it. I seen really good bands go down the tubes, the Pale Fish, best thing since the Beatles, but they fucked up. We gotta all take the same ride, we gotta—"

She turned around to face him. "So we should all hold hands or something?"

"I'm serious! Listen to me, dammit!" But she'd listened and heard enough. She turned her back on him and felt a heavy steel door slam behind her. Then she heard his voice cutting through that door. "Just get this Real World shit out of your little rabbit hole brain," Eddie railed at her, "or else they'll blow up your kid and then you'll be really safe!"

And Pepper was over the back of the seat smashing her fist again and again into Eddie's face and any part of Eddie she could hit. She heard herself screaming, and then she was pulled away flailing like a many-legged bug, and Tonya's voice rang in her head, "Give it up, honey. Let it go." She felt strong thick arms squeezing the holy living shit out of her. And at last she gave it up.

A moment later, or an hour, Pepper opened her eyes to find Tonya's dark eyes six inches from her own. Somewhere she heard Sergei Rupp droning about post-quantum theory as reciprocal causation, the shadow of a tree making a tree as the tree makes the shadow and both make the sun, and Mabel telling him to shut his trap. Then Tonya's voice as if under water. "We need to keep things calm, honey, okay? Start a fight here and we morph into World War Three." She caught a bray of news—

INDIANA STATE TROOPERS REPORT FOREST
FIRES A HUNDRED MILES ALONG THE
MICHIGAN BORDER. ALL HIGHWAYS ARE
CLOSED.

HAROLD, THE PRESIDENT BLAMES IT ON TOO
MANY TREES.

"Forest fires?" Tim exclaimed. "That's where we're driving. There's no fire. The highways are open." But he couldn't see the flames in the troopers' eyes.

Mabel McClafferty stumbled forward. "I got these damn

packages I gotta mail pretty soon or they're gonna spoil."

"We'll be in Chicago tonight," Tim reassured her.

"I'm gonna write a letter to the goddamned editor," Mabel announced to the firmament.

Pepper met Tonya's eyes. "You got muscles," Pepper said. She didn't know what else to say. "I never fought with a woman before."

"You don't know what you're missing," Tonya smiled.

Pepper pulled back. "Nothing personal, but I happen to be straight, okay?"

Tonya smiled. "Not to worry, honey. Straight chicks throw curveballs. I'll pass." Her dark eyes twinkled like the moon on wetlands. Pepper wasn't sure what to trust, but she leaned into the embrace so she couldn't see those eyes.

"I can't stay on the same bus with that guy. We're getting off in Chicago."

"That sucks. The kids are gonna be really sad."

Pepper fought against her tears. "Well that's just too bad. Right, let some guy take care of me. *Hey, honey, we'll protect you. Hey, honey, you're safe with me.* Why does that guy piss me off so much?"

"Maybe it's love."

"Fuck you." She jerked back, but the arms held her. They held her as Mom had never held her. Firmly, but like a baby. She couldn't speak, she could only be embraced. She felt a soft brush of fur on her leg, and Bailey curled like a bracelet around her ankle. She wept, then drifted off.

She was stumbling across a godforsaken desert, with some huge decision to make. The time had come, the bills were due. But it didn't matter. There were arms around her, and she was safe.

Chapter 6
Lessons of History

As the battered blue sardine can rolled across America, the paradigm shifted into overdrive. Record numbers of homeless families died in the streets, so the President ordered mass inoculations. Investment bankers shredded their portfolios: the President privatized the IRS. Doctors ripped catheters from the uninsured: the President quarantined the University of Wisconsin. "We will hold firm," declared President Pert, and he did. "Our actions will be decisive," he said, and they were. His approval ratings rose steadily. Little kids in the House of Horrors clung to Daddy's hand.

The drive to Chicago was uneventful except for lightning streaks in the daylight sky, white on white. At the back of the bus Loki and Jessie stared northward out the window. Fires seared the horizon now.

"Let's play Blue Terrapin," suggested Loki. "A million bad guys are chasing us, but we win."

"You can't if there's a million of them and just us."

"Agincourt." The children looked at J.G. Babcock.

He glanced up from his book. "Sorry to intrude," he said, "but the Battle of Agincourt, 1415, is analogous. King Henry's army was small and exhausted, the French had thousands of knights on horses, heavily armored. But it was muddy, the horses were scared, the English shot arrows, the French panicked, and Henry was a hero. Except what was he doing in France? He belonged in England."

"How did you find out?" Loki asked.

"I like history. Well, not that I like it necessarily, but I study it."

Loki turned to Jessie. "So we can shoot arrows and scare their horses."

"If they got horses," said Jessie. Loki considered this complication.

Babcock loved to watch the children play, but he knew better than to intrude further. Something about their playing was— The word that came to him was *sacred*. Something about intensity, simplicity, belief. Their voices cut through the Gordian knot. He'd always been disturbed by the Gordian knot. Alexander had seen that puzzle with the same strategic acuity that sent his deadly phalanx into the Persian heart, but why could he not have cut the knot of his own ambition and made peace? Might we not still have called him "the Great"?

Studying history: Babcock recalled vividly the moment he'd given himself to this path. He was seven. He and his sister Allegra liked to hide in an old refrigerator box out behind the garage while he recited stories his teacher read in school. That day he'd told her about a little shepherd boy, though he hated stories about little shepherd boys. They always learned lessons from their wise old grandpa and J.G. didn't have a wise old grandpa. Then he told Allegra about the clever little girl in ancient Egypt who made a magical cat from lint. He hated stories about clever little girls because he loved his sister but she wasn't very clever. Then Allegra asked, "Did they have lint in ancient Egypt?"

He was appalled. He'd never failed to answer Allegra's questions. Next day he asked his teacher but she got mad, so from that day he began to read. He got his mother to check out books on ancient Egypt, then books about anything. He needed to know the answer, but there were no historians of lint.

Thereafter he devoured whole libraries. His questioning broadened, of course. His sister didn't actually ask, but he told her answers upon answers like popcorn. Sometimes he failed: he'd once started to read a book about famous mass delusions, but his mother had taken it back to the library and he never knew if we ever came out of the mass delusions.

Seeing the streaks in the sky Babcock wished he'd finished that book. And he longed for some grand insight into the meaning of history, of conquest, of human strife, of stories told to sisters. Maybe there was no meaning, just the same old merry-go-round of atrocity followed by sunrise.

Yet around him he saw another merry-go-round. In his teens he began to detect an oddity in the tides of humankind: people kept on doing stuff. Amid the fall of kings and the thundering hordes, people ate lunch, petted their dogs, got sick, got better, fell in love — oh how they fell in love. His sister's eyes burned as he told her.

Now, in this singular flight from nightmare, he saw a slow gravitational alignment of body to body, the dance of Eros. The couple named Eddie and Pepper were sitting apart, but the dance was there. The chubby girl hovered near the young driver, though clearly the old man had his eye upon her. The children were wrapped in their own discoveries. And in the seat ahead of him he heard the first clucks of a mating call.

"I am Sergei. I sit here by you, yes?"

"Well, yes— Do you not have a— Irma Jean Clemson."

"Irma Jean Clemson." There was a pause. "You enjoy trip?"

A longer pause. "Well, I need to get back home. I teach third grade. And you?"

"Theoretical physicist."

"Oh." Irma Jean Clemson pondered. "Does that mean you have theories?"

"Yes!"

"You have the most intriguing accent."

"I am fusion reaction." Dead silence. "I say this with humorous intent."

She spoke, trying to raise her voice above a whisper. "You were wonderful on the elevator. You saved us. I was terrified, but I felt like Laura in *Little House on the Prairie* when they cross the river and almost drown. And they leave Jack behind, but then he swims across and they're so happy."

"You live in little house?"

"Oh no, I wish I did. It's a book. My favorite book. I feel so close to Laura."

"My teacher of third grade was Frau Blumenkohl," the physicist mused. "I could see her breasts aroused."

A sharp intake of breath, then Mrs. Clemson spoke brightly, as if to her third grade class. "Oh? How old were you then?"

Sergei giggled. "I was fully formed."

At dusk the bus pulled into the Indiana Dunes and stopped at a picnic ground for dinner. Again the setting up tables, hauling down food, dividing into crews, lively chatter. Babcock watched Loki helping Jessie with a carrot peeler. Sergei Rupp and Irma Jean Clemson were slicing red peppers together. The rhythms of Eros never ceased.

Perhaps this was the real human history, Babcock thought as he chopped cabbage, this daily foolery, and Attila the Hun was just a sidelight. No scholarly attention was ever paid to the washing of dishes or even the cleaning up after the slaughter. There was comfort in the simple fact that life went on. After the famine or plague or massacre, life peeked up out of the gopher hole. With your family dead and only one chicken left, its tattered feathers singed, you began slowly to do the necessary things, and years later you remembered how to laugh. He'd read it time after time, never understood it till now.

When dinner was ready he joined the line for the stew, took a full plate and a little dish for salad, and sat on the edge of a picnic bench. Tim asked if he could sketch him. He nodded. The stew, yes, this was the lesson of history. Eat stew when stew is offered. Tim continued sketching.

Mabel stood nearby, gulping from her bowl. She asked Tonya if what she heard on the news was real. "They all say the same thing, so do they make it up together?" Not waiting for an answer, she wandered off to scold the defunct McClafferty.

Tonya smiled at Babcock. "Well, J.G., maybe it's true. Maybe all your history just gets written by six little guys in funny hats who've made up everything since the Norman Conquest." Babcock winced. He had worked less than a week for the TV news. Now that too could be added to his list of failed professions. *Sorry, sis.*

Pepper had been eating absently, staring into the distance. She picked her teeth, asked Tonya for a piece of dental floss. Tonya wiped her hands, dug in her bag. "We never used dental floss in Oklahoma," Pepper said, "although I guess the rich bitches did. What'll we do when we run outa dental floss?"

"So you're getting off in Chicago?"

"Damn right."

They were back on the bus. Risking roadblocks, Tim cut back to I-90 to make better time. He flicked the windshield vid. The ghostly newscasters reported on a Boston pizza parlor where a patron claimed an anchovy had come alive. Tim punched off the vid, unsettled. By the sad round-faced man with the compulsive smile — Mr. Babcock, was it? — whose woeful eyebrows rose when he looked at his portrait and Tim, too late, saw its cruelty. By Jodi's relentless hovering, a pattern where needy young women had a fierce attraction to him, then left him cold. By Smoky's insistence that the trip should just go on.

You didn't just go on. Check any disaster movie. You assessed the threat, then the hero proposed a hare-brained one-chance-in-a-million plan that only a brilliant screenwriter could conceive, and humanity was saved. That's the way it worked in what passed for consensual reality.

But Smoky had maintained that since they didn't know what to do about the looming terror they might as well act as if there wasn't any. It wouldn't be the Blue Terrapin experience without a stop in Chicago at Smitty's News, and tonight was the night. Smitty's News was a little blues bar on the North Side of Chicago owned by a guy named Arturo, and there was some story about the name that Tim hadn't really listened to. They were to arrive for the first set about ten p.m., party till two, then drive all night to La Crosse and spend the day holed up by the Mississippi — just the thing for celebrating the Last Judgment. And with that, Smoky had gone for a nap in the back of the bus.

"Hey, people!" Tim heard a woman call out. "Anybody need my cell phone to call family?" It must be the squat dark woman, the little boy's mother, Tonya, her name was? Why, Tim wondered, did she think people didn't have cell phones? She must be telling them to do it. "You want to call your sister? She must be worried."

"No," said the cheerfully doleful Babcock, "we're very close."

The crazy lady spoke up. "I got too many relatives for that. None of the McClaffertys could control themselves. Or the Jensens. I was born Mabel Jensen. I forgot about that." Amazingly, she fell silent.

"Jodi? You're Jodi, right?"

"There's just my parents," the chubby girl murmured, "and they said I don't exist. So they don't exist. That's one thing we've got in common."

"Pepper?"

"I told you, my family's here, my family's Jessie. Anyway we're getting off in Chicago, get out of this mess."

"Mommy!" The little girl burst into tears. "No, Mommy, no, Mommy, no—"

"Shut up!" Pepper's voice rang like a slap. "Fuckin' shut up!" Jessie whimpered, then ran to the back of the bus and buried her face in a pillow.

"Goddammit," Eddie muttered from across the aisle.

"Sorry I asked," Tonya said, staring at Pepper. "Nobody else?"

Mrs. Clemson explained that she had her own phone and would call when she, well, or if, well, she didn't want to call so late because Walter might be in bed and he needed his rest. And Sergei Rupp stated that he had sons and daughters, he had ex-wives and secretaries, but he had nothing to say. "They alive, that is good. I alive, that is good. No quantum entanglements."

Tim felt Tonya standing behind him. "How about you?"

Yes, of course he should call Mom and Dad in Arizona. But he just wanted their silent presence, and you couldn't do that on the phone. Movies or books he could talk about for hours, but love meant silent presence. He wanted to call Janis, whom he'd lived with for five years until last month when she'd told him she needed to move to Duluth to find herself. He wanted to call his friends, who loved his cartoons, and ask what was happening in Brooklyn. There were so many people he loved and he'd never told them, never really had words to tell them. Maybe now it was time to tell them.

"No, thanks," he said, and flicked on the vid. Oddly, he liked smarmy old Harold & Rosalie. There was something appealing about a stupidity that had reached its quintessence. His mom and dad used to do imitations of them, and in those moments around the dinner table it seemed that lunacy might be held at bay if only the laughter held out.

> AND WE'RE HERE AT CRISIS CENTRAL AROUND THE CLOCK. NEW POLLS SHOW A MAJORITY OF AMERICANS HOPE THAT THE END OF THE WORLD IS NEAR.
>
> ARE WE PLANNING OUR VACATION, HAROLD?
>
> AIR STRIKES ON FIVE CITIES, BUT THE WHITE HOUSE LABELED THE ACTIONS "PRECAUTIONARY."
>
> THE PRESIDENT'S APPROVAL RATINGS CONTINUE TO CLIMB. "HE'S DOING STUFF," THEY SAY.

He flicked it off. "Scuse me," Pepper called to Tim, "are we gonna be in Chicago pretty soon?"

"Hopefully," he said.

At the rear of the bus Jessie was curled on the bench seat sobbing. Loki wanted to comfort her but he didn't know how. It seemed strange to hug her the way his mom hugged him when he came out of nightmares. He imagined some day when he was grown Jessie would be crying and he wouldn't know what to do except ask if she'd like some coffee. Except he didn't know how to make coffee. Everything seemed impossible. If he ever learned calculus it might help. It had lots of applications.

"You won't get off in Chicago," he told Jessie.

"Will too!" Jessie wailed.

"No. You know why?"

"Why?" she sniffled.

He groped for something itching his mind, then blurted, "Cause we look out the window and we don't see Chicago."

Jessie smothered a sniffle. She looked at him sullenly, then turned to the dark window. "Where's Chicago?"

"An old bum folded it up and put it in his pocket." Loki pointed out the window. "Look, he's walking off down the street, but the street is in his pocket."

Jessie pressed her nose to the window, then yelled, "Loki does magic!"

"Don't tell."

At the front of the bus, Chicago weighed heavily on another mind. Tim checked Smoky's dashboard note, worried he'd missed his exit. He strained to see a road sign. "So give me a clue," Jodi spoke from the seat behind him. "Are you stand-offish with everybody, or do I have the special honor? Just curious."

"What? I'm sorry," he said, "I'm just distracted." He saw another sign, checked Smoky's note again. The silence was heavy. "Jodi, sorry, I need— Smoky's asleep in the back. Would you tell him I need to talk?" The bus lurched as he shook his accelerator foot to dislodge the pouncing ferret.

She stood up. "I don't like to be called cutie pie," she grumbled as she went up the aisle.

As she passed, Mrs. Clemson felt an unsettled sadness, like the day Kathy Bogardus started banging her head on the chalkboard. She raised her hand, then realizing there was no one in charge she put it down. Taking a deep breath, she spoke aloud to the passengers outlined in twilight. Her voice startled her. She'd never heard herself speaking loudly to adults.

"You know— I've always found that when the children are upset it's good to sing a song." No response. "And maybe we're all a bit upset because it's been quite a long day. Is there something everyone knows?" Dead silence. "Loki, what's your favorite?"

"*The Itsy-Bitsy Spider.*" He knew that was Mrs. Clemson's favorite.

And she knew she was making a fool of herself, but there was no going back. "Good. Can we do that then, everybody?" She started to sing.

> THE ITSY-BITSY SPIDER WENT UP THE WATER
> SPOUT,
>
> DOWN CAME THE RAIN AND WASHED THE
> SPIDER OUT—

Loki joined in the song, then Babcock. Sergei turned around in his seat, stared at Irma Jean, and began to sing.

> OUT CAME THE SUN AND DRIED UP ALL THE
> RAIN,
>
> AND THE ITSY-BITSY SPIDER WENT UP THE
> SPOUT AGAIN.

The song began its repetition. Smoky stumbled down the aisle, leaned on the back of the driver's seat, snorted to clear his head. "So? What's the big news?"

Tim spoke under his breath, his eyes fixed straight ahead. "I think we might have to change plans."

"Where are we now?"

"So I was on 80/90, then the Skyway, and that's into 90/94, right? Then 55 splits off, then 290, and we get off around Addison, across to Division. What you wrote?"

"So?" The song recycled its giddy despair.

> THE ITSY-BITSY SPIDER WENT UP THE WATER
> SPOUT,
>
> DOWN CAME THE RAIN AND WASHED THE
> SPIDER OUT—

Tim spoke evenly. "Well, now we're definitely on I-90 to Rockford."

"Rockford?" Smoky exclaimed. "What the hell did you do?"

Tim shrugged. "I drove through Chicago. Directly through Chicago. But Chicago wasn't there."

The Itsy-Bitsy Spider droned on, Sisyphus climbing the drain spout toward the promise of stars.

Chapter 7
Old as Sin

Rosalie had seen it coming. Harold was going insane. No red-rimmed eyeball-bulging insanity, but a trim square-jawed thoroughly professional insanity you could only spot in a man who'd been breathing on you for twenty-five years. At this moment he was hunched over the anchor desk whimpering, but she knew that when the light blinked he'd square up, flash a grin of deep concern, and spout utter nonsense.

He wasn't reading what was on the prompter. Nor was she. She tried, but she couldn't help it: when he started to babble she could only follow. They had been there round the clock, days maybe, only leaving the anchor desk to sit on the toilet or peek out a window at the iridescent streets. The staff and crew went through the motions for the five-minute summaries, then rushed into the corridors to reinforce the doors.

The light blinked. Harold straightened, grinned, stared into Camera Two. Rosalie froze, felt a sharp cramp in her gut and her throat seared with bile. The cameras popped on and everything went red.

> AT THE TOP OF THE HOUR. ALL MAJOR
> NETWORKS ARE REPORTING LOSS OF
> CONTACT WITH NEW ORLEANS. PORTIONS
> OF CHICAGO HAVE BEEN SPOTTED NEAR
> WACO, TEXAS.

"Harold, what the fuck is going on? What are you talking about? That's not what it says, you're not making sense—" Rosalie's mike went dead, an intern pulled her away from the anchor desk, and the cameras tightened their grip on Harold.

> THE PRESIDENT ORDERS MORE CRACKDOWNS,
> AND YESTERDAY THE SUPREME COURT
> SHED THEIR ROBES TO SUNBATHE.

"Harold, please, honey! Stop it! Please! Please!—" Three interns were holding her. One patted her hair and murmured comfort while another shoved a sweater into her mouth.

> THE DOW JONES POSTED HEAVY LOSSES, AND
> THE NASDAQ IS RUNNING OLD BASEBALL

SCORES. AND HERE'S A GOOD ONE, ROSALIE.
THREE NEW GUYS CLAIMING TO BE ELVIS
PRESLEY. TWO WERE PRONOUNCED DEAD
ON ARRIVAL.

"Hmmm . . . prrppph . . . Fuck yoffhhhhh. . ."

AND WE'LL KEEP YOU POSTED AS LONG AS
OUR COFFEE HOLDS OUT.

"Nrrrfffmph. . ." Blinding light penetrated her eyelids. She heard Harold ask if they needed to do a retake.

"No, we can edit."

When she opened her eyes the lights were off and the crew was on its break. The horsey intern named Wesley was putting on his sweater. The intern named Grace was stanching a nosebleed. The cute intern named Tammy was giving Harold a backrub. Oh, thought Rosalie, she's the one he's fucking.

Harold sat like stone. Tammy gave up, smiled forlornly and accepted a cup of coffee from the long-haired young cameraman. Oh, thought Rosalie, that guy's fucking her too. Good. When Harold finds out he'll feel very old.

"Feel better?" Harold asked.

Rosalie nodded. "What happened? Did we finish?"

"We're fine."

"Is something going on I don't know about?"

Harold slumped. "We're feeling a lot of pressure."

"Where is everybody?"

"They're watching the doors. People trying to get in. They won't say who, or even if it's just pizza. Not a peep." Harold was crying tearlessly. When his nose ran it meant he was crying.

"Harold, I don't think I can do this any more. I think I might start screaming and never stop. I might try to kill you on national TV."

He turned to look at her. For a moment his face dissolved, then he regained his jaw. "No problem, hon. You're a pro."

Smoky pressed on. His limbs were stiff. He'd known trouble was brewing when these people came aboard. Now he wasn't thinking straight. They'd continued across Wisconsin at night and stopped at the little park by the Mississippi, but why hadn't they stayed under that little forest canopy during the day and then traveled at night? Now it was broad daylight with long stretches of Minnesota farmland and not a cloud in the sky, perfect weather for drones. Smoky recalled a cockroach, flush with Olympic prowess, making its scamper across the bare Formica counter of Betty's Cafe, an instant before Betty's swatter came down.

Maybe not a problem. No sign they suspected the Blue Terrapin of mortal sin. But he felt a tremor from the ferret curled in his lap. Bailey tended to pick up vibes. Smoky glanced around and saw the passengers' faces pressed against the windows staring southward at the sky. A black helicopter shadowed the bus. With what intent? Would he be able to talk his way out of this one? Suppose the helicopter was not in a conversational frame of mind?

Three helicopters now. He remembered a passenger — who'd left the Air Force to become an alcoholic — describing the instrument panels on the Binkies, as he called them. The deadliest hardware had the cutest names. "You don't see any people," he'd said, "just little flares of pink and yellow on the screen, those are your targets, anything that moves. It even keeps score. You never miss."

The Binkies pulled ahead a quarter mile, then hovered confronting the bus. Smoky could see their racks of missiles, nipples erect.

A sharp jolt. "Shit," said Smoky, "we blew a tire. Sorry, guys." The bus limped onto the shoulder and bounced to a stop. The raptors hung perfectly still, and Smoky strained to see the distant flashes that would blossom around him into circuses of fire. Many old friends would mourn for him if they ever knew, but they wouldn't ever know. *That's all, folks.*

As the bus hiccuped off the road the helicopters wobbled then froze again. A rain of small glinting objects fell, striking the highway a quarter mile ahead. Then, with no further ado, the Binkies broke formation, rose to the west and lost themselves in the cumulus. "Beer cans," Smoky announced.

The passengers stood by the road as Tim and Smoky fixed the tire. Life was anticlimax, it seemed. Smoky pondered whether he should say something more to the passengers, then dismissed it. If they hadn't felt their neck fuzz bristle, they were mercifully nearsighted.

Over the years he'd faced other crises, of course. An eighteen-wheeler barreling straight at the bus. A guy pulling a pistol and blazing away until he saw that it wasn't loaded. Freak-outs, fist fights, a suicide, divorces, a busload of people with the trots, and a misplaced two-year-old. He took it in stride, expecting the worst so that anything less than Hell would come as a neat surprise. He called that looking on the bright side.

But he suspected that his crusty-geezer act was wearing thin. Easy to fool the passengers that there was a steady hand on Starship Enterprise, but how long could he fool himself with tough-guy bravado? He was faking himself to himself. His long grizzled hair was Smoky, but his bowels were Arnold Lunz.

Back on the road, he turned off I-90 and angled southwest along country roads toward Yankton, South Dakota, where he normally stopped at a small county park with lots of foliage. On the seat opposite, Mabel McClafferty clutched her packages. "I got stuff to mail, can't sleep till I mail it," she said. Smoky reached to flick the vid, decided against it. There was a limit to the news your kidneys could filter.

Mabel could never tolerate dead air. If somebody else wasn't talking it was her duty to take up the torch. "I grew up in Chicago," she said, and Smoky knew that if he even grunted he'd get her whole life story. Once that spigot was open there was no way to turn it off. On the other hand he was sick of listening to music, same songs over and over, *Hey baby, hey baby. . .* Baby never seemed to give a shit. So he grunted, and Mabel was off and running.

She grew up in some neighborhood that had white people, she said, and some buildings were medium-sized, so it wasn't the center of Chicago or out where the houses were short. All cities are like tents, tall in the middle and then they flatten out. "They probably do that on purpose."

She'd had friends when she was little, but they always moved away when she wasn't looking. Her mom yelled a lot, but mostly at Pop, so she loved her mom. And there was an older sister who lived in Seattle now and a younger brother, but now he's older than her and lived in North Carolina or South Carolina, whichever one was on top.

Smoky glanced at Mabel and chewed his lip — a survival strategy. As a small boy he had horrible nightmares until one night he found the exit ramp. The octopus had swallowed his feet and was working its way up when he gave a small jerk that jumped him into reality. Reality had seemed safer at the time. In later life, as reality itself began to exude a sucking sound, he chewed his lip. With this lady he might have to bite clear through it.

Mabel rolled on. Her dad had a career involving bathtubs. Her mother had worked in a beauty parlor but was pretty ugly herself and mostly did fingernails. Once she did Mabel's hair and it came out like fingernails. "They weren't great parents, but we always had a turkey at Thanksgiving and a Christmas tree and firecrackers on the Fourth of July till my brother put a cherry bomb under the cat."

High school was hard. "They said in the old days kids were smart cause they studied Latin, and if you spoke Latin you could speak anything, even Chinese, so they put me in Latin. I learned *amo, amamus, amat,* but I never used it cause I never had a date except for a skinny guy that asked me to come along to the carwash. Later I went on dates, and I had to bite one on the eyebrow. Little boys are okay, but then they start getting dumber, and then when they're as dumb as they can get, you marry one."

Smoky leaned forward, scanned the sky for helicopters or anything at all. He'd heard it all before. His mom had talked about a TV show she used to watch called *Queen for a Day.* If you had a better sob story than the other contestants you got a new refrigerator and a year's supply of beauty kits. He'd wondered if Queen Elizabeth got a new fridge every day. He bit his lip harder.

"I wanted to be a nurse cause people are always going to get sick so I'd always have a job. But I'm glad I didn't, cause now they say it's cheaper just to croak." She had worked as a waitress and on the assembly line for something they killed people with. "And a Chinese laundry, but I couldn't follow a word they said even though I'd took Latin." She was glad to get married and stop working, except that McClafferty never could hold a job so she had to work. "That's life," said Mabel.

Kermit McClafferty. She met him at a bus stop when he asked her for a bite of her peanut butter sandwich. "I married him even though he looked like that frog puppet." They moved to Cleveland to stay with her uncle, but then her uncle moved to Alaska and she heard a song about Philadelphia, which also had a baseball team, so they moved there.

"We never saw a baseball game. I stopped counting the years. Worked in a hospital mopping floors, which was kind of like being a nurse. Sometimes McClafferty worked, but most of his energy got took up going from the TV to the fridge, and then he developed the occupational disability of being drunk. We heard the South was cheaper so we moved to DC, but then he got killed by a bus. Didn't surprise me. He always said *Holy cow!* whenever he felt like it," she explained darkly.

Why had she stuck with the guy, Smoky wondered. This lady's inner landscape had the rationality of an Escher print, but it sparked a yearning. He'd longed for one of his past lady loves, anyone, to have been nuts enough to stick with him, but it never went that way. He bit his lip again. He was starting to sense continental drift.

"The thing about life, I read this on a plastic soap bottle," she said, "that life's not about having stuff or buying stuff, it's about being able to pay for it. Only I don't think I remember that right, cause they want you to buy that soap, don't think they don't."

Smoky caught a glimpse of the mile marker as Bailey scuttled back onto his lap. He glanced at Mabel, stocking cap low on her forehead, still clutching her parcels and her left-over sanity.

"They say you repeat everything," Mabel said, "but I hope I don't ever repeat Sunday School. Once I mixed up the apostles and the epistles and I got in a lot of trouble with that."

This opened the subject of religion. No wonder the Feds were pursuing her. She carried dangerous information.

It was after supper. The sun had just set and the fading light silhouetted tall thunderheads reflected in the dark river. The park in Yankton was just as Smoky had remembered. Trust the Midwest to stay more or less the same, if you don't count Chicago. They were concealed among a track of woods like a Mohawk haircut that led down to the Missouri. They had aired out the bus, drained the nightmares, and were getting ready to head across South Dakota by night.

It had been a lazy day, the passengers hardly speaking, but after three square meals they seemed to be slowly returning to life. Babcock shambled around collecting dishes. The children played quietly among the trees. By the fire Tonya strummed some lost passenger's guitar, and Smoky could see Pepper and Eddie, across the fire from one another, staring into the coals as if wanting to be swallowed. All were drifting on the cicadas' rhythm and the tang of the gumbo.

Smoky did good gumbo, but after gumbo there always came a hollowness. He sighed and stared into the black of the forest. He sat there, not wanting to get off his ass and head somewhere, but if he didn't stir they'd sit here all night and that meant driving in full daylight across open plains just waiting for the swat. He pulled out his wallet. On his knee he stacked the relics of a past life: six UniQards.

He knew he should have kept his connections. Years ago he'd been involved with people dealing psychedelics. They'd seen it as a spiritual imperative, despite the onset of pigocracy, to keep gateways open. But when Don was arrested and Jake was killed — by mobsters or cops or girlfriends — Smoky split the scene. Yet he'd held onto these bogus UniQards. Maybe a habit acquired from his mom who'd always hoarded coupons or travel tips on hemorrhoids in the Himalayas. Last night proved her wisdom.

He'd been rattled by Chicago, and just past Madison the fuel gauge bottomed out. When he pulled into a station he couldn't have made it six feet further. He inserted his UniQard in the pump. Zilch. Of course that happened all the time: people were locked out of their homes, humiliated at the check-out stand, trapped in parking garages, strip-searched and beaten, all because of some cybernetic butt-fuzz. Just the price you pay for Our Way of Life: the envy of the world, we told the world. No sweat, call 666, give some Mongolian felon your DNA specs, and they'd punch you through — if you could get the phone to work without your UniQard.

He needed fuel. Methanol, hydrogen, gasoline, carrot juice — he'd provided for all options when he rebuilt this baby. But what if he'd been identified? Suppose he was wiped? Did he dare send a message to tell the Feds *Here I am*? That's when he remembered his bogus stash.

The first fake UniQard was warped. The second worked. He tanked up on corn syrup and rumbled out of the station even before the machine spat out the receipt. The turbanned attendant waved bye-bye. This card should be okay for a while, but they always caught those things eventually. It was constant warfare between the systems designers and the hackers, but both sides respected each other, both made good money at it, and he knew some who even sent each other Christmas cards.

The President had vowed to tighten security and for once he seemed to have meant it. Just before dawn Smoky had flicked the vid and caught the end of the top-of-the-hour. The terrorists were reported to have taken a Pakistani station attendant hostage and set him afire. The service station had been carpet-bombed and a massive manhunt was under way. Then the news lady screamed that her breakfast was running across the anchor desk, and the news cut off. Pretty impressive to think that all the pumps in America were wired into Washington, Smoky thought, and most of the toilet stalls as well. He'd have to switch the cards around.

"So did they wipe us all?"

Smoky looked up from his reverie. Jodi was munching an apple. She gazed across the fire circle where Tim sat sketching. "I saw your little dance with the pump last night. I'm not sleeping real good." Tonya continued strumming.

"We'll be okay, depending," Smoky growled, stuffing the cards in his wallet.

"My dad was in the CIA, still is, maybe. He's pretty high up for an asshole."

"You've got a way with words." Smoky looked into the fire. This kid was fat and fat was fine, but not if she didn't want to be.

"Basically they can pinpoint within about three seconds whenever you use your card. They can wipe it right then, although they won't if they want to track you. If they got ID's for us all then we're effectively dead. They'll wipe us. No further relationship to civilization."

Smoky stared at the fire. She offered him the apple. He declined.

"Bogus UniQards, great. But it's the government that issues those. It's a revenue stream, plus they keep tabs on smugglers and stuff to get their piece of the action. Daddy'd tell us stories at the dinner table, all the terrible stuff he was saving us from. Factory in Borneo made running shoes for some multinational, paying kids a nickel a day to work twelve hours, maybe a dime if you sucked off the foreman. But what they did, these kids got a witch-doctor to put a curse on the running shoes. And all over America, Europe, Japan, these joggers are jogging into rivers, off cliffs, straight into trucks." Jodi tossed the core into the fire. "So Daddy traced it and they bombed the shit out of the factory and ten square miles of jungle. Made the world safe for joggers."

If he listened to more of this, Smoky thought, he'd jog into the fire himself. Change the subject. "You know," he said, looking up at her, "*cutie pie* isn't a term of disrespect. It's French for *that's interesting.*"

Their eyes met for a moment, then she glanced away toward Tim. "Your partner's really stand-offish."

"He's just learning the route. You gotta learn, hey, she wants a little more speed, so shift gears and give her some encouragement."

"How old are you?" she asked, gazing at him.

"Old as sin." He smiled.

"I better help with the dishes." She trudged away.

Smoky rubbed a mosquito bite. He must be getting pretty desperate, he thought, to start flirting with some sour pudgy kid who carries depression with her like a sandwich, munching on it all day.

Then he remembered Lana. That was it. It was here by the river. Same place. Same woods. Same godforsaken bus.

Lana was the tallest woman he'd ever made love with. She must have been six-two. Gawky, all elbows, early thirties, and carried herself in a perpetual panic. He wasn't attracted to her much, but he struck up a conversation just to make her feel better. It turned out she'd been married briefly, now she was back in school for library science. Just for something to say he'd asked how she liked being tall, and soon there were tears, then hugs, then the meeting of eyes, then the slow walk down to the woods in the dusk with a couple of sleeping mats.

Lana was no ball of fire. She was as awkward horizontal as vertical. It was like caressing a pile of lumber. At such times

Smoky was thankful for a vivid imagination, and with some fantasy of a gigantic female arthropod he managed to live up to his part of the deal, but it was touch and go. He fell into a straight 4/4 rhythm and his mind was wandering back to the bus's cranky fuel pump when Lana started to shake.

No moans, nothing that signaled passion. Just a tremor, then choppy little spasms like Mexican jumping beans. He'd had his eyes closed to hold the fantasy, and now when he opened them her eyes were doe's eyes, huge and serene, staring directly at him. She spoke in a whisper, "I hope this is okay with you." Her arms gripped him in a bear hug of appalling force, and then the quake began.

Her face never changed. The doe eyes held him in their serenity as the desert floor moved under him. He'd felt an earthquake once only. It shook for twenty seconds that seemed like hours, a shaking deep in the muscle of rock, the roar of the mountain's mouth, a giant rising in dreams, and then dogs in the distance howling out their hearts. Now it was Lana who shook and shook, then finally stopped her shaking. Her arms released him and they lay there a long time after. Smoky didn't know if he'd come or gone or even if there was passion. Those eyes never changed. After a while they got up and went back to the bus and said thanks, goodnight.

That was their only time together, though in the next days they were friendly and sometimes talked about books. Once was sufficient, it seemed. That had been on the eastbound trip and she got off in New York City. In the twenty years since, whenever he'd been there, he watched for a woman's head above the crowd.

Now, flirting with Jodi, was he hoping for history to repeat itself in a shorter condensed edition? Trying to recapture that time when he could frisk off into the woods without erectile qualms? Trying to distract himself from the thought of imminent death? History didn't repeat itself, he knew, it just found new ways of entertaining us.

Near the bus he saw the children sitting under a tree. For kids they were very quiet. He suspected that now they were speaking to each other telepathically or trying to. He'd known that to happen. Or talking to the trees the way trees talk. Very slowly.

Mabel McClafferty sat on a log across the circle from Smoky and stared at the fire. Now he couldn't help but feel her thoughts like loose potatoes in the back of a pickup rumbling over the ruts. For a moment she felt — he felt — a flapping of wings. She nodded off, then jerked awake. She'd been wide-eyed all night, then all day. The Midwest always made her antsy, she might have told him. People left their cattle out in the fields doing anything they wanted to do. They advertised tractors on the radio, as if she didn't have enough to worry about.

She knew she didn't fit on the bus. She was invisible. People could stand next to her having their conversations like she was wallpaper, maybe that wallpaper with big ugly roses in the north room of Grandpop's farm house where nobody ever went because it was so dark. It was no fun watching the fat girl mooning over the old hippie or the little scrawny science guy giving the tight-assed teacher the glad eye. That girl Pepper didn't fool her one bit, talking about how she couldn't stand Eddie. It was like a soap opera around here and Mabel couldn't stand soap operas. Dopes with great hair-dos having a miserable time. It was that hair-do thing again. You gotta earn your hair-do, was Mabel's view.

She thought too much. That's why she talked a lot. Because as long as you talked you didn't have to think. Nobody could talk and think at the same time, or at least they never did. She'd kept trying to call the President, but he must spend a lot of time on the can since she always got some flunky. Or maybe the problem was telephones. Her aunt didn't believe in telephones cause they're not in the Bible — she found airplanes in there but no telephones. Mabel noticed a hawk circling overhead. Might be the one that ate her cat. Unless that was a pigeon. Pigeons were mean where she came from.

"I'm sorry I yelled at you." A soft male voice interrupted Mabel's ramble. Somebody was apologizing to her. About time. She looked over her shoulder. Nope, it was Eddie behind her, talking to Pepper. More soap opera.

"No problem," Pepper said curtly.

"And I'm sorry you wanted to get off in Chicago, and I'm sorry about Chicago, although I don't think you missed much, I mean the whole blues scene is really in Cleveland now, if you can believe it. What can I say?"

"I don't know, Eddie, what can you say?"

"Well, I'm just trying to say that I'd really like to stay with you. Real world, all that." No response. "So I mean maybe all we have in common is a phone bill, but I really liked being with you, I mean we've both got a temper and strong feelings which makes it hard, I mean, sure, but maybe that's good cause then we don't inflict ourselves on somebody that can't handle it. And we're talking about survival here, and maybe other guys told you they were reliable even though they were fulla shit, and I am also fulla shit but I'm definitely reliable."

He paused. Pepper's fist was flat to her thigh, white knuckles by firelight. "Good." Her voice was low and trembling. "So can you just stay away from me right now? Just right now. Just go." Her own words stabbed her like slivers of ice. Eddie hesitated then turned and walked back to the bus. Pepper stood rigid in the flicker of the fire. It was over and done with.

Somewhere between her teeth and her gut Mabel felt a sharp twinge. Heart attack, heartburn? She put her hand on the top of her head and awaited further notice. Then she realized: it was sorrow. She grieved McClafferty. The time he grew a mustache. The time the toilet exploded. The time he sat on the cat. Only one thing he offered her, but the most precious: they could laugh together.

Her hands made a slight flutter. "I oughta be a hawk. Better'n Social Security."

Smoky pounded his forehead gently to get rid of Mabel's echoes. He knew he should get on the road. He'd never taken NoNarx, always faked the tests, so he was probably the sanest person here. But he'd felt his own reality slipping. He'd done acid, peyote, other Daddy's Little Helpers, but he'd never realized how tenuous a grip Reality held on the body politic. Reality was a group consensus, a tribe's decision to take their trip together. But now it was more like one of those candidates squeaking by from a scant turnout at the polls: we elected the moron, but nobody really believes it.

Maybe you had to hand-knit Reality with whatever bent needles you had at hand. Maybe that's why he had found his way to this forest where he'd lain with the gawky earthquake and now was flirting with the chubby depressive. Reach out and squeeze each other the way Shadow squeezed fruit at a fruit stand, not to judge it so much as to know it. Shadow: he wondered if he could find her, find that place. He tried to picture her, but she kept her face turned away to the dusk.

Jodi came out of the darkness. She carried a sleeping mat from the bus, walked to him resolutely, stood facing him. "I'd like to get to know you," she said. "Is that okay?" Damned if I know, Smoky thought. "I mean," she added, "I never thought I'd live past the age of fifteen and now I'm twenty-three, so this is progress."

His plan had been to drive through the night. Darwinian instinct required it. But another instinct stirred. He rose, touched her breast lightly, and brushed the loose bark from his backside. When you drive off the map you just have to follow the road. They walked into the woods.

In her dressing room Rosalie stretched on her couch, sipping a cheap Scotch. It was all she could find. Somehow she felt cameras on her so she tried to smile but gave it up. The room was peaceful. The new halonic lights were cold, blinding, but they'd piped in the old-fashioned fluorescent hum to make it feel homey. She'd taped over the vids so if she started hallucinating at least she'd know it was hallucination.

Three days ago she'd flushed her NoNarx without telling Harold. She imagined the pills descending into deep sewers where the great monstrosities lay — Leviathan, Moloch, those — and seeping into the dreams that fed the oceans. Then great blotches came upon the face of the deep, vast bruised waters purged of all life. And then no oceans but only oily puddles shimmering on concrete. Where were the oceans now?

For a few minutes Rosalie's mind wandered over the myriad ways of dying. Then she fell asleep and dreamt an untroubled dream of eating chocolate pie.

Chapter 8
Mormons and Mind Melds

ONK ONK. Little Green Men more this is Johnny. We are all Johnny but this is the me Johnny. I love you.

We watch vid Rosalie go bugshit. We are nuts but Rosalie bugshit. Harold is funny but not Rosalie because she is not. We wish if Harold will do the Tammy.

Biloxi3 is on the fritz and farts not now. Other Johnny tell Boss reality happens or not anyway. Boss bang staple on table Johnny's flipflop down. Boss is your Solomon for wise.

Rosalie is your hated bitch to Gruk2Bic. Boss think send killers or cutters. But I tell Boss good she live so everyone hope she die. Hope is good, an Earth joke. Take me to your leader, is the movie. You can't get what you want, is the song. Earth is fun.

We like Pepper and Eddie best. Sad no fucking now but do that more they better. We like Pepper on top of Eddie and bounce. Pepper loves her bitty girl so people cry. We never cry before.

Mad scientist of movies not your Doctor Rupp. We think he shall fuck stiff teacher lady good. Mrs. Clemson is your artist like Beethoven, with the song. I cried about the spider. It is my life. Mr. Babcock we all like him hope he die so we will cry some more. I so however do not hope. Earth is not Gruk2Bic.

Brown woman is too your Solomon for wise but the brains is Mabel with boxes. We write down her sayings and make tattoos. It is good to slip in education. We all want killing like Bonnie and Clyde but not now people on bus. They are family of us. We kill yesindeedy family here but Earth is not Gruk2Bic.

Gruk2Bic loves Earth is greatest thing. No riots now or they would miss the show. Little Green Men starve but see French toast. They slave holy shitload but Mrs. Clemson sings. They give us their kids to do because they see the Loki Jessie happy safe. Gruk2Bic is all peace knock wood. I wonder why knock wood.

Boss does not kill me nosireebob not now. Or nail me

down and never let me die. He laughs at all my jokes. We do girls together and boys on holidays. He does it first since he is Boss and then I finish them but I do not finish them but the finishers do. Boss will make me Boss when he decides to shoot his head.

So I love Planet Earth and want a pen pal. I tell you all the history. Some day history happens then you be like me. We are all Johnny or going to be. I want French toast but kill my wife this morning. We are the spider climbing up.

From here on in, the narrative is in serious question. None of the participants could trust their own senses at the time nor their splintered memories later. Action-adventure plots rely on humdrum Newtonian physics and square-jawed guys or gals, but in the times herein detailed the laws of cause and effect had been voted out of office. The possibility that a happy ending might be cobbled together from the shards of Armageddon can only stand as evidence to humankind's powers of fantasy. Yet if the ensuing reportage seems far-fetched, is it any less so than history?

Sergei Rupp, like Pepper, had always been a devoted fan of mad scientists. As a child shuffled between refugee camps and palaces, transatlantic jets and ox carts, he found security in two worlds only: mathematics and horror shows. Through his formative years he cheered the hyperactive bespectacled geniuses — heirs of Dr. Frankenstein — who unleashed zombies, giant ants, death rays or carnivorous spaghetti upon the long-suffering planet. He never saw them as villains. The venom they spewed was only dialogue they were forced to speak by Hollywood, and their crimes were simply the pushing of boundaries in a world that could never understand. Someday the world would see their true worth.

At the age of eight he had an elderly tutor who, when he wasn't molesting Sergei, taught him the calculus. The sex was unpleasant — he hated the smell of tobacco juice — but to his impressionable mind it eroticized mathematics. An equation gave him an erection, and as a teenager he devoured the hard-core math journals. Thereafter he pursued numerals and Eros assiduously, honing a genius for both.

Mathematics led implacably from Eros to Dread. The slippery improvisations of sex were challenged by the orderly structure of horror shows, where premise led to consequence. He was whipsawed between the lubricious temptations of topology and its terrors. He stumbled through the labyrinthine castle to find the singular locked closet of X, then flung open its door. He heard the pathetic whine of functional domain and codomain bound in masochistic enslavement to each others' black-leather whims. Over the concept of zero, with its death stench of infinity, loomed dark greenish skies torn by thunder. Yet always his loins felt the urgent thirst of the equals sign — that wrenching lust for oneness with the Other.

As a child his first nightmares were of Venn diagrams, those neat overlapping circles that illustrated set theory: A intersecting B, B intersecting C, C intersecting A, and the center of ABC a deep dusky cleft. He felt himself as multiple beings split by the circles pulsing and dissolving. Then the circles moved into congruence, all part of all, same face, same eyes, same purple sweatshirt, one common cry.

His dream was happening now. People were melding into croaking frogs, gangsters, or huddled masses whose cities flung themselves like frisbees. As he slouched against a window at the rear of the bus watching the dark chunks of Utah dissolve in the moonlight, he began to feel less like the mad scientist and more like a hydra-headed blue creature with wheels and two glittering eyes about to take wing, when suddenly he was jarred awake as somebody poured a beer on his head.

The bus was in riot, music blaring, passengers weaving up and down the aisle, raucous laughter. In the midst of it all they were singing a mad anthem in honor of J.G. Babcock, who sat dumbfounded. Then he heard a voice within the din, a story being told. Who was talking here? All the fragmented babble, and one voice within.

Here's the story, sports fans. Getting near Salt Lake City we're down to two sacks of granola, a hunk of Polish sausage, four eggs, and one dish sponge. Tonight we score food or starve. Big supermarket called Buddie's south of Salt Lake. We skirt the city on back roads that would shake the fenders loose if the Terrapin had fenders, then hook into Buddie's from the south.

Park in the lot, divide into teams, two to a shopping cart, each with a list. In twenty minutes the carts converge at a checkout line. A skinny red-haired clerk whose badge says HI I'M STANLEY! checks out the first cart, checks out the second, checks out the third, fourth, fifth. The screen totals two thousand bucks.

Hand him a UniQard. Blank. Try again. Nothing. Try mine. Zip. You take cash? Stanley is baffled. Nobody's ever offered cash. Storm clouds gather.

Stanley walks away to look for the manager. Two minutes, they'll call the cops and Buddie's will get carpet-bombed. But over there a clutch of people — the manager, clerks, customers, security guards, and now Stanley — all listen in rapt attention to J.G. Babcock.

He's been standing there reading the customer service policy at Customer Service. He's never met a Mormon, but the manager has that classic freeze-dried look and Babcock starts talking simply, unstoppably about the history of the Mormons — the golden tablets, the trek westward, the persecutions, the seagulls, the temple rising, the lives of their great-great-grandsires, their broods of offspring, their legacy.

Babcock has those Mormons in tears. We stand there, then quickly we waltz past the checkout stand, roll across the parking lot, toss five cartloads into the bus, run back to grab Babcock as his hearers embrace each other in joyous communion, and burn rubber.

"There's a big mouth on that man," says Mabel McClafferty.

Someone handed Sergei a can of beer. No one had spoken: the story had spoken itself from the dark heart of the interweave like foam on the head of the beer.

Sergei broke out in a sweat. Breathlessly he forced his fingers to scribble an equation involving UniQards, beer, and the Collective Unconscious, with a side trip into his own subquantum DNA, and it all added up. He rose crying something in Russian that sounded like "Dorm chickens urinate!" Eddie and Tonya wrestled him into a seat and held him as his breathing slowed to a rhythm of huge gasps. "Phenomenon of UniQards—" he hissed.

"UniQards? They didn't work," Eddie offered. "Major fuck-up." *Fuck-up fuck-up fuck-up*, the echo resounded.

"We're wiped." Jodi's shrill voice sliced through the babble. "They don't have to bomb us, they just go into the data banks and wipe us. We don't exist."

"Wiped! But not by others wiped!" Sergei took a sharp suck of air and began expounding the mathematics of dissolution. He scribbled large symbols on his pad, muttered, exclaimed, gesticulated, and the passengers caught a string of indecipherables: "Dimensional correlative . . . transition T . . . velocity V . . . Boltzmann's constant . . . coefficient of Heisenberg matrix," a burst of profanity about Heisenberg's unmerited fame, then "Density D . . . identity I . . . UniQard K . . . Pauli exclusion principle," then ripping a number of sheets from the pad, "Here! Then this! Then that!" and he flung the last shreds of the notepad into the air. A portentous silence, then his fingers mimed an enormous equals sign. "At level of seventh dimension, we become each other."

"I used to throw up in algebra," said Mabel McClafferty.

Through the low rumble of the Terrapin they understood. They themselves were wiping their identities, melding into one another, and the proof was that otherwise they couldn't have comprehended a word of Sergei's rant. These few days, they realized, each passenger had had flashes of, what, inner connection? empathy? collective itch? Moments in the presence of another person when they felt a vacuum suck into the other's soul. Tim staggered to his feet. He'd passed his two-beer fall-down limit an hour ago. "He means we're becoming one big blob," he mumbled. "We're gonna be oatmeal without any raisins. Our dreams are all inside each other, and— How do I know it?"

He was looking at Jodi. She met his stare. "So tell us," she said. "How do you know?"

"I felt everything you did."

"What? Who? When?" Jodi shouted.

"Last night. In the woods. With that old bastard."

"What are you talking about?"

Tim was crying. He tried to shout but could manage only a whisper through his beer-tinged weeping. "I was inside him. I felt what he did."

"It was great," Eddie exclaimed in wonder.

"Yes it was," said Babcock.

Jodi turned a murderous red. "Oh shit, did I have every guy on the bus dreaming about me?"

"Not just dreams," said Sergei.

"Not just guys," said Tonya.

The Terrapin rumbled across the night. Smoky snorted out a chuckle, then choked it off. Over his shoulder he saw the travelers sodden with fog, heard them breathing in unison. With a sharp cramp his gut told him that while ego dissolution in a hot tub was dandy, on the freeway it might get ticklish. Evolution toward human oneness was much to be desired, but evolution speeding too fast was called explosion. He pulled onto the shoulder, came to a shuddering halt, moved up the aisle clasping passengers, shaking them awake. "Hold on, people. Stay with us. Get hold. Stay steady."

"Vindication of Hoxhi!" cried Sergei.

Smoky moved back down the aisle, grabbing, shaking. "Hold onto your names. What's your name? Name!" They looked at him blankly. "Tell me your Christalmighty name!"

"Edward," Eddie whispered numbly. "Christ, I haven't used that for— Eddie!"

"My name is—" Babcock began.

"Mag. Mona. Muffy—" Mabel struggled. "That's a tough one."

I'm— Who am I, I'm— Oh God— I'm— They struggled to remember what their mommies called them.

"Jodi. Jodi. Yes."

"Mommy, what's my name?"

"Jessie!"

The collective voice began a chant.

> EDDIE. EDDIE GRABOWSKI.
>
> PEPPER MCBRIDE. JESSIE MCBRIDE.
>
> TONYA. TONYA BROWN. LOKI ZELL.
>
> JAYDEN GRANVILLE BABCOCK. MABEL MCCLAFFERTY. RUPP! RUPP! RUPP!
>
> IRMA JEAN— IRMA JEAN— CLEMSON, PERHAPS?
>
> JODI HOBBS. TIM RIVERS. SMOKY.

Over and over, and then the chant split apart into separate voices calling out names as sole possessions, an omelet of egos regurgitated.

Smoky stood vigilant until the voices trailed off, then sat back in the driver's seat, started the engine, and the bus settled back into post-party, post-panic torpor. Someone picked up the beer cans. Others made up bunks, as if sleep were an actual possibility. Sergei wiped his glasses with his shirt tail. The wave had passed, unless it was only the first contraction of labor.

To the grinding heartbeat of the Terrapin and a few scattered murmurs, one by one the passengers accepted the mantle of slumber. Only a few beds had been made up, so they leaned in the seats or stretched on the benches or floor mats as if night were only a mood swing, not a planetary enchantment.

Pepper fought to keep above the surface of sleep, bobbing up from dream to catch a breath of wakefulness. She heard Eddie breathing in the seat behind and prepared for another sales pitch.

"So here's how I see it," he whispered.

Pepper turned her head slightly as if to listen by accident. Why couldn't she shut the goddamned door and keep it shut?

"Say if we create all the nightmares out of our heads," he continued, "then why couldn't we dream some reality we can trust? Where there's love you can trust? Because people always come back to one plus one is a good idea."

She was silent a long time, then spoke. "It's not a matter of dreaming, Eddie. My heart's dried up. I've gotta stay strong for Jessie."

"Heart," he mused. "You ever seen a heart? I miked a video of an open-heart surgery. It's this huge honking hunk of meat. Amazing muscle. This surgeon, funny old guy, says something like, okay, just try to flex your bicep as hard as you can, seventy times a minute, never stop, how long could you keep it up? World-class athlete, maybe ten, twenty minutes, and he wouldn't move his arm again for a week. But that's what the heart does, twenty-four seven, seventy, eighty years."

"Love is not a hunk of meat."

"It's muscle, hon. It keeps us knowing who we are. Eddie. Pepper. Jessie." He pointed to her hands clenched in her lap. "I like stubby fingers. They do things."

"I got stubby fingers?"

"I'm saying that as a compliment."

She began to weep softly. "What do you know about hearts?" she asked. "You run sound for lousy bands."

They sat in the silence of the Terrapin's rumble, each staring at some blurred future traced in the particles of night. Finally Eddie replied. "True." A pause. "So?" The unanswered question wrapped them together in shut-eye.

Smoky drove into the night. Strangely, he could hear the two of them whispering halfway back in the bus. Was his hearing becoming more acute from abject panic or some other quirk afoot in his head? Remember, he told himself, that life is comedy. Busing through Utah with a dozen strangers trying to remember their names. Hearing people speak of love, that old joke that everybody's heard but keeps getting repeated. He should have delivered news of the impending catastrophe as a punch line to rock the Terrapin on its suspension system and bring them all to one final pulped-ego guffaw.

Other voices. He'd have to find the earplugs he'd bought when radios started playing hip-hop. Telepathy had not totally retracted its claws. In their dreams the sleepers heard Babcock's voice.

Amazing, those people in the supermarket actually look to history for meaning. They find joy in it. Like survivors hiding under the rubble and they find a carrot, maybe? I wonder if someone's written a history of joy. Interesting challenge but where are the primary sources? I do speak to my sister more easily now than I ever did before. And she answers me.

Pepper dreamed into the webwork.

A history of joy. That'd be something worth the study. Even if you had to memorize dates for the test.

But Jodi's sourness spoke as well.

How do we survive? Count on bedazzled Mormons? It's the same old two-step. Get up, pee, brush your hair, have a cigarette. The taste is the same whether after sex or just before they put a bullet in you. Maybe that's the comfort. We rumble through space till it's time to toss us in the salad. What happens when we get to San Francisco, or if?

Pepper tried to blur the voices. She remembered playing war with her brothers. *Bang, you're dead. No, I killed you first.*

I'm dying, get help. Fix fix, now I'm okay. Hand grenade, look out, throw it back. Fantasy so easy. She'd played that game with two husbands, creating little comic book worlds, and then the pages ripped out.

Once she'd seen a movie about hippies on a farm. They had a beautiful life till it all went to hell. She saw weeds growing around the abandoned house, the rusty tricycle by the wading pool, and their stricken faces when they all knew the party was over. At that time, of course, she'd thought they were idiots, kids who believed in the Tooth Fairy, but she never forgot it. Laughter around the dinner table or a childbirth in half light, a rightness about it, a ripe fruit she'd never tasted, never knew it existed, though she longed for the tang. And on this trek there were moments — tossing groceries onto the roof, washing dishes at sunset, seeing Jessie snuggle in somebody else's lap — when she felt that rightness.

Jessie, wide awake, tugged at her sweater. "Mommy, look," she whispered. She pointed out the window, above a dark ridge. "The moon came all this way with us."

Chapter 9
Stronghold

"The President called. He was crying."

"Who?" Rosalie thought he was joking, but these days she could never tell.

"The President. He's in a subterranean bunker. Serious problem with constipation."

Harold signaled to roll the prompt to check it before broadcast. Funny stuff was appearing there, jokes that could get you killed. He felt Rosalie's glazed eyes on him. Lotta water under that bridge. He hated himself for hoping she would die.

"Don't you think I haven't thought the same," Rosalie mumbled.

Staring into the eye of Camera One, Harold saw them. The bright blue bus was crossing the eastern grasslands of South Dakota passing a roadside souvenir shop shaped like a plaster brontosaurus. Somewhere in his mind's intestines he had assumed total command. He felt his five stars biting into his shoulder. He grunted for an air strike. Rosalie sobbed, long seconds passed, then a squadron of F-9's streaked out of the stratosphere, spat out their rage, and the bus was a ball of blue fire.

He glanced into Camera Two. No, the bus still moved westward through the grasslands. The brontosaurus was toast. Harold had never outgrown his lack of eye-hand coordination.

Six o'clock, the Terrapin pulled into Stronghold. Smoky knew that something was very odd. A number of things, in fact. After stocking up supplies outside Salt Lake City they'd made a sharp dip southward to give the computers something to worry about, then a straight shot across South Dakota. Problem was, they'd already been across South Dakota. That's how you got to Utah. As a kid he'd had a puzzle of the United States and no way could you fit South Dakota where Utah was supposed to go even if they were both pretty square. The passengers hadn't noticed, and Tim wasn't speaking to him. They'd probably slept through grade school geography, and they were all from back

East except the Oklahoma gal, who seemed to have other stuff on her mind. But Smoky was unsettled.

As liberal-minded as he liked to think himself, there were basic propositions he had trouble with. Chicago disappearing? States playing a shell game? The Interstate Highway System on acid? If the Great Plains states were this flipped out, what could you expect of San Francisco? But who was he to question the unfathomable? That's what got him evicted from Shadow's ineffable vulva.

And now they were traveling on Benedict Arnold's UniQard. That was Eddie's doing. Once, he told Smoky, he had actually been employed in a straight job, resulting in three-per-day credit card solicitations qualified for a credit limit of three million bucks at 30% interest compounded weekly. In retaliation he'd returned the form, name crossed out, signed *Benedict Arnold.* In two weeks came Benedict's MasterCard. Never used it, but nice to know it was there.

Then America started its evolutionary jitterbug and old plastic gave way to new, so with his bogus MasterCard and three hundred bucks he'd won in a poker game where the other players were drunker than he was, he acquired Benedict's UniQard. Maybe a reasonable hedge against the future, Eddie figured, to have an identity outside the reach of Realists or Reality. So, as Smoky's cards bit the dust, Benedict Arnold fueled the ship of fools.

Smoky couldn't shake that lingering anxiety about states rearranging themselves just because they felt like it. Still, if a couple of states vanished out of the middle of the roadmap the long haul would be that much shorter, with no loss of scenery. He would vote out Indiana and Nebraska.

They had supplies enough for a week, so Smoky thought it might be best to hang out in the remotest spot he knew. That was Stronghold. Just before Pine Ridge you turned off Highway 18, through Wounded Knee, Porcupine, Rockyford, then Highway 2, then onto a little dirt road past the cafe where the old sisters used to serve their succulent Indian tacos, off-road onto a bumpy track that soon became a faint smudge across the parched sage. At the point where the directions ran out and you had to give up all pretense of knowing your destiny, you were there.

A narrow spit of prairie maybe the length of a football

field, jutting into nothingness. Flat, flat, flat, and then on three sides a plunge into chasms chewed out by giants — vast gnarled wounds in the earth with columns of sandstone rising up the colors of rattlesnakes. Then, as far across the gulf as a rifle could shoot, the prairie continued without a ripple.

The moment he pulled to a stop Smoky realized that his survival instinct had shrunk to the size of the Social Security check he'd get if he reached the age of eighty-five. Stronghold was the worst possible choice. Idiot! Spend the night frolicking with a problematic nymph, drive a bright blue bus in broad daylight with squadrons of airborne sociopaths homing in for the kill, and decide that the safest place is open prairie, no water supply, backed up to sheer canyons. You just had a hunch that this was the place to be.

The passengers were stirring. Smoky set the brake and opened the door. The smart thing, maybe after supper, would be to head to the little town of Wall thirty miles to the north and blend among the tourists. They could enjoy the sprawl of Wall Drug Store, a legend advertised into existence, and decompress a bit. Fix supper, then cut north into the Black Hills. Think like a crab louse, he told himself, stay back in the bush.

Jessie looked out over the chasms, gripped her mother's hand, and asked, "Mommy, did the dinosaurs eat it?"

"It's called the Badlands, honey. That was the Badlands we went through a while ago and these are some more."

"Why are they bad?"

"Now don't you go close to the edge, okay?"

Jessie felt her mother's grip tighten. "Mommy!" Too tight.

Pepper kneeled and embraced her. "I'm sorry, honey. Mommy's having a hard time right now—" She trailed off. Jessie knew that cloudy look that came to her mother's eye when she remembered stuff that she'd never tell Jessie. Pepper sighed deeply. Jessie gazed over the wasteland.

"It's called Stronghold," Pepper said in a perky tone. "Remember that little house a ways back. The driver said there used to be two old ladies lived there, they had a cafe and the bus would stop there. But there's nobody there now." Her voice drifted off.

"Mommy, what's a ghost dance?"

"I don't know, honey, where'd you hear that?"

"The old ladies said it."

"There aren't any old ladies."

"At the cafe."

Pepper was about to lecture the girl about telling lies, but the words that came out would be her mother's. She rubbed her eyes. "It had to do with the Indians. They did a dance."

Jessie looked into the darkening sky. "There's a man looking at us. Is he a ghost?"

Pepper took her hand. "Let's help with dinner."

Harold ducked behind his desk. He knew he'd been spotted. How could a small child see him two thousand miles away? But then how could a news anchorman be promoted to Army Chief of Staff? He couldn't explain his epaulets or the receptionist calling him General. He felt a power he'd never felt before, however richly deserved, a massive power filling his newly-pressed shirt. He patted his hair and marked the little girl for interrogation. If she survived.

Someone was reading the news. It sounded like himself. Rosalie crouched with him behind the anchor desk, her helmet askew. Why was she wearing a helmet? He tried to glance at the prompt but couldn't stop staring directly into the camera's wormhole. He heard himself sounding smoothly apocalyptic.

> BULLETIN: GOVERNMENT FORCES ARE
> CONVERGING ON THE TERRORISTS
> SOMEWHERE IN RURAL SOUTH DAKOTA.
> THE FANATICS ARE BELIEVED TO BE
> TRAVELING BY BUS. THEY ARE ARMED AND
> DANGEROUS.
>
> DRUMS, CAN YOU HEAR THE DRUMS?
> HAROLD, THE DRUMS!

Thank God they were still a team.

Jessie looked around for Mommy and saw her by the door of the bus watching Eddie set out the cookware. Mommy had told her about making babies. If people loved each other they hugged and rubbed together, and the woman had a baby. Maybe that's what Mommy and Eddie did. It would be nice to have a little brother if he didn't stink like Mrs. Kowalski's baby. She wondered how many times you needed to rub together.

And Mrs. Clemson and the mad scientist looked like they might rub together too.

Jessie wandered about. She could never stay still for long except with Loki. With him a stillness formed around them like an eggshell, and they were the baby chick with two beady eyes, and Loki was one beady eye and she was the other, and the baby chick was fuzzy and safe.

But Loki was reading books he'd found in the luggage, so Jessie wandered about. She never thought about wandering, she just couldn't help it. A dozen times in the city she'd wandered off from her mother, made her way through legs and canes and huge old ladies with shopping bags. She'd been buffeted and tripped over and confronted by snarling Pomeranians. She'd hear whisperings of amazing worlds and wondered if she would come to know them. Then from nowhere Mommy's hand would reach out, grab her, shake her: "Don't you ever do that again!" And she'd cry and Mommy would hug her and lecture how all kinds of terrible things could happen, but she never said what.

So Jessie rambled in the dusk, watching her long shadow melt into the other long shadows. In the world of long shadows she was a grown-up. Shadows never got mad at each other or yelled. When they came together they blended like when Mommy poured maple syrup on vanilla ice cream for her birthday. It seemed like that would be a better way of making babies. Not rubbing but melting.

The young bus driver sat on a camp stool sketching the crazy lady. Jessie wandered over to watch. She liked to see his squiggly little cartoons. They didn't look like the people but looked like how they felt. His cartoon crazy lady was tilted into a waddle, her tiny eyes in deep hollows, and she had a beak. Right now the real lady was walking back and forth holding a small boxy thing and wiggling her elbows. The drawing showed wings. It was silly but that's how her shadow looked. Jessie stared into the sky, but the hawk was gone, maybe taking its nap. The story lady had told about a hawk that ate a rabbit. It had to do that, being a hawk. Still, Jessie had cried.

"What's a ghost dance?" she called out in a tiny voice. Nobody answered. Mommy was talking to Loki's mother, but

Jessie didn't go too close. She didn't want to be hugged any more today.

"Any luck?" Pepper asked as Tonya clicked off her cell phone. Tonya shook her head. "Hey, I wonder if you have any tampons? I got caught short." Jessie didn't know what those little white things were supposed to be. Her mother said they were for when she was older, and she wasn't supposed to spin them around on their strings or throw them at the cat.

Tonya grinned. "Wow, less than a week and our cycles are starting to match. It's kinda tribal." She dug into her shoulder bag. "Eight years ago I got on this bus, Blue Terrapin, to Mexico. Loki was a year old. Days went by, I came home, I was different." Jessie saw the dark-skinned woman gazing at her mother, who was staring across the field at Eddie. So many secrets. "You seem kinda preoccupied," Tonya said.

Pepper frowned at her, then softened. She stammered something about her luck with men, how it all looked so good on the platter, and when would she stop going into heat like a pimply adolescent eyeing that bulge in Reggie's jeans? Her voice became fragile. "Well, maybe you got the right idea. You kinda play both sides, huh? Maybe it's a little bit easier with women?" Her eyes met Tonya's. Jessie felt their shadows melt together.

The dark woman's face went hard. "Honey, you're very cute, but I don't jump for the rebound." Near the bus a lantern blazed. They stared at each other, and then — Jessie couldn't tell who did it first — they smiled.

Lights flared: Action News on the air. Rosalie sat bolt upright with her mouth in ecstatic rictus. Harold stared into the camera's mad red eye. He saw the distant enemy milling about, washing dishes, folding tables, repacking the bus. Two children sat by the edge of the gully looking out. He discerned no defenses, no weapons of mass destruction. Too easy, he thought. It looked like a trap.

> HAROLD, REPORTS FROM SIXTY COUNTRIES:
> AMERICAN TROOPS ARE KILLING EACH
> OTHER IN RECORD NUMBERS.
>
> AND A BATTALION OF MARINES IN PAKISTAN
> WERE AMBUSHED AT NAPPY TIME.

Harold whispered the coordinates, lowered his polarized goggles into place, strangled a sob, and awaited the screams.

Jessie saw her mother's silhouette against the jagged red horizon that bled like when she'd gashed her foot on broken glass. Behind her, she heard Smoky's voice. "So what's got your tail in a knot?" He was speaking to Tim the cartoon guy, and in her mind's eye she could see what his sketch of the sunset might be, torn flaps of skin in deep shadow.

"You bastard. She needs more than a screwing from some stringy old letch."

Jessie knew she wasn't supposed to hear this. She held her breath so she could hear better.

"My friend, we did what adults do. And we had a good time doing it. You want something, ask for it. You knew how to do that, once upon a time when you were nursing, but it must've slipped your mind. Reality is very cooperative with all requests, my friend."

Jessie remembered nursing. Was the old man saying that people could nurse any time? You just had to ask?

Harold crouched in the sandbagged bunker among the shards of the anchor desk. What wrecked it he couldn't recall. On a monitor to his left he saw himself as an action figure manipulated by monstrous hands, a best-selling retail item under heavy assault by the foes of freedom. Rosalie sat rigid, her face in hideous grimace, staring at the charred corpse of Kim, the intern with heavy tits. Cameras ringed them like vultures. Above, the Earth in its party hat flashed its toothy smile.

As the cue light flashed, Harold began to read the prompt, something about a boost in consumer confidence as people rushed to spend every last buck. The Dow Jones was in free fall, but Walmart reported record sales. He rattled absently through the headlines, his mind preoccupied with spelling the word *logistics*. Once as a kid he'd won the city spelling bee and couldn't stop shaking for days.

The terrorists, part of a vast conspiracy, were pinpointed in a corner of the Pine Ridge Indian Reservation behind a heavy defense perimeter, holding children as hostages. The Seventh Armored Cavalry was moving in that classic pincers maneuver that had destroyed Koreans, Iraqis, Mohicans, you name it. They always died like flies.

"We're counting on you," the President had whimpered. Harold was up to the task. He'd been a sportscaster once.

Jessie wandered to the group of men standing by the bus. Eddie held a small black box and a screwdriver. The mad scientist looked over his shoulder, and the old driver smoked a squishy cigarette. A lantern sat on the ground, making their faces look like the goblins in the book the story lady wouldn't read to them.

"Here it is," Eddie was saying. "Our GPS tells us where we are, but it also lets the goon squad monitor the signal. So we jimmied it—"

Sergei interrupted. "I do theory, he does application. We are ungodly alliance."

"So now it locates us where we're not. They're reading us twenty miles north. Way off they're blowing up cows, billboards. You can see the flashes. Kinda neat if you grew up on science fiction."

"What freaks me is they cut off radio traffic," Smoky muttered. "We oughta go. Answer to anything is go. That's the American way. Move it."

"We should stay," Eddie countered.

"Fix my clock radio, why doncha?" called Mabel from a distance. "It grew up with me. All it gets now is these beeps, like little green men."

"Why do they go after a bunch of goofy pointless little people? It's not reasonable." Jodi sat on the steps of the bus, clipping her nails to the bone.

"It's reasonable," Smoky grunted. "All killing today is reasonable. There's a clot of very talented people out there who will make you a persuasive case that you should be dead. They'll even give you a free trial offer." He took a long draw of his smoke and announced his intention to depart.

A furious dispute ensued, drawing in the others from the fringes. Tim, who had always been deferential, was vehemently opposed. Exasperated, Smoky declared they'd take a vote. "Okay, so who wants to go and who wants to stay to get bombed by the dawn's early light?"

"I say we stay," Eddie said. "We've got water enough for a couple of days."

"Go right now," countered Pepper.

"I'll second that," added Jodi.

"Mosquitoes," rasped Mabel. "Let's go."

"Is that drums?" Tonya glanced into the dark. "I dunno. It doesn't make any sense to be here, so maybe that's a reason to stay. Try to think rationally, that's like using old road maps. Might as well stay."

Sergei launched into a lecture on inertial force as an active dynamic, concluding from the mysterious eros of subquantum strings that they should stay. Mrs. Clemson timidly seconded his decision. "Got one!" Mabel announced, wiping her forehead.

"That's five to four," Tim said. Everyone looked at J.G. Babcock.

"Well, one consideration would be—" Babcock began hesitantly, his voice skittering like a panicked rabbit. Then he saw his sister's loving eyes still full of belief. He took a deep breath. "—would be our location," he said. "Stronghold was the place of the last major Ghost Dance. A number of tribal bands gathered here, and there was word of cavalry approaching—"

"Get to the point?" Smoky turned away in exasperation. The ferret was perched on his shoulder nipping his ear. He swatted and it leapt onto the bus stairwell and disappeared.

"What's a ghost dance?" Jessie asked in a voice so tiny she couldn't hear herself.

Babcock continued quietly. "The tribes debated whether to stay at Stronghold or to leave. Some stayed, some left. As it happened, those who stayed were safe. Those who left encountered the major cavalry unit. They were disarmed and marched to Wounded Knee."

"History. Is history. Forget history." Sergei waved his hands as if erasing the chalkboard.

Babcock winced. "I'm sorry, but history is reality. We are facing reality."

"Reality is construction."

"No no no!" Babcock cried. "History is the choices that have been made and the consequences of those choices. We are now driving through a landscape of those consequences, if you would care to notice."

"It is child breaking toys. Is mess of old men's poop. Is die like sheep."

"History is our language. It's all we have in common."

Sergei waved his arms. "Blind armies. Slaughter of first-born. Heaps of boots. Bloody meat."

Mabel mumbled something about meat prices.

Through his glasses Sergei's eyes bulged with sights of atrocities swallowed whole. He beat his chest as if assaulting his heart. "Lessons of history! Taught by psychotics!"

Babcock's thin flute voice rose to a fierce squeak. "History is our language of meaning. If we lose it then we babble. We build a world from babble."

"Better babble than curses."

"Curses rise from lips where words have no meaning."

"My friends!" Smoky called out in the voice of authority. He quietly pointed out that as far as he could tell they were wandering from the point of the discussion. And that both Rupp and Babcock were in favor of staying, so what was the argument?

"Six to four," Tim said. Smoky gave a vague gesture, went around to the other side of the bus to piss. The group dispersed to make up their bunks or to watch the last gasp of sunset.

Jessie saw her mother walk out toward the cliff. She was sorry that Mommy felt bad, but already she knew there would be a time when she would be free of Mommy, free of all sadness, free of the fear that she'd grow up to be like Mommy and hate Mr. Henry and all the other sonsabitches. She felt somehow that this bus was taking them away from the sonsabitches to a land where there was not one single sonsabitch. Then she'd see Mommy smile again and laugh her laugh, that rare birthday laugh like maple syrup.

Loki finished his books and came to find Jessie. They sat together in the grass. She wanted to ask him about ghost dances, but she was afraid he'd tell her something scary.

"It means that this place has ghosts that do dances," he explained without her asking, "so all the bad men will go away. There's bad men around us here."

"How can you tell?"

"I get a picture on the back of my eyes."

"Mommy says that isn't real."
So he told her what was going to happen.

A squadron of jets from the 2nd Attack Battalion homed in on the tourist mecca of Wall, South Dakota, raining a sleet of phosphorus, followed by a wave of B-4's dropping Motherlover ordnance that excavated the town to a depth of 300 feet. Site of the famed Wall Drug Store, the town attracted thousands of tourists annually, but an official at the Pentagon press briefing noted that this was not high season so collateral damage was below estimates. As he quipped to the press corps, "No bodies have been recovered."

According to a later White House communiqué, the town of Wall with its notorious drugstore was a suspected terrorist stronghold — "Who else would want to live there?" — and thought to be the destination of the mystery bus. Other sightings were reported in Council Bluffs, IA, Tampa, FL, and Kabul, Afghanistan.

Harold watched the fireball rising. He'd made no mistake. It was only a diversion to make the terrorists think the Feds had goofed so they would let down their guard. The real assault would come at dawn.

The last gasp of twilight was nearly gone when Jessie saw her mother walk back from the lip of the boundless gulch. She went up to Eddie, who was tinkering with Mabel's ancient radio as he crouched by the lantern, and squatted down beside him. Jessie heard their hushed voices in the crisp dark air.

"You trying to make that old thing work?" she asked, trying not to say what she needed to say.

He sensed that she wasn't there to talk about clock radios, but it was a safer topic. "I could make it work if there was something for it to pick up, but those bandwidths are dedicated to drone strikes now. That's why she gets the beeps. None of 'em carry a tune."

"Eddie," she said, "what I'm trying to say—"

"Right, okay, say it."

"Right, okay. You're a nice guy. I like you. It's best if we could just be friends."

He stopped work, put the ancient radio down on the

plastic mat in front of him, and stared at it as if it had spoken. "Friends. I've heard that before. A number of times, in fact."

"So have I. So, right, I don't mean that. I mean I want to break up whatever this is and get rid of it because I've got very strong out-of-control feelings about you. Call it love, lust, rage, whatever, I can't deal with that as part of my life right now. I'm a realist, Eddie, and if I had the chance to vote right now, I'd vote for those fuckers because they got one thing right, and that's the fact that the world is shit and you're shit and I'm shit, and I don't want to believe that, I want to believe there's love and I want to love you and I can't and I never will!" She started to cry. "And please do not touch me because I will kill you if you do!"

Jessie watched from the darkness. Her mother stood there sobbing the way Jessie did when Jessie cried, her hands at her side, face ugly, snot-nosed, tears like acid. She cried for a full minute. It was like seeing Mommy naked. Then it passed and there was only the sound of her breathing.

Eddie spoke in pain, but quietly. "If you've got somebody you can be that honest with, maybe you should think twice about it." He stood looking at her. Pepper turned and walked away.

She called to Jessie. It was time for bed. They went into the bus and crawled into the bunk together.

"Mommy, why don't we take our pills any more?"

Silence. "Well, honey, sometimes you think something's good for you and it turns out not to be."

"Then how do you know?"

"I don't know how you know," she said, lost. "You don't know. How do you ever know? Go to sleep."

A long breath and the chorus of bugs. Then a low rumble, a flash of distant lightning, a slight earth tremor. Flurry of hushed voices outside the bus, then silence.

"Mommy?"

"What now?"

"Do people nurse if they want to?"

"No. You nurse when you're a baby. You're not a baby. Go to sleep."

The bugs recommenced their chorus. Jessie saw two shadow figures come up the aisle, might be the mad scientist, might be Mrs. Clemson. They fumbled about, gathered mattress pads and blankets, stumbled down the aisle and into the night.

"Mommy?"

A long intake of breath. "What, honey?"

"I know what's going to happen tomorrow."

"Honey, I'm sorry, I know you're scared, but Mommy's tired and upset, and I'm scared too. People don't know what's going to happen tomorrow. That's what tomorrow is, where you don't know what's gonna happen cause it's tomorrow." She caught herself on the verge of screaming. At last she said quietly, "So what's going to happen tomorrow?"

"Loki told me."

"Oh. What does he say?"

Jessie pretended to go to sleep. It was her very first time for having secrets.

Chapter 10
Ghost Dance

Pepper's dreams ran rampant. Penned up for years, they snarled and bounded over the broken barbed-wire fence. All night she stumbled through the hallways of Sapulpa Senior High searching for her locker as the helicopters circled. No, it was her bedroom closet, she was looking for shoes when Alec grabbed her hips and then he was on top of her and she bit down on Eddie's hand. No, her own hand. She'd hurt her baby boy again, he wouldn't stop crying and dammit he had to learn and she pinched him and he screamed and she bit her hand. Not her hand, her mother's hand. She spat out the runny half-cooked eggs and her mother slapped her again and again and she woke.

Her eyes were wide open to the night. It was only a dream. She was drenched with sweat. Jessie slept beside her, a limp rag doll. Someone snored gently in the front of the bus. She sank below the surface waiting for the alarm to ring. She tried to close her eyes, but the dreams began their spiraling. The thought of going to work today made her sick at heart. No, she wasn't going to work. She was on a bus with her daughter. She was thirty-six years old. She was going to die.

The dawn seeped in upon her. Jessie stirred, needed to pee, so Pepper tore some paper from the roll, bundled her out of the bus to find a private spot. No trees, no shrubs, only sagebrush and table-top flatland up to the chasms. They stumbled across the weedy sandstone, far enough from the bus for decency's sake. "Where's the bathroom, Mommy?" Jessie asked, and Pepper gestured: everywhere. At last they squatted down together in the sharp Dakota morning under the ghost of a moon.

Pepper rose. Maybe fifty yards to the south she saw two figures silhouetted against the dark distant mountains. What happened in the next moments she could never comprehend. She found herself standing no more than a breath away from Irma Jean Clemson and Sergei Rupp. Jessie stood beside her.

"Is that Mrs. Clemson?" Jessie whispered, but the couple paid no attention. They stood in the prairie dawn wrapped in blankets, he with his hand on her curving hip, she absently stroking his elbow. Pepper trembled as they spoke.

"It's very beautiful here," said Mrs. Clemson.

"Yes, Irma Jean Clemson."

"What are you thinking?"

"To have you again."

Irma Jean Clemson looked around to see that no one was listening within ten square miles. The woman and child ten feet away were only a chill breeze fingering her hair.

"Well," Irma Jean faltered, "I imagine that you've been intimate with many women. Wild women, I would expect. Of course it's none of my business, I was just speculating—"

"And you." He touched her breast through the blanket. Pepper began to weep. She stood, drawn like dew to these lovers' presence. Was this to be the world now, where there were no distances, where one could stand within others' intimacies and bathe in their love? Something in the Bible, she recalled, about people invited to a wedding and those came who were ready to be there. She never understood what the preacher meant, but she longed to go to that wedding. She was there now uninvited, unnoticed but welcome as the sun.

Oh Jessie, she wanted to say, *this is what it is. This is what God put in the bank for your college education.* But those words weren't ready to come. She only stood there weeping while Jessie looked at the couple as she had looked at the chimps at the zoo sucking each other's fingers.

"You know, it's very interesting," said Mrs. Clemson, fumbling for some redeeming educational purpose, "I've only been with my husband before. Isn't that interesting? I think it is. He's a very nice person. His name is— Isn't that interesting? His name is Walter."

"My secretaries had husbands, yes."

"I'd like to call him, actually. I don't know why I can't. He'd tell me I was imagining things. Perhaps I even imagined our being together, so to speak." She tittered, then sobbed, then gasped. He clasped her.

"You have fierce wet flow of imagination."

Mrs. Clemson caught her breath. Pepper hugged Jessie tightly, praying the twosome wouldn't get graphic. Then the strangest thing happened. Her hands relaxed. She remembered an old song, *Let It Be*. Why did she like that song and hate that other song that said the same thing. Okay. Let it be.

"You know, I'm really more like Laura in *Little House on the Prairie*," Mrs. Clemson (nee Irma Jean Struble) whispered. "Her sister Mary was good, but Laura was naughty." Sergei cradled her face, put his fingers at the corner of her mouth. "I haven't been able to stop thinking about that book. It's so strange, at the moment we— My most intense moment, I mean, when, you know, I was just very, I— I think I actually saw it."

"We will live in this little house and I bite savagely at back of your neck."

She hugged him hard. "No one ever did that. That felt really good."

Then Pepper found herself back at the bus, and Jessie ran off to find Loki. The chill was fleeing the dawn, and the tables were set for breakfast. She looked up at the sky. It was a leather patchwork of mauves, siennas, ochres, ceruleans — colors whose names she'd seen on crayons but never known.

She saw Tonya at the grill frying bacon. Tonya's lips were moving. Pepper couldn't hear the words but knew they were the ghosts of memories. She was inside Tonya, in Tonya's mind, where the edges curled up around themselves. An old woman's face, the most wrinkled face she'd ever seen. A huge gray rat squatting in a cast iron skillet. A bush of white blossoms. A laughing fat man stripped to the waist, drinking a Coke. A basin with a wet spongy thing that Pepper knew, though she'd never seen such a thing, to be an afterbirth. And a sexless face, thin-lipped and hollow, dead. She caught herself. Was she going nuts? Would Jessie be left without a mom? "Jessie! Jessie!" she cried out but couldn't tell if the cries ever left her lips.

Then Tonya wasn't there. Now Pepper was standing near Babcock as he ate a bowl of granola. She was inside Babcock, the loneliest place on the planet. She heard his absent sister speak with a voice like eggshells. *Like eggshells*, some poetic geezer said — Pepper had to read him in high school. But now she understood that poetic geezer. Like eggshells. Babcock's sister said, *It's morning*, and Babcock nodded. *Every day since the Third Millennium BCE*, he joked, and discoursed on the ancient Sumerians. Then Pepper knew that there was no sister, only a sister gone, yet he was closer to her than ever.

"Jessie!" Silence.

She stood again in the orbit of Sergei and Irma Jean. A cloud had passed over them. He was no longer ringing the bell for Round Two. She was telling him the full story of *Little House on the Prairie*.

This was like yesterday's panic when they found their edges blurring, names fragmenting, souls running together like an iridescent oil slick on asphalt. But no, it wasn't the same. Pepper's edges were sharply etched in the morning chill. This was a new sensation, this interpenetration of souls. Would it bleach out with the rising sun? Would it persist? Would it shape the world anew?

Pepper saw the others eating their eggs or granola or toast. It felt thrilling, as if she weren't really there. She was here, then over here, like air, like her girlhood dreams of flying. She found herself standing behind the bus watching Loki and Jessie a few yards away as they sat on an outcrop of sandstone in a dialogue too liquid for words. They gave no notice to Pepper's presence. Perhaps she was only another shadow washed out by the glare of the whitening sky.

Jessie was six. On the flat rock she placed six pebbles in a circle. Her fingers fumbled the pebbles, slowly mastering their alphabet of grace. *Alphabet of grace?* Was that from a poem Pepper remembered or some ad for shampoo or a language she knew because she'd never learned it?

More pebbles. Now Jessie looked older. About thirteen, same curve of the nose, her hair now a blonde waterfall down to the small of her back. The delicate beauty, but then Pepper saw the firm tight set of the jaw, that implacable will. Pebbles, and suddenly late twenties, bobbed red hair, smell of roses, pregnant. Forty, in a rumpled sweater, dark hair in a pony tail, and those tired fierce eyes.

Pepper was slipping. Something flickered across the sunlight, and she grabbed a steel rung of the ladder up to the roof of the bus. Jessie faced her now, a wrinkled woman with a great flaming wave of hennaed hair, those same fierce eyes, and the sweetest tilt of a smile.

Hello, Mom, said Jessie.

Pepper felt herself slipping off the face of the Earth. She'd wondered who would be next to go. She was next. The rough steel bit her fingers. She had known this moment as a child staring into the night sky and feeling herself slipping up toward the diamond pinpoints. Her fingers slipped from the rung—

And clutched Eddie's jacket lapel. Its denim seam chafed her fingers. His hands wrapped her firmly, the way she'd held the broken hawk. She never knew when he'd appeared or how they found themselves embraced in the lower bunk of the bus. He held her firm and never moved, held her in the reality that both had cursed. She sobbed out her rage, then her terror. At last, when she'd sobbed herself empty, she began to fill.

Thus it was that Eddie and Pepper were asleep in the bus when the buffalo came.

Sitting with Loki, Jessie turned sharply and called out her question again. "What's a ghost dance?" Loki might have told her, but she seemed to be expecting no answer, as if she'd found a question she could spend a lifetime calling into the wind.

It was Babcock who answered, glad for a question to answer, though he knew she was asking much more than he could ever tell. "Ghost Dance, okay. . ." He knelt and spoke to the children. "So the Indians were starving. But Wovoka— Actually his name was Jack Wilson also, but— Wovoka had a vision. They would all be happy, and their ancestors would come back, and the buffalo. The buffalo would come again. What they had to do was be honest and peaceful and everyone dance a dance, the Ghost Dance." He demonstrated a slow sidewise shuffle toward salvation.

Above the horizon the spots appeared. In his studio command post, Harold had ordered a dawn attack. Kim, the heavy-titted intern who'd been dead the night before, brought him a cup of coffee. He pressed his fist into her butt crack and she let him. Rosalie dug in her purse looking for something sharp to slit her wrists. She found her lipstick. She took off its cap and slashed. The black spots grew.

"So thousands danced the Ghost Dance, tribes all over the West. And the bad men were scared and said it's against the law. But the Lakota came here, right here to Stronghold where we are now, and they danced and sang a song, *The people are coming home, the people are coming home.*"

The sky began to shiver and craze. Smoky was first to see it, a webwork of black shatter lines, then huge swart jags between the jangled pieces of the puzzle, as if some thick-fingered adolescent had jammed the sky together.

> ELEMENTS OF THE FIFTH MARINE BRIGADE
> ARE MAKING THEIR WAY NORTH,
> REPORTING HEAVY LOSSES FROM FRIENDLY
> FIRE.

> STEALTH BOMBERS, SO QUIET YOU CAN'T
> EVEN HEAR THE BOMBS. LOOK AT THOSE
> HELICOPTERS, HEY?

The black spots became helicopter squadrons by the hundreds, thousands, a rabid legion of hornets rising from their trampled hive. Harold dug himself deeper into Kim, who stood holding the coffee cup, her bovine gaze locked on the studio clock. Rosalie slashed her wrists repeatedly with Ruby Red.

"Oh shit," said Smoky.

Loki and Jessie rose and began to dance in a circle with Babcock. "So the bad men were afraid of what the Indians were doing," he said shuffling on. "They brought in soldiers. And then a little ways from here at a valley called Wounded Knee the bad men put up cannons. And back here one of the chiefs was afraid and decided to leave. And they went to Wounded Knee and that was horrible."

Loki abruptly stopped the shuffle. "Why does history always end bad?" he asked. "It wouldn't have to."

"No, I guess it wouldn't have to," Babcock said. He'd never thought of that.

"Can't they stay here and do the dance?" Loki was about to cry. He was nine years old and he wanted Mom the way all the Indians wanted their mothers. He began to shuffle the other way, counter-clockwise, turning back time. A mutual lurch and the others followed.

> HIT 'EM WITH ALL WE GOT.

Like blowflies, Smoky thought. They were coming in clouds like blowflies over the carcass of a possum, its wounds open like red spring roses to the buzz.

> WAVE TWO, PREPARE FINITO. NAPALM.

The helicopters were louder. The adults were standing around the bus like pillars of salt. Smoky felt his bowels loosen and clenched his buttocks. *Go out gracefully, Arnold,* he prayed to himself. Mabel fumbled her clock radio to find out what was happening. Mrs. Clemson mumbled the Twenty-third Psalm. Sergei giggled and sobbed. Tonya started toward Loki, but he was dancing. *Let him dance, let him go out dancing.* She wept.

GIVE IT TO'EM, HORNETS! HARD!

"I better tell Mommy," Jessie whispered.

"No, dance!" cried Loki.

The helicopters came in one mighty wave, their rotors intoning a single curse. Clean-shaven ordnance officers cocked thumbs to shit expletives of fire. The tiny band stood transfixed. Jodi, sobbing, threw her arms around Tim. "I know," he mumbled. The dancers danced.

Then in the East the buffalo appeared. They came like a thin veil of dust on the sun. "Over there," whispered Loki, "See? All over the sky." The bleary hallucination spread like an oncoming thunderhead.

The tides intersected. Buffalo by the millions stormed the sky, and their hooves came down. The copters were swept away like crumpled leaves, rotors crushed, fuselages exploding with the silly pops of toddlers dancing on bubble wrap. Pilots fell from the heavens crying for their mothers.

CHARLIE, DO YOU READ ME? CHARLIE?

OH CHRIST! WE'RE SUPPOSED TO WIN!

One indrawn breath. The sky was blank. Kim set the coffee cup down on the anchor desk and walked away. Harold touched the face of the empty monitor screen. Rosalie stared at the lipstick on her wrists.

No sound but a faint breeze through the sagebrush. Babcock, Loki and Jessie had ceased their shuffle. In the depth of the lower bunk Pepper murmured the name of the man who held her. Silence lay over Stronghold for the space of half an hour.

Then Mabel's clock radio blared. Some golden oldie.

Near dusk the passengers finished packing the cooking wares. In the aftermath of apocalypse no one had thought of doing the dishes. All day they'd wandered about slack-jawed, waiting for something more to happen, but nothing did. Around suppertime someone started supper. Smoky suggested they leave around dusk and drive at night. Nobody disagreed.

Loki sat at the gully rim with Jessie. Words came to them sometimes, or through them without speaking, but now they watched the sandstone liquify in deep ambers and blacks. They had died so many times in the past few days, Jessie thought, that now they knew how the dinosaurs felt. "The story lady wouldn't read us a book because it was scary," Jessie said. "But I thought of all the stuff that could be scary about it and then I was really scared." Loki didn't see the point, but he nodded.

He looked back toward the bus. Mrs. Clemson stood with Sergei Rupp. She was in a long coat and carried a travel bag. The scientist brushed her forehead with his lips. She offered her hand. He took her hand for a moment, and then she turned away.

Across the distance Loki heard her murmured words. To Babcock, "Excuse me, I greatly enjoyed your comments on history." To Smoky, wishing him well. And to himself in a whisper at a distance of thirty yards, "Loki, you're a good boy. Very creative. Be careful."

Are you going somewhere?

"Oh yes indeed."

At last they broke camp, and the bus rolled at a stately pace across the grassland to a secondary road. As the Black Hills loomed before them the full moon rose. Dimly, by the moon, they saw mile after mile of burned-out forest. Scrub trees sprouted among monumental spikes of whitened trunks. A few tall pines towered, their stripped branches drooping like tattered bottle brushes. The devastation continued into the night.

By fits and starts the passengers converted the lofts for sleeping, climbed into berths or sprawled on the mattresses front and back. Dreams blew in from the window slits or crept out like spiders from cracks in the flooring. Not dreams, exactly, only wisps of dreams, sound bites of dreams, dream stutterings, whispered promises that the true dreams were on the way.

Two in the morning, Smoky pulled to the edge of the road. "We're at a hot springs," he called out. "I thought I remembered it. Just down the bank. You don't have to if you don't want to, but it'll get some grit out of your system. Highly recommended. No bugs."

No response, then a few people stirred, feeling the grime of the fearful days. At last, one by one, the groggy throng crawled out of their berths, shuffled blindly over the bags and sandals in the aisle. They grabbed a towel or a heavy shirt to dry themselves, descended the steps, and stood astonished.

The sky was crystalline. Eddie, who had his contacts out, said it looked cloudy. Then he saw that it wasn't clouds. It was the Milky Way, a galaxy strewn across the sky like the mist from a waterfall, the stars trumpeting *We are suns!* The passengers stumbled down the bank to the spring, stripped their clothes in the dark, lit only by green glow sticks that Smoky floated on the surface of the pool. They sat waist-deep in nakedness. Then they toweled off, climbed back, and the bus turned westward again, whipped by the wind.

Smoky decided to wait until dawn to tell the others. There was no going back to Stronghold, and he knew it would do no good. Irma Jean Clemson was gone.

Loki lay beside Jessie at the rear of the bus. Their eyes were wide in the night.

"Did you see her?" he asked. Jessie made a faint sound. "I saw her. She was going across the grass, and there was a little house way far away and that's where she was going. Did you read that book, Jessie?"

Jessie sniffled.

"And then she was younger. She was my age or maybe a little younger. And she didn't have her coat on then, or the suitcase. She was a little girl. And she was happy. I never saw her happy before, but you saw her, Jessie, she was happy."

Jessie spoke. "And then the little girl, she waved at the house. And there was a family there. And a dog. And the mommy and daddy waving, and they said come home."

"And the ferret, it was with her, in her pocket. Cause it was scared of the hawks, cause there's hawks in the sky, but you don't want to live on a bus, cause even if there's people who love you you're still a ferret."

In their night eyes, Irma Jean Clemson was skipping, laughing and skipping to the little house on the prairie, singing out all the love inside her she had never known was there.

Chapter 11
Shadow

All night the passengers' dreams strained at their leashes, fragments splintering off, ricocheting across the crests and canyons of the West. Geography passed, as it did in seventh grade, without reference to latitude, longitude, or your parents' divorce. Dried river beds wove a web across the map, and the Terrapin forged the rapids.

Rocks piled up like candle wax, the colors melting and running. Salt Desert, Monument Valley, mountains sinking like a ship — the Titanic, or maybe not the Titanic, maybe some other big ship sinking in the desert. Zion, Ship Rock, Arches. Sunrise. *This is backwards, guys, it's all backwards, we shouldn't be here, we should be somewhere close to—*

Mid-morning, the thin ribbon of concrete led straight to the horizon with no seductions of curvature. Bright sun. No concealments in this country. Smoky saw high wisps in the sky. If the copters appeared he could ram down the pedal and jack up the speed maybe ten miles an hour. As a kid he'd thought about writing a science fiction story about a guy running across the face of the planet fleeing from sunset. But he hadn't written it. He was never big on stamina.

The night's magic had drained. Those pinball visions had vanished at sunrise, a topographical melt hardening into day. The passengers were only passengers, yawning and grunting, digging through blankets and rubble for sweaty underwear. They seemed to know their names. They had not blended into a stew of psychotic protoplasm, no exploding heads or unseemly special effects. There was still a crack in the second window back on the right-hand side and a sticker above the windshield: *Beware! Attack Driver!* It had been there for years.

The concrete gave way to asphalt, the asphalt to gravel, and Smoky headed the bus south-southwest. Mid-afternoon. It shouldn't be more than forty-five minutes if he remembered right. How long had it been? Twenty-eight, twenty-nine years? Ten, fifteen? Thirty, forty? The longer he lived the closer he came to a deeper understanding of everything but Time. He recalled giving someone directions to Shadow's place. Simple: just turn any direction on a road without landmarks, any road that was worse than the one you were on. When it couldn't get any worse, you were there.

Nobody's wristwatch was working, so they mostly told time by their bladders. Twenty minutes on gravel, he pulled over beside an outcrop of rock, directed guys to the left, ladies to the right, himself claiming the senior driver's privilege of pissing on the left front tire. For a few minutes he stood in the fierce sun to watch a crow circling to check the menu. His leather hat was too hot, but it shaded his eyes and looked romantic. It might hold Jodi for a couple more nights.

After the buffalo wingding, which had to be seen to be disbelieved, Smoky had dug out his leather hat with various gimcracks fastened into the band — a feather, a small crab claw, an earring from a gal named Hilda, and other incriminating items. He would retire it every few years for its sheer impracticality. No circulation, so your head sweltered in the sun, and rain took all erectile vigor out of the brim, which slowly descended over the eyes and ears. But in recent years he couldn't be long without it. As a senior citizen, a.k.a. geezer, he needed something to stay visible to the world. Especially now when life seemed to be a passing whim.

The passengers were silent as they boarded the bus, save for Mabel muttering, "Quoth the raven, Nevermore. . ." The bus pulled out and the crow abandoned hope. No one asked Smoky where he intended to go, and he would have been hard put to tell them. He drove on. No signposts, no roads, no power lines, no calling Triple-A. He checked the fuel gauge: down to a quarter. Shadow had her own supply tank and could refill him, but he wasn't sure of the distance. Twenty miles of desert waste, then he saw a road toward distant foothills off to the left. A weathered fence post stripped of its fence stood to the far side. He turned onto the road and came to a halt.

A coyote sat in the road staring at him. Smoky took the bus out of gear. Normally he'd beep, then edge ahead slowly to make it clear to the critter that he weighed seven tons and was in no mood to negotiate. But this was the road to Shadow.

Loki stood up from the seat and stared at the creature. The coyote's mouth moved as if chewing or mumbling a threat.

Smoky sensed that if he asked the kid about it the damned kid would say something creepy, so he didn't ask. After a minute the coyote trotted off the road and disappeared in the brush. It was just a coyote.

He drove on. A few minutes ago he would have said it was mid-afternoon, but now it seemed later. It was hard to give up the notion of Time: you'd always relied on its torture or its promise. The dirt road bent around a deep dry gulch that seemed to go on for a lifetime. Smoky felt better now, driving curves.

He thought about Shadow, the first time he'd seen her. He couldn't remember the year — they all blended together like leftovers in the back of the fridge. He'd been driving the Terrapin for a couple of years when he quit on an eastbound run after getting in a fistfight with the other driver. He caught a Greyhound in Indiana, headed back to San Francisco bruised and confused. At a truck plaza near Winnemucca they'd stopped for a freak hailstorm. As he stood under the restaurant canopy he heard a woman's low voice beside him. "How'd you wind up looking like that?" Like what? "Scared shitless."

He didn't turn to look. He stared at the hail and the asphalt steaming like a tennis court in Hell. Finally he heard her chuckling and turned to look. Dark eyes focused on something beyond him. Chiseled nose and cheekbones, tight-drawn sun-brown skin, maybe part Indian, maybe just desert leather. Forty-ish, in a man's red plaid workshirt and blue jeans. She held a sketch pad.

She was an artist. She lived fifty miles from the truck stop, just coming back with groceries. Without beating around the bush she asked him to come with her and model for a week. She'd feed him and he could sleep with her if he wanted to. And then she would put him back on the bus.

He was stupefied and terrified, but he felt obliged to follow where it led. He wasn't calmed by the fifty-mile trip in her battered pickup with most of the floorboards out. He wasn't relieved by shambling into her ramshackle house and seeing the explosion of freakish art. He wasn't soothed by the supper of tangy stew with animal parts he couldn't recognize. Bits of her last lover?

It was only as they began to make love that she looked at him. Looked at him sharp to the soul. As he popped into her in his clumsy urgent way, her eyes pierced and filled him with a joy beyond bearing.

Even in his thirties he didn't know much about control, so he lasted about ten seconds. Later he got more skilled and fancied himself a cocksman, at least until about sixty. But with Shadow he was never really in control, any more than you control a river. You swim in it, drown in it, dissolve, then find yourself lying on the bank newborn. He had come to risk a week and he stayed six years. Drowning in Shadow.

Then it ended. There was that fear of roots, that urge to push on. He started driving up to Hancock and coming home drunk, stashing a case of bourbon and running through it too fast. Never an argument, never a fight except the tiff about the turtle. She simply closed her eyes to him and it was done. He hitched to San Francisco and back aboard the Terrapin.

Over the course of the years he'd stopped back several times to see her. Always a friendly greeting, a delicious stew, but never sharing a bed. She would speak of her recent lovers, but whenever he visited she was alone. She would mention illnesses and the ravages of age, but he could see none of it. She was ageless.

It had been more years than he could remember. What led him to her now he didn't know. Not curiosity or lust or even terror, no. A need to bring his friends to her presence? His friends? He hadn't thought of them that way. Passengers were passengers. Sure, you'd share jokes or a romp in the sack, but at the end of the line they were candy wrappers tossed into that throw-away landscape called America. *Friends?*

Near dusk he turned left down a tire-track, lurching over sage and stones. From the rear Mabel's voice: "Is this Hell?" Over a low rise he saw the house, a low sprawling cluster of out-buildings strung together by the ramshackle years. No lights in the house. Junked cars, the same pickup, a defunct refrigerator — typical Indian or white-trash decor. But then he saw the circle of stones.

Flat stones on edge, three to four feet high and twenty feet apart, circled the house in a three-hundred-foot diameter. Some Druid lover with a tractor? He pulled into the barren yard. The passengers stared out the windows. He heard the boy whisper to the little girl, "Look at the stones."

She stood on the porch, white hair tight in a bun, wearing a dark workshirt and blue jeans. She appeared to be holding a butcher knife and staring past the bus. Smoky opened the door, climbed down and walked toward the house. The passengers saw him stand with her for five minutes, ten. They seemed to be speaking, but it wasn't certain. Then he turned to the bus, beckoning them to enter the rambling shanty.

At first, in the dim fractured light, it seemed that the walls were laced with dark vegetation. Then they saw the sculptures. Formed of papier mache, deep amber sun, and the blackest black. Human and animal. Figures the size of Barbie dolls. The faces of children, dwarves, soldiers and laughing women, the screaming and the blind, apoplectic fathers and maddened artists, the snarling mouths of the losers and the dull plod of the conquistadors. A woman nursing. A tangle of lovers held in gigantic hands, and woven into the orgy were grocers offering olives and grapes. A wall of the faces of mothers waiting for their sons.

All the figures were linked by hands or legs or noggins conjoined, limbs branching out like the fingers of trees. They formed a spiral dance through the rooms, crossing the walls' broad flatness, then looping low behind an old sofa into a corner, where suddenly they climbed upon one another like a tumble of beetles ascending some rich corruption.

None were separate. All danced one dance.

They were crudely formed but with sudden sharp details: an intricate face, a finely hewn hand, an exquisite seashell, the wound in a breast, a flagrant bouquet of genitals. There were housewives on tiptoe, naked postmen waltzing, deformed children frolicking at a picnic where—

Young men were killing a dog and shrieking in crazed exuberance. You turned away to—

Politicians waving slices of pizza over faces that hungered and cursed a line of soldiers advancing across a window with taped cracked panes and methodically cutting throats, bleeding—

Down wallpaper with faded sunflowers, the trickles converging to the hand of a midwife inside a woman spread in childbirth, birthing—

Long swaths of paint, colors daubed crudely across

dozens of figures pell-mell. Faces were splotched in whites, reds, blacks, yellows — humans assigned their races as if by chance.

There was no attempt at display, no lights to illumine the curvatures. It seemed to be some odd whim of Shadow's, like an old canvas left leaning against the dryer in the utility room, a priceless Rembrandt as meaningless as laundry.

She had made soup for a dozen people. They didn't know how she had expected them, but she had places set, scattered through three adjoining rooms. A tray beside a ratty armchair, two places on a burl coffee table with camp stools, a peeling white kitchen table pulled up to a sofa. Oddly it felt as if no one lived in these rooms. Perhaps there were other passages to some hidden chamber where the heart dwelt.

The passengers filtered through the rooms in silence. They were directed piecemeal to the places set with bowls of pungent soup and warm loaves of bread. They sat and began to sip, glancing up from time to time at the dancing walls.

Babcock glimpsed Napoleon and his generals clutching for a handhold to keep them free from the grasping ivy of defeat. A grieving Empress Josephine bore an unsettling resemblance to his sister.

Sergei viewed a galaxy of women whose undulating forms traced a slithery topology existing nowhere in the universe but in his fingers.

Mabel's eyes were on the butt-heads: her boss at the used car lot, her fifth grade gym coach, all the stuffed-shirt lard-bottomed CEOs on the elevator up and down forever. "I see ya," she snorted.

Jodi sat by Tim, who glanced distractedly over the figures. At every bend he saw tall gawky men entwined with chubby women. Their eyes took the same journey, then met. Mabel slurped her soup.

For Tonya it was a vast sarabande of lovers, all the beings who had ever joined with her — male and female, demons and saints, robust and wan. Some danced through bright patches of light, others moved in the shade. A waitress, a cop, assorted hippies, a rare-book librarian, a hunchbacked elf of a lover with bristly ears. The mellow couple who accepted her skittish embrace. The walleyed Young Republican with a thunderous dick. And Benny, polymorphous Benny, whose irises changed color as myriad gods in daily rotation possessed him. Her lovers spiraled off into rooms unknown. What she hadn't done with her body probably wasn't survivable.

Pepper saw her hellish family, mom, dad, brothers. No faces, only crumpled cardboard chewed by rage, a wad of paper raping a wad of paper in a world swarming with faceless waste. Only Jessie had a face she could see, and now Eddie — she had begun to see Eddie's face and it terrified her to see it. It was that horror movie where the heroine rips off the demon lover's face and sees what's real. But what if Eddie's face was really his face and there was no escape from love?

The same for Eddie. Daily he shoved his way through the human blur, and whenever he looked into another's eyes it was only a matter of time before it smirked and dissolved. Now he stared at Pepper, memorizing her nose, her ears. She looked at him sharply and then their eyes met, held. She felt her mouth soften. That moment married them.

"What is it?" Jessie whispered.

"People," Loki replied. "Somebody sculpted them. It's all papier mache. We did it at school. But not like this."

The children concentrated on their soup. "Too zingy," said Jessie, but she finished it.

Smoky devoured his second helping. Corn chowder, jalapenos and cognac, he guessed, with maybe some lizard parts. He saw everyone staring at the walls. *What the hell are they staring at?*

Dreams, said Shadow. *I keep them all here, the ones that've never been dreamed. Endangered species, you know. Yours have all been dreamed? You must have been living a pretty special life, or a very sad one, if you don't see my artwork there.*

Smoky didn't understand nor did he want to. Shadow's magical stuff always rubbed him raw. He sat at the yellow Formica table in the tiny kitchen alcove while she ushered the passengers to their bedding places. He saw Tim and Jodi heading off together. Thank you Jesus, he thought, maybe the kid would start speaking to him again. Not easy to have a co-driver who glared at you as if you'd screwed his pet cat. He stared at the barren walls.

Shadow returned. She sat across from him in a high-backed wicker chair he didn't recall. The table he knew from repairing one of its heavy grooved legs. He wasn't a great carpenter, but once he fixed anything it sure as hell didn't wobble. *You did a good job on that,* Shadow said.

You shoulda let me paint it, Smoky replied, *I hate that mustard color.*

You decided you didn't want to look at it any more.

You decided you didn't want to look at me. Had he said it out loud? She smiled. They sat in silence. Smoky knew what was going to happen. He would hem and haw, then start talking, and when he began he would tell her every wrinkle in his soul. He would talk till dawn.

So he talked. He couldn't hear his words. He knew he was speaking of his life, the women, the miles, his hungers and satisfactions and shames. He spoke of standing in the chill sunrise of a Winnemucca truckstop crying out for Shadow till a trucker got pissed at being waked up and knocked him flat. She grinned at that.

He spoke of the time wandering in Omaha, of all places, when he'd tripped for eighteen hours and saw everyone as babies. On the sidewalk crawling, dancing together, stumbling, falling, rising, crying, crowing, babies kissing and making love. Babies in intercourse, doing it there in the street. Teenage babies, young married babies, career-track babies, middle-aged babies, grandpa and grandma babies. *I still see it that way,* he said.

Shadow was mostly silent, but once in a while she would interrupt. *Is that true, Arnold? Arnold, really? Poor Arnold!* Don't call me Arnold, he wanted to say. *Smoky's the name of your hat,* she said. *Without that hat you're Arnold.*

He fingered the weathered leather brim. *All my life I've tried to live up to my hat. You're telling me I haven't made it?*

You've made up a great character. Now you need to go back, pick up poor little Arnold, take him along for the ride.

He stared at her leathery face and it seemed to take on patterns like patches of feathers in variegated hues. *Come to bed now,* she said.

They were in bed. One candle burned. He was in her only a moment when he felt a spasm of sperm and fought against coming so soon. But what he'd known as coming was only the faintest whimper of coming. Now his coming began. A coming from the marrow, the sap moving up the sequoia, the sperm only spume on a mighty tide, a flood of great rivers, the Amazon, Ganges, the Nile. *What the hell,* he mumbled, and then he saw her eyes open full and heard the waters roaring into her channels from every cell of his being. They flowed and flowed as he gave himself up to the current, beyond pleasure and beyond a name. Only at dawn did the rivers run dry.

In other rooms the passengers dreamed their undreamt dreams. Those dreams had been exiled, imprisoned, and now they moved in each person's streets, searching to get their bearings. One dream hunkered in a doorway and tossed out popcorn to pigeons. A dream advertised keys-while-you-wait and ground out keys to the labyrinth. A dream found a flute and began to play. A dream went naked to school. A dream found warm flesh and laughing eyes. On the walls the statuary liquefied. The walls began to clear.

In the morning they stumbled awake, wandered into the kitchen. There were pots of coffee, coffee cake, and hunks of curious fruit. Shadow moved about clearing bowls from the night before. She seemed younger, they thought. Smoky sat at the table hatless. Jodi gave him a hug, and Tim nodded to him.

They ate in silence, sometimes glancing at the bare walls as if to see something vaguely recalled. "Did they run away?" Jessie whispered. Loki was silent.

Smoky refueled from an underground storage tank behind the buildings. It was some mix of ethanol, gasoline, soy milk, and beetle juice — a test for the fuel cells but they'd manage. Shadow kept the tank full for any lover who was low on gas.

The passengers straggled onto the bus. Tim sat on the bench behind the driver's seat and watched Smoky standing on the porch with Shadow. They stood without speaking. At last Smoky turned without embracing her, strode rapidly to the bus, climbed on, set his coffee cup on the dashboard, closed the door, and put the bus in gear. As it pulled out the passengers waved to Shadow. She raised her hand in blessing.

The bus jerked and bounced on the ruts. In the daylight it was clear that the road was unused, overgrown with brush, almost totally impassable. Tim leaned forward to Smoky. "Hey, I'm sorry I was kinda crazy," he said in a low voice.

"No problem."

Tim groped for something more to say. He wished he could draw a cartoon strip and fill in the balloons, and then everyone could read it and understand. He was only beginning to discover how much there was to discover and how far away he was from discovery, and the distance filled him with awe. "Your friend is really beautiful," he said.

"She is."

Tim hesitated. He didn't want to push things too far, but it felt as if more words were needed to heal the rift. "I noticed you weren't saying anything on the porch before you left. Was everything all right?"

"We don't run our mouths a lot."

"Well, but is everything okay between you, I mean? I mean, it's none of my business, but she's just really amazing, and so I was wondering."

Smoky sighed, then snorted a laugh. "As good as it can be, anyway. She died in 1992."

Chapter 12
Approaching Apocalypse

At dusk the bus crawled along a road cut straight through the parched hills. The sharp dip into southern Utah meant that they were funneled inevitably toward Las Vegas. No one wanted to risk a populated area, but all roads seemed to go there. Smoky realized that all the secondary roads on his map had been wiped by flood, bumped by a wrinkle in time, or simply erased by progress. The Terrapin seemed doomed to worm its way through Vegas.

Pepper remembered Vegas. It was her first escape from home, age sixteen, as soon as the swelling subsided from her jaw and the belt mark across her face was dim enough to cover with makeup. Her dad had been paid the day before and still had a couple hundred bucks in his wallet — those were the days when people used cash — so she waited till late night when he'd passed out, took the money, walked to the freeway, and stuck out her thumb.

Two days later she arrived in Vegas. She'd been raped by a trucker, but he'd tried to be nice about it. First time she'd ever been raped away from home, Pepper thought. She remembered seeing a mosquito land on the guy's shoulder right in the midst of the fray and swatting it. There was always some comedy.

She was there eighteen months living hand to mouth. Then she got a break. Some twerp saw her waiting for a bus, thought she was a hooker and asked her what her price was. She was so mad that she named an absurd amount. He actually paid. Later she found it was half the going rate. When she lost a waitress job she spent about four months pretending to be a hooker, making good money.

Of course she assured herself that she wasn't the real thing. She found guys in supermarket lots or coming out of the carwash. Poor suckers, they thought they were fucking a genuine whore, when she was only pretending. Then she met a Mexican named Ricky and forgot to charge him, and that's what got her pregnant.

She came back to Oklahoma four months gone. Her dad

met her at the door, swung at her, and she nearly killed him. She wasn't a kid any more. After that, things were more peaceful around the house. She got her problem taken care of.

Pepper looked out the window at mile after mile of barren rock. *Pretending* to be a hooker? No wonder this country was flying apart. If a sixteen-year-old kid could twist language into a braided rug, what could the heavyweight thinkers do? NoNarx wasn't the cause: it was just the lube that made the screwing slicker.

She turned to Eddie. "I was a hooker in Vegas," she said. He flicked his music off, removed an ear bud, asked her to repeat. She held her breath. Could she tell the truth when he could actually hear it? "Never mind." Not yet. She knew what his reaction would be: acceptance. She wasn't ready for that.

After the night at Shadow's, Pepper's mind was clearer than it had been in months. Now and then she felt a shimmering blink of paranoia, but it passed. Still, when she tried to think about the future, there was a crazy mix of frequencies that turned her thoughts into kitty litter. Every cloud had a silver lining, but every silver lining was double-edged.

Las Vegas — that leach field of America's sepsis — was in full spasm. Along the roadside were towering holographic images of the great entertainers: Sinatra, Madonna, Rush Limbaugh, Col. Sanders, all the greats. A billboard advertised free money. The classic casinos along the Strip still stood, but they were dwarfed by the 90-story Elvis Grand, formed exactly as the King would have been if he'd been shaped like a hotel and pockmarked by windows. Lasers projected mushroom clouds in rainbow hues. *Birthday cake on the desert! Look how bright the money is!* Disquiet gripped the passengers of the Terrapin. Could they weave their narrow passage through this bristling swamp of fun, fun, fun?

They turned onto the Strip. Fierce digital jollity blared through the dusk. Lasers, holograms, strobes, pulsars throbbed to subsonics and shrills — but the streets were nearly deserted. A burly policeman leaned against a lamp post clad only in hat and pistol belt tightly cinched under his pale beer belly, crying. Ahead, a tour bus was parked in front of Elvis' two-story big toe. Elderly tourists in feather bonnets emerged with tomahawks and digicams, lip-synching to canned laughter echoing from the buttocks of the King. On the side of their bus an ad-flat showed a sweaty purplish President Pert mouthing, "Get Real."

Pepper pressed her cheek to the chill window glass. As the Terrapin crawled into the suburbs she saw block after block of elegant bombed-out homes. A family sat on the manicured lawn outside a charred ruin watching a blank TV. By the curb a dog chewed a plaid shirt sleeve with something inside. A tiny boy threw rocks at the dog. Was this the new world? Reality come home? A comic book for psychopaths? Jessie's legacy?

Eddie put his hand on Pepper's shoulder. She flinched but let it rest there. Maybe he was worried that she was going nuts. Not a bad idea if she could find a babysitter. Maybe they could sit together in a cage picking fleas off each other. The bus coughed into high gear as it reached the ragged outskirts of Vegas.

The news was on the vid. The shapes hovered on the windshield, the camera zooming in on the Beloved Couple's bloodshot eyes. They no longer bothered to report the meltdown. Who could tell what was true? The Hell's Angels were riding tricycles. The Joint Chiefs of Staff were hosting a Tupperware party. At San Quentin the prisoners and the guards couldn't sort out who was who. As an emergency measure the President tried to release smallpox upon America but couldn't find a pen to sign the orders. A fat little girl in an ermine coat exploded during a spelling bee. A Boy Scout troop attacked the city of San Diego. Or maybe not.

Jessie was tired of nobody talking out loud. All this chatter in the air, but you couldn't tell who said it. Loki was clinging to his mother and it was no fun looking out the window, so she wiggled away from her mommy, sidled up to the front of the bus, and sat on the floor. The driver who drew cartoons was sitting on the bench behind the old guy. Action News was on the windshield and that was pretty funny, so she watched it. The news man sat up stiff and talked like he'd just swallowed something. The lady kept throwing up but pretending not to.

YOU KNOW, FRIENDS, WE'RE DOING THIS FOR YOU. WE COULD BE AT HOME IN BED. IF WE KNEW HOW TO GET THERE.

OH SHIT, HAROLD.

ROSALIE, JESUS CHRIST.

"The lady said *shit*," Jessie called out, "and the man said *Jesus Christ*." No response. That scared her. Mommy always yelled at her when she said stuff like that. "The lady said *shit*, Mommy," she repeated.

"Jessie, hush!" Pepper called from the back of the bus. Jessie was relieved.

> ROSALIE, THIS JUST IN. TROOPS REPORT STIFF
> OPPOSITION IN PASADENA FROM PEOPLE
> RESISTING BEING KILLED.
>
> HEAVY LOSSES, HAROLD. THEY JUST KEEP
> LOSING STUFF.
>
> THE NEW YORK TIMES REPORTS THAT
> REPUBLICANS AND DEMOCRATS PROPOSE
> A NEW COALITION GOVERNMENT. UNITED
> UNDER THE SLOGAN, "SPLIT THE LOOT."
>
> THAT WAS HAROLD BEING FUNNY.

The lady threw up again. Jessie was tired of that. She ran back up the aisle and hopped onto the seat beside Babcock. His eyes were closed. Jessie liked Babcock, but not when he was weepy.

"Why are you such a big sad lump?" she asked.

I always wanted to be the hero.

"Talk out loud," Jessie pleaded.

"Okay," said Babcock and cleared his throat, but it was a long time before he spoke. "I've always wanted to be a hero. And we were kinda heroic, I thought, ganged up against evil. But it's all so horrible. The best thing about history is that it's finished. But then you discover it isn't." He wiped his tears.

"You've got a little bit of snot," said Jessie.

"I miss my sister."

"Is she dead?"

Startled, Babcock looked at her. A whiff of terror crossed his face, then he squeezed forth a smile. "Well, yes. Long time ago. We were kids. I suppose I miss being a child."

She hated it when grownups talked like that. It was supposed to make you feel grateful for being a child. Like when one of Mommy's boyfriends gave her a cross-eyed bunny doll and asked her how much she thought it cost. Jessie left Babcock with his nose pressed to the glass and crawled into the seat behind Eddie and Pepper. She liked to listen to them think.

Nobody was used to their thoughts being heard, so they didn't know how to think in words that kids couldn't understand.

How soon are we? asked Pepper.

San Francisco, said Eddie, *two hours.*

What are we gonna find there? A big party in, what is it, Golden Gate Park?

I dunno. San Francisco is unpredictable under the best circumstances. I had a gig in San Francisco once. Drummer fell off the back of the stage. We never found him.

It's nuts, Eddie, it's crazy. We should stay up in the mountains somewhere.

Eddie put his arm around Pepper. She leaned into him. "End of the trip, whatever," he whispered aloud. "Move west, then there's no farther west." His face shifted with shadows. Jessie's face crinkled. The trip was coming to an end.

"Maybe we're making this up," Pepper said. "It's not really happening. Just a high-stress day in the bowels of Granny Bell. Or we fell into bed and I got freaked and dreamed the whole thing. I never asked for this. I never wanted a relationship, Eddie. I didn't want to want sex any more. I didn't want to have my skin peeled back and go through that meat grinder again. Christ, I keep feeling I've got some mad little rat inside me that's gonna go off like a bomb and take us all with it."

"Well, that's good cause that means you're in charge. What would it take for you to consider not blowing us up?"

To Jessie, her mommy looked like when she was telling Jessie she couldn't have a piece of candy just the minute before she let her.

Pepper was silent. Her mind raced over the journey. Climbing stairs, the elevator's screech, the great maw of the Badlands and the sharp rush of Eddie's breath, the dance in Shadow's walls. And it came to her that the moment when the passengers were dissolving into one another, when she had clung to her name, to *Pepper McBride* — that was the moment when something changed. She emerged with her name, but it was only a name. She might carry Pepper's scrapbook around like a throw pillow found at a rummage sale, but now she was a country she'd never traveled. What would she find on her shores? Gems, shells, plagues, or some fruit whose juice and flesh and savor she'd only dreamed?

"Okay, Eddie," she said, "I'll take the ride. I've never been as honest with anybody as I am with you. If we can do that I'll take the ride."

Eddie stroked her cheek. "I'm kinda scared shitless."

"You say the sweetest things."

Outside Bakersfield Smoky decided they'd better eat, as they still had hours to go, so he pulled into the parking lot of a defunct shopping plaza and persuaded people to set out some leftovers. The passengers sat or milled about, silent, dutifully munching. It was hard to speak the first word: too much to be said. Tim sat motionless, holding his pad and pencil as if there were nothing left in the world to draw. Jodi tried to imagine the plot of the Stephen King book she'd never finished reading. Babcock wondered what would become of his sister then remembered that she could come along, wherever. Sergei recalled a tall red-haired secretary who had moved west years ago. She might still be interested, if alive.

Tonya and Pepper stood together observing their children, twenty feet away, looking at a bug on the concrete. Without thinking, they put their arms over each other's shoulders and leaned together, two mothers watching their kids watch a bug. It felt right. Then Loki rose, and Jessie bounced up joyously beside him. With the beatific smile of a knight holding the Holy Grail he held out his hand toward the women. On the back of his hand, poised contentedly, rode the stately tarantula.

As they climbed aboard, Mabel McClafferty stood behind the bus looking southward, her arms stretched out to her sides. "I wouldn't mind being one of those hawks," she mumbled, wriggling her fingers. "I see stuff." The bus started up, pulled onto the highway, and rumbled into the dusk. Mabel flexed her arms slowly up and down, feeling the beginnings of flight.

It was dark now. Smoky was driving. Normally at this point in the journey he would call ahead to confirm his arrival time and make calls for anyone who needed to connect with friends or confirm arrangements. Tonight he just kept driving. No sign from any passenger of plans for life in the future.

From Vegas they'd taken the I-15 to Barstow, bypassed L.A. with back-road jogging to Bakersfield, up the 99, cut over to join the I-5 in the middle of nowhere, then the 280 toward the Bay Bridge. He had thought he might go roundabout to catch the I-80, just to crest the rise and see that golden city laid out ahead like a million stars. A sight worth seeing, maybe for the last time ever, but that's what made him decide on the 280. He wasn't ready to think about *last time ever.*

In the hours strung together like paper dolls, Jessie heard soundless voices caroming through the bus. *What happens? Call home. Lay low. Just live. New job. New name. Find money. Stop driving. See the dinosaurs.* That was her own brain talking.

"Jessie, be quiet."

"That wasn't me," she lied. "Somebody else wants to see the dinosaurs." A long moment. "Can we, Mommy?"

Loki was across the aisle from her, clinging to Tonya. He saw the lights ahead and started to get up, but Tonya held him. Jessie wanted to grab him and hold him until he looked deep into her heart, but she didn't. *I can't see it,* Loki said, *but there's something in the middle of the lights, maybe a carnival or like a house of mirrors or millions of people—*

I see it, said Jessie, and together they were seeing echoes, hearing the smells, smelling the music, touching the glittery shadows, tasting the wind. Catching a glimpse of a future, a rampant phantasmal dream they could only dream together.

"We can't get there now," Loki turned to her. "There's something in the way."

Then — after three thousand miles, detours, dystopias and recapitulations — they were on the Bay Bridge. "We're on the Bay Bridge, friends," Smoky said. "Something up ahead." The passengers stared forward through the windshield. They saw brilliant searchlights ahead. The sirens began.

Of the next ninety seconds they later remembered only the sick terror, the taste of sour milk, the hot eyes of the searchlights, and Babcock's voice in a high gentle lilt rising over the sirens, telling the history of the Oakland Bay Bridge. Jessie, as an old woman, would remember every word.

"The Oakland Bay Bridge is— Actually in 1924 there was a study that determined it was impossible. Earthquake faults, the depth of the bedrock, all that. But in 1929 President Hoover formed a new commission, and by 1933 the contracts were finalized."

Loki strained to see inside the lights.

"It opened for traffic in 1936, four and a half miles long, eight and a quarter including the approaches. Two bridges actually, with a tunnel through Yerba Buena Island, the widest bore tunnel in the world. Chief engineer was Charles Purcell." There is a use to history, thought Babcock, if only to fill the silence.

Eddie heard a high-frequency hum. It never fails. Incipient feedback, he thought.

"They sank steel tubes fifteen feet in diameter, filled with compressed air, installed anchors for cables, guided them into place in the mud. Then the digging apparatus went down the pipes, down to the bedrock, two hundred feet."

Jodi stared into the lights, her mind a blank. She held tight to Tim's hand and to Smoky's thigh. Tim remembered his parents' faces looking down at him in the crib. At the back of the bus Sergei, bereft, remembered his first wife's face but couldn't remember her name.

"They drove piles into the rock, created a dam to lay the foundation, wove cable, thousands and thousands of wires spun into a cable two feet thick."

Tonya held Loki. Pepper held Jessie. Eddie held Pepper. Sergei held his breath.

"And in 1989 an earthquake collapsed a section of the east span, but they rebuilt with significant improvements that subsequently cost billions to improve."

Smoky glanced at the vid. Action News was streaming live. He saw the Blue Terrapin from above crawling solo over the stark nakedness of six westbound lanes of the Oakland Bay Bridge. The fierce cold armaments of America — all that was left of it — were poised for the kill. The bus burrowed headlong into a blinding blaze of light.

BROGSNIT.

The bus had stopped. The passengers stared through the windshield. A Little Green Man stood in the roadway, phosphorescent amid blackness.

"He says congratulations." Loki's voice.

HIDOOLY WAWA.

"He says— I know what he says: *'Congratulations, you are a hit.'*"

"How do you know?" Jessie whispered to him.

"I'm retarded."

RITZ.

"'*Everybody loves you.*'"

WONGA.

"'*Across the bridge is bad stuff.*'"

NORTZ.

"'*Do not cross the bridge.*'"

Jessie cried out to the creature. "Can we have a big house and we all live together and love each other?"

DOO DOO.

"'*That would confuse our audience.*'"

RAZZA RAZZA, BEETZ.

In a distant galaxy the hastily repaired Biloxi3 — known otherwise to two children of Earth as the Galactic Improbability Generator — was goosed to a wattage consuming forty-two suns per second. The Little Green Man apologized to the passengers for rescuing them from certain death, but it was by popular demand. The series had been renewed. Then a flash of light.

HOT DAMN.

Which meant that it seemed to be working.

The bus continued its trek across the bridge. The passengers opened their eyes. The Little Green Man was gone, and so were the lights of San Francisco. Tim leaned close to Smoky. "This looks different."

"Yes it does."

"But we're still on the bridge."

"Break it to'em slowly," Smoky murmured. "This is the George Washington Bridge out of Manhattan. San Francisco is a long ways ahead."

Chapter 13
The Series Continues

America is a half-eaten muffin left on a park bench, pecked by pigeons. An insomniac's stuttering dream. A folded road map left in spilled coffee, the colors bleeding. The wound of a mangled liposuction. Washington's portrait with the eyes cut out. A mixed metaphor with a split infinitive, participles dangling. A blurt of electrons from yesterday's news. Wishful thinking, neatly wrapped with a bow. A sales pitch howling through riverbank pines. Not much to write home about. But you have to start somewhere.

Harold and Rosalie sit at the news desk puffy-eyed and bereft of juice, but they're still pros.

> TOP OF THE NEWS, ROSALIE. THE FBI REPORTS THOSE BUS-RIDING TERRORISTS HAVE BEEN APPREHENDED IN MACON, GEORGIA, CLAIMING TO BE THE CHOIR OF THE EBENEZER BAPTIST CHURCH.

> PORTIONS OF THE UNITED STATES HAVE BEEN LOCATED, AND IT'S BACK TO WORK FOR THE SURVIVORS.

> UNCONFIRMED REPORTS THAT THE PRESIDENT IS CONSCIOUS AND ANSWERS TO HIS NAME, BUT CONTINUES TO BE INCONTINENT.

The passengers stir. "Are we alive?" "What happened?" Smoky glances in the rear-view mirror. Say it straight out, he thinks. "Yes you probably are. You're on the Blue Terrapin outside New York headed west to San Francisco once again. Maybe more than once. We'll stop at a rest stop, convert to bunks, and breakfast on the shore of Lake Erie."

The passengers barely react to the news. They sit with the patient look of migrants through all millennia, the storm lifted, the journey continuing, but no predicting tomorrow.

Sergei scribbles. An equation bares its teeth. He rises to his full shortness and cries, "What it is!" Dead silence. Finally Eddie says, "Well, what?" But Sergei is back into his equation. He no longer finds the multiplication tables entirely reliable.

Smoky watches the vid. Harold has slumped in his seat, waving his hand like a cop the traffic ignores. Hey, people, he seems to be saying, no point in our telling you lies. Just look out your window, make up your own.

Pepper looks at Eddie. He shrugs, then smiles. She has a flash of her uncle's cattle being loaded for the slaughterhouse, imagines them shrugging and smiling. "Is it that much of a problem?" asks Eddie. "Being nomads? We did it for millions of years before we found that nice piece of property we could kill for. C'mon, don't look at me cross-eyed, I'm just saying we've survived up till now. Doesn't qualify us as action heroes, but you're alive, I'm alive, and the kids. We drive till we get there, then see where we are. Could be worse."

Pepper puts her hand on Eddie's shoulder and lets her forehead rest there. Everything he says sounds so depressing, yet she can't help but feel his crazy glee. Maybe she can get used to it. She remembers as a teenager how much she'd hated beer till one night she'd dreamed of drinking a tall cold mug. After that the hops beckoned.

The Terrapin moves gently through the darkness. Suddenly Pepper shudders. She remembers some movie: people on a bus who'd had a really close scrape and thought they'd made it out okay, but in fact they were all dead, heading off to Eternity. They didn't know it till they realized that no one was hungry. If you were dead you wouldn't be hungry. She feels a dread rising. "Are you hungry?" she asks Eddie.

But Eddie is looking over his shoulder. At the back of the bus there are figures in the aisle, caught in the flashes of headlights, suspended in disbelief. One lurches forward, a big burly guy with a hook nose, wispy chin beard and baseball cap. A scream from Tonya: "Benny!"

Benny charges down the aisle with a booming "Tonya!" and suddenly Tonya is a rampant dachshund bounding into his arms. They kiss vehemently as she tries to squeeze out the words "This is Benny" between lips, teeth and tongue. Then Loki tackles Benny, and they tickle each other madly as Jessie leaps onto the pile.

"I was playing a gig in Austin," Benny says, once he's tickled Loki into submission. "Masses of people packed in this little bar, and I'm getting so high on the energy I realized I hadn't drunk anything, or eaten—" Pepper clutches Eddie's hand. Benny looks deep into Tonya's eyes. "Then I thought about your chicken gumbo, baby, and then I thought about you, and zappo! This is some kinda experience!"

"You're taller," Tonya says.

"I'm always taller without a mustache."

The passengers look on as if inexplicable reunions happen every day. But Pepper's dread freezes her. It's all illusion. They died at the bottom of the elevator shaft.

"Eddie—" Pepper begins to weep. She understands now. She sees the face of Orpah Butterbaugh, a classmate who drowned, the first dead person she'd ever seen. And then she hears Jessie's voice calling "Mommy." She will have to look down into those wondering eyes and know that Jessie is dead.

"Mommy?"

Pepper can't speak.

"Mommy?"

A gasp. "What?"

"Is there something to eat? I'm hungry."

Next morning, by the shores of Lake Erie, the French toast slathered in maple syrup firmly establishes that the passengers are not dead. Appetites are unbounded and voices loose with laughter.

Besides Benny there are four new passengers. An African-American nurse whose mind wandered while placing a catheter. A skinny teenager who'd hacked into an FBI computer model of the Blue Terrapin flight and empathized too strongly. A Mexican gardener who arrived on the bus without his pants, for reasons he was loath to reveal. And a buxom Austrian masseuse who had just set eyes on the Statue of Liberty when the Biloxi3 kicked in.

Sergei introduces himself to her. "I am Sergei. I explain scientific aspects. You have beautiful breasts." Then, swept by a wave of universal kinship, he turns to the throng in the food line and proclaims, "You all have beautiful breasts!"

J.G. Babcock explains to the unsettled Mexican gardener that westward migration is a universal archetype. In the great migrations, when it all crumbled to dust, people had only known to go west. The gardener listens gleefully. He can't understand a word of English, but the voice speaks acceptance.

Tonya sees Benny eying Babcock. She knew he had funny tastes in guys, but *Babcock?* Well, that's no business of hers. She wouldn't look twice at a guy who wasn't bi.

Jodi sits between Tim and Smoky watching them eat breakfast. They are both edgy with this negotiated friendship, she knows, but for the first time she isn't hungry. For her first time ever she's full.

To Smoky it's the start of one more trip west. Maybe, hatless, to Shadow again. For Tim the challenge is ears. He can draw superlative noses, but ears are an unfathomed labyrinth.

Pepper takes a second helping of French toast, just to be certain. She sees Eddie looking at her, puts her plate down, and nods okay. They'd found a small tent in the baggage and he'd pitched it at a distance from the bus until evening, the time to leave. They crawl in, and soon they are coupled.

In the aftermath of the Bay Bridge the passengers have mostly lost their unsettling telepathy. They speak what is needed, a bit louder than normal as a hedge against intimacy. But as Pepper merges with Eddie she hears the children. She saw them at dawn silently feeling their root systems intertwine. Now she hears their unspoken speaking.

You see the crazy lady? Jessie asks.

Her name is Mabel, Loki replies. He doesn't like French toast. He'd hoped for biscuits. Maybe tomorrow.

You see her?

Where?

Up high, Jessie whispers, *in circles.*

He looks up. It's a hawk.

It's the crazy lady.

Yes, Loki sees, *it is.*

Jessie giggles. *She's got sharp eyes.*

And a beak.

Then they speak together in their souls, and Pepper hears them as she commences her slow deep joy.

We'll be safe.